rude girls

Vanessa Walters was born in Barnet in 1977, and continues to live in North London. She was educated at Queen's College, Harley Street, and now attends University College London where she is reading law. *Rude Girls* is her first novel and she is now at work on her second.

VANESSA WALTERS

rude girls

PAN BOOKS

First published 1996 by Pan Books

an imprint of Macmillan General Books
25 Eccleston Place, London SW1W 9NF
and Basingstoke

Associated companies throughout the world

ISBN 0-330-34349-1

9 8 7 6 5 4 3 2

A CIP catalogue record for this book is available from
the British Library

Typeset by CentraCet Limited, Cambridge
Printed and bound in Great Britain

For my mother

chapter
one

Paula slapped the table. 'I'm telling you for the last time. Eat your cereal!'

Two small eyes glared up into two large ones. Will met will. The strong overcame the weak. The boy started to eat his cornflakes.

The doorbell rang. Paula looked up from her breakfast. 'Finish your cereal, Fabian, while I get the door. Must be Janice and Shree.'

Paula hurried to open the front door of her flat. Sure enough, Janice and Shree stood there laughing and excited.

'Share the joke nuh,' said Paula, smiling as her friends jostled into the sitting-room of her small flat.

'It's just some stupid boy who was speeching Shree,' said Janice, shaking her head in mock sadness as she flopped down into a chair.

'Dat bwoy did look sweet, tho',' said Shree, putting on her Jamaican accent.

'Sistah, ya looking fit star,' mimicked Janice. 'Something haffe happen between mi and you.'

'What did Shree say?' Paula asked as she settled herself on the sofa.

'Come, nuh! Come help me feed my seven childs dem and pay de rent and den t'ings can run fe me and you. Lord, me never seen a man run so fast in my life,' Janice said. All three girls laughed.

Shree, Janice and Paula, best friends since the beginning of time, were all nineteen and unemployed. Laughing together, they looked as if they hadn't a care in the world. Shree, the prettiest of them, had shining black shoulder-length hair, perfect coffee-coloured skin and a curvaceous yet petite figure. Her eyes slanted upwards, framed by long curly lashes. She had an aura of fragility about her. Janice possessed a long face with big eyes and lips. Whenever she smiled, revealing a perfect set of white teeth, she became attractive. She was tall, dark and skinny, with her hair scraped back into a bun. More reflective than her friends, Janice was a secret dreamer – almost the opposite of down-to-earth Paula. Light-skinned Paula had a good-looking though hard face which was framed by a short bob. She was of medium height and solidly built, with large breasts and thick, muscular legs. Paula didn't talk shit or take it.

Paula rolled off the sofa and turned off the television. 'What time you call this anyway? Comin' around my house big eleven o'clock. Hackney Downs will be done the time we reach there.'

'Calm yourself, woman,' Shree said as she started unpacking the box she'd brought from her flat on the nearby Radford estate. Tongs, combs, gels, hairsprays, hair extensions, hair oils, all of it came tumbling out on to the floor. The three women rubbed their hands. 'And now to work!' Paula always did Shree's hair, Shree did Janice's and Janice did Paula's.

'Your hair is so lovely,' Paula said enviously as she combed out Shree's hair. After she had tonged the front and back, she tied the hair in a pony-tail. Paula gelled Shree's baby hairs and curls before she fixed a gold scrunchie around the black one already in.

'All done.' Shree stood up and twirled. She was dressed in a red cat-suit over which she wore a black mohair cardigan. Small gold earrings, two large gold chains and gold bangles on her wrists set off the outfit. The Jamaican flag was painted on her nails.

'Gwaan, rude gal!' Paula whispered, and Janice nodded. 'Stand up and let's see what you're wearing, Janice.' Janice took off her white denim jacket. She was looking extra sexy in a black sequinned bra-top with matching hotpants.

'That looks wicked, Jan,' said Shree. 'Come and sit down and I'll start on your hair.'

Shree sat down on the sofa and Janice sat at her feet. 'How are you gonna do it?' Janice asked.

'I'm separating your hair into two, with one pony-tail high on your head and a bun at the back. Pass me that hair-piece on the floor next to your foot, Paula,' ordered Shree as she parted Janice's hair with a comb and fitted the long, curly hair-piece on to Janice's own hair with two elastic bands. Then she applied gel to the back and pulled the hair into a bun, securing it with another elastic band which she concealed with a red bandana.

'Mmm, that looks kriss,' Paula said, crossing the room to look at Janice's hair. 'That piece looks real.'

'That's the idea,' said Shree.

'Mummy, Mummy, Mummy.' Fabian came trotting into the room.

'Hi, Fabian, come here, honey,' said Shree, smiling.

Fabian ran over to Shree. He was big for three years, with a very light brown complexion and chubby like his mother. He had a cute face, with large brown eyes and an irresistible grin that revealed his dimples. Shree lifted him on to her lap and kissed him on the cheek.

'I finished breakfast,' he said solemnly.

'I love the big three on your T-shirt, baby. Did you have a good birthday?'

'Yeah. I had cake an' pressies an' Mummy took me to the cinema,' said Fabian importantly.

'What did you see?'

'Umm, *Fan – fan – um – Fantasia.*'

Janice was sitting on the sofa beside Paula. She leaned over and pinched Fabian on the cheek. 'How's my Fabian after all that excitement?' she asked.

'All right, but Mummy's been naughty.' Fabian pointed an accusing finger at Paula.

'Oh no, what did Mummy do?' asked Shree, pretending to be shocked.

'She shout at me an' bang the table.'

Paula kissed her teeth at this, but then she smiled. 'Okay, I'm sorry. I'll take you somewhere nice on Sunday to make up for it.'

'Mummy, am I coming with you today?'

'No, you're going to spend the day with Granny.'

Shree gave a snort and Paula shot her a warning look. Fabian's face fell. 'I don't wanna stay with Granny. Granny beats me.'

'Well, if you weren't so bloody feisty Granny wouldn't have no need to slap you. Just sit down quietly and watch telly or go and play in the garden, all right?'

Fabian nodded, 'There's a sweet-shop on Granny's road.'

'Yeah, Fabian,' Paula said. 'You would remember that.'

Paula went into her bedroom to dress. She put on a crisp white beaded dress, leggings, white trainers and gold earrings. 'You don't think I look too fat?' she asked when she reappeared.

'No, you look big but that's an advantage. Men don't go for thin girls any more, like Janice,' said Shree.

'Hey, don't push it, Shree,' Janice said indignantly.

'Calm down, Janice, it was just a joke. You'd better hurry up with my hair.'

Janice picked up the curling-tongs as Paula sat down on the chair.

'Do you just want it curled?'

'Yeah, but tong the fringe as well as the sides so my face doesn't look so square.'

'It's a good thing you've got the weave in, all this curling and you'd have no hair left,' said Janice, beginning to tong the sides. When Janice had finished, she stepped back and looked at the result. 'Yes, that looks good.'

Shree gathered up her things and Paula went to get Fabian's overnight bag while Janice helped him put on his jacket.

'Have you got your raving clothes, Paula?' Shree asked. Paula pointed to Janice who was carrying Paula's and Fabian's bags.

*

'It always takes so long for the lift to come,' Shree complained as they stood on the landing outside Paula's flat.

'You can take the stairs, if you feel that way. It's only two floors,' Paula said unsympathetically. Shree huffed. 'Not with this box,' she said.

Finally inside the lift, Janice held her hand over her nose. 'Why does the lift here always smell so foul?' she asked, grimacing.

'It's because of that drunkard who lives on the third floor. He's always being sick in the lift,' said Paula as the lift doors closed.

Outside the building, they put their bags in the boot of Shree's convertible mauve Astra.

'Did I remember to Chubb-lock the door?' Paula asked anxiously as she sat down in the back with Fabian.

'Yes, idiot. What's happened to your mind?' said Shree.

'Too many things to remember, also known as motherhood,' Paula said. 'Turn up the sound, Shree. I wanna get in the partying mood for the all-dayer.'

'You don't need to get in the mood,' Shree said, laughing. 'You get in the park and the atmosphere just hits you.'

'Imagine,' sighed Janice. 'Boys, music and more boys.'

'You're too boy-crazy, girl. I'm only going there for the sound systems. Choice FM might be there and they always play the latest records,' Paula said.

'I'm not boy-crazy, but it wound't be any fun without them. Besides, you only go because you always win the dancing competitions,' Janice argued defensively.

'The whole area's gonna be there if it's anything like last year; all the people from our old school, all our friends, just about everybody,' Shree said.

'Here,' said Janice. 'Play this new reggae tape that Elroy made up. It's wicked.' She produced the tape and Shree put it in the cassette-player and turned it up loud. Several people, as high up as the eighth floor, came out on to their balconies to see who was making so much noise. Shree drove off around the back of the sprawling grey blocks which loomed large and gloomy above the inner-city skyline.

A little later they were caught up in slow-moving traffic. Then as they waited at some traffic lights, a car pulled up alongside, emitting slack music. The girls turned to see a large black Mercedes, chocka with boys ugly as hell, a bit older than themselves who were probably going to the same all-dayer.

A man poked his head through a side window and grinned nastily, revealing blackened and gappy teeth. His face had craters in it and a cigarette dangled precariously out of the side of his mouth. 'Where you heading, girlies?'

'Nowhere wid you, suh,' Paula said, laughing but very firm.

'Check the teeth nuh!' Janice whispered, and immediately Shree was convulsed with laughter, but she recovered quickly when she saw the looks the men from the Mercedes were giving her.

'Sweetness, crossover.' This was from somewhere in the back seat.

'Ah who you a call "sweetness"?' Janice asked indignantly.

'Not you, babylove.' A second head as ugly as the first poked out the side window. The man eyed Janice's cleavage. 'But I'm sure we could – uh – arrange something.'

The lights changed and Shree sped forward, leaving the Mercedes way back.

'Man nuh have no manners,' Janice said. Paula and Shree murmured their assent.

Paula didn't get on with her mother. There was love but no affection, Paula's mother being as brusque as her daughter was. Fight after fight had led Paula to make her own way in life, her own decisions and her own mistakes. Paula stroked her son's hair. She didn't regret anything she'd ever done.

They pulled up outside a small terraced house in Tottenham. Janice stayed in the car while Shree helped Paula get Fabian's overnight bag out of the boot. Paula walked up to the front door with Fabian. She pressed the buzzer. Her mother opened the door. When she saw who it was she sniffed before turning and walking back to the kitchen.

'Pickannies! Pickannies! Pickannies! Dat's all me ever gwan see. Children having children and den me haffe bear the burden. Me can tek this no more.'

Inside the house it was humid and gloomy. Paula glanced up the shadowy stairway to where her room used to be. She followed her mother into the kitchen, dragging a reluctant Fabian behind her.

'So how's it going, Mum?'

'If it's not "going", is you gwine tek care a me?'

Paula's mother laughed as if she'd cracked a huge joke. 'Gal can't even take care a her own pickanny but she a take care a me now.'

Paula heated up under the insult but remembered who was taking her son off her hands for the day. She bit her lip. Her mother saw the effort and laughed cruelly and without humour. She poured herself a cup of tea. Paula dropped Fabian's overnight bag on a chair at the table.

'Well, I'm going now, Mum. Back sometime tomorrow. Thanks.' She kissed her son and then ran out into the sunlight.

Inside the kitchen Paula's mother wagged a menacing finger at Fabian. 'You gonna behave yourself, boy?'

'Yes, Granny.'

The sun beat down and for once it was hot. Driving up the hill to Hackney Downs it seemed like they were part of a nationwide migration. Cars, cars, cars. People just piling into the all-dayer as if they didn't want to miss a second. Shree parked the car in Capworth Way, a deserted side street off a road leading up to the park. There was no sign of life in the side street. The garage and the shops which lined one side of the street were closed and on the other side the rubble of a demolished housing estate was hidden by a high wooden fence.

'What are you parking it here for? It's so lonely, anyone could try and steal the car and nobody would see,' Janice said.

'You worry too much,' was Shree's reply. 'It's broad daylight and anyway there's nowhere else to park. By the time we have driven around looking for a space in another street, this one will have filled up.'

Janice and Paula looked dubious but they didn't say anything as they got out of the car. The three of them strode confidently into the Hackney Downs park. They looked one hundred per cent and they knew it. Everywhere the three girls turned they recognized someone. 'Hey, Tyrone. Shamaia. Veronica. Sabrina.'

The all-dayer was alive and kicking. All the females were krissed out in their cut-up leggings and new-style weaves. Sequins, gold, lycra. The sun reflected off everything and the effect was dazzling.

'Stepping up, girls!' A good-looking youth passed them and slapped Paula on the shoulder good-naturedly. Paula smiled her greeting and moved on. It wasn't Hackney's first all-dayer of the summer but it was the biggest and most successful. Heady with the happy atmosphere and loud music, Paula almost felt like a thirteen-year-old again, with few worries and no responsibilities.

The park was a large grassy expanse dotted with a few trees. By the main entrance was a sectioned-off play area for children. Tall trees and dense bushes fringed the edges of the park while beyond, three high-rise blocks cut a sharp contrast against an azure sky. The park was filled with people, fast-food waggons and stalls that sold whistles and other trinkets. Sound systems were scattered throughout the park. Mostly reggae. The deejays had set up their equipment on long wooden tables, making barricades between them and the crowds with their enormous speakers. You couldn't walk for fifty yards before bumping into yet another sound system.

The three girls walked up to a crowd of spars they sometimes moved with. They said their hellos. Everyone was discussing clothes or men or raves. Some of the girls flirted with the deejays running the nearby sound system. Boys, noticing the concentration of funky-fresh females, flocked to that particular sound system.

Janice rocked from foot to foot and sang along softly. She loved the reggae tunes. Everyone was really getting into it. Even the little kids. She turned to Paula. 'Maybe you should have brought Fabian. There's enough small kids here.'

Paula shrugged. Janice didn't press the point. A man came up behind her and put his arms around her waist. Janice let herself be led. She whined with him slowly. She liked to dance and this man had nice strong arms. Paula said something to Shree and they both pointed to Janice and laughed. Embarrassed, she detached herself from her dancing partner. 'I'm not in the mood. Dance later, right?' Without waiting for an answer, she ran off to join her crew.

'You lot are too damn rude,' she said, laughing.

'Come,' urged Paula. 'Let's see what's happenin' over them sides.' She pointed to the more crowded side of the park. Neither of her friends had any objection.

Shree was in her element. Girls threw her envious looks and eyed her clothing with hostility. From the men there were shouts of 'Fitness!' 'Sexy!' 'Boyaka!'

Crossing the park, Janice tapped Shree on the shoulder and pointed to a group of yardies standing around by a couple of big trees. 'Hey, Shree, isn't that Derrick over there?'

Shree scanned the group which seemed to be dominated by a handsome middle-aged man wearing a white Kangol cap and a white click suit. Shree smiled. 'Yes. Let's go and say hi.'

Shree and the other girls ran over to the group of men.

'How's my girl?' Derrick hugged his daughter and then stood back to look at her. He eyed her red cat-suit sceptically. 'Me see you a track man today.' But he said it as a joke and all three girls laughed.

He turned to Janice and Paula. 'Y'all right, ladies?'

Paula and Janice smiled. 'Yes, Derrick,' they chorused. They liked Derrick. Most women did. He was a real charmer.

'So how's de car me gi' you? Don't forget to clean it every week. I hope you never park it in some lonely street today, there mus' be 'nough car t'iefs about.'

'The car's fine and you worry too much,' Shree said, nudging Janice to stop her laughing.

They engaged in light chit-chat for a short time.

'Janice, Shree tol' me that you is living on your own now.'

'Yeah. My aunt's letting me have her flat while she's in Jamaica.'

'So how you find it?'

'It's wicked. I really love having my own place. I have more freedom.'

'Jus' tek care of unno self,' Derrick said, smiling. He asked Paula about Fabian and gave them each twenty pounds, because as he said, 'You are all my daughters. If I look after one I look after three.'

The girls thanked him and then left Derrick to his business. They merged into the crowd at the nearest sound system. The deejay on the mike stopped the tunes and announced, 'Now we're going to have a bogling competition. Me want all you ladies out there and all you men who think say none can test you. Me want you to come into the centre. We've got a couple of albums here to give away.' He withdrew a crumpled note from his breast-pocket. 'Oh yeah, and a twenty pound for the first prize.' He held it up for all to see. 'Who out there want this twenty pound?'

The younger girls started screaming, 'Meee!', 'Over here!'

'Dance for it!' shouted the deejay and the competition began.

Shree and Janice could dance well but Paula was in a class of her own. As people were knocked out of the competition by the judges, a circle formed around those left. Shree and Janice were soon eliminated so they gave themselves up to cheering on their best friend. Paula did the armstrong, the clapdance, the butterfly. Any dance which popped into her head, she did it. Three competitors left. Paula bogled on her head. Two competitors left. Paula whined on the floor. Then she'd won. Everyone was clapping and cheering and shouting.

'Boyaka,' screamed Shree and Janice. This was echoed by others in the crowd. Paula straightened up and brushed off her clothes. Worn out but exultant, she ran up to the stand to collect her prize. The deejay handed the twenty-pound note to her with a grin. 'All fruits ripe, seen,' he said, eyeballing her figure. Paula, blinded by the untold amounts of gold in his mouth, couldn't think of a smart comeback, so she just said thanks and walked back to her friends.

In a corner of the park nearer the high-rise blocks, there was a small fair with a few rides and stalls. The three girls, tired of dancing, walked over to the fairground to see what was about.

It was quite good. The prices were a bit high but the rides were fast and furious so they thought, why not? Paula ran up to a ride aptly named the Mary Rose and paid her fare and jumped on before her friends could protest. Janice and Shree looked at each other quizzically. But they followed anyway. The ride was shaped like a ship and when it started to move it swung from left to right, increasing in speed and swinging more violently so that at times it nearly turned upside-down. Janice opened one eye and laid out beneath her she could see all the sound systems in the park. Some people watched the ride, amused, laughing and pointing. Janice closed her eye again in distress.

Paula just yelled and waved her hands along with everyone else. 'It's a good thing I'm not soft like you, Jan. I don't feel it when I go on these things.'

No one answered. Janice and Shree were relieved when the ride stopped and they were able to get off.

'Come on, let's have another go,' said an enthusiastic Paula, already heading for the front steps once again.

'No, Paula. I feel dizzy,' Janice said, holding on to Shree.

'The second time it doesn't feel so bad. Hurry up, so that we get good seats.'

'I think Janice has a point.'

'So, do you have a better idea?' Paula asked stubbornly.

'Well, we could walk around for a bit,' Shree suggested.

'All right, but I don't see anything else to look at here.' Paula kicked at a stone.

They wandered around the stalls and arcades. Men came up to talk to them, always the usual things. 'Looking nice, gal.' This was then followed by, 'You on the phone?'

Sometimes boys just said, 'Yush' or 'Young gal' or even 'Oi!' These times the sisters didn't even bother to look back.

Suddenly Shree stopped in her tracks. 'Shit.'

Walking towards them were the beasties that had been so fresh with them at the traffic lights, looking even worse outside the car than in. They had seen the girls and were speeding in their direction. The three girls ran behind a ride.

'What are we going to do?' Janice asked.

'They'll be here in a minute, they know where we are,' Paula said.

'Last few seats,' yelled the operator of the Mary Rose.

'That's it! Let's get on that ride,' Janice said, pointing.

The three girls dashed across the fairground, pushed some other people out of the way and climbed on to the ride. They giggled as they saw the boys standing where they had just been, looking around for them in confusion, but Janice and Shree's laughter turned to screams of dismay as the ship began to swing.

While they were on the ride Paula, the only one with

15

her eyes open, noticed there was a growing concentration of people on the far side of the park. Many people were heading in that direction. As she looked around she noticed the other rides were being cleared in a hurry, while the fairground workers looked worried. The operator of the Mary Rose wasn't looking too happy either and as soon as the ride stopped he threw open the gates. 'Everybody out this side.'

Paula's eyes gleamed with excitement. With one hand she grabbed Janice's arm and with the other she grabbed Shree.

'What?'

'What?'

'Come on!'

Janice and Shree sighed. It was so often the way with Paula. Headstrong. Determined. They always had to follow her. But Shree had also noticed something was up so she didn't argue.

By now everyone was following everybody else. Worried parents and older people were taking themselves off home. If there was going to be trouble they didn't want to be caught up in it.

'I think we should just go,' Janice said, but the other two didn't pay any attention to her.

'Hi, did you hear the gunshots too?' A dark-skinned, lanky girl, wearing denim shorts and an orange T-shirt, joined the group.

'There weren't any gunshots or we would have heard them, Chantelle,' Paula said.

'Where were you?' Chantelle asked.

'We were over at the fairground,' Paula said.

'Well, of course you wouldn't have heard the gunshots, you were right over the other side of the park, near the entrance, and there was all the fairground music. I have been down this end all afternoon,' Chantelle explained.

'So what happened then?' Paula asked.

'Well, most people were just standing around talking and dancing, when there were two shots and then everyone stampeded to see what was going on.'

'Who did you come with?' Shree asked the girl.

'Oh, I came with Tanasha but he was so eager to be where the action was that I let him go ahead. You know what men are like. I was just looking around for someone I knew. It's a good thing you came along.' The others nodded and the four of them continued in the direction of the crowd.

Janice noticed a police van speeding in the same direction as themselves and frowned. She knew from experience that with police usually came trouble. They reached the thickest part of the crowd and came to a standstill. Chantelle got the attention of a tall man in front of her who could see what was going on. 'What's happened?' she asked.

'I think someone's been shot or killed, but I'm not close enough to see properly,' he replied.

Paula, not being as tall as Chantelle or Janice, was getting impatient. She motioned for the others to follow and pushed and fought her way through to the centre of the crowd where they found a small space and something of an emergency.

A large black woman was screaming and cussing. Tears were flying down her face. At her feet a large man lay semi-conscious. Blood seeped from his side, forming a dark streak on the grass. Another woman knelt beside him and held his hand. She spoke softly to him.

Two uneasy-looking policemen kept the crowd at bay. They seemed not to see the scene in front of them and kept looking around to make sure the police van was still close by. The four girls looked at one another in shock. None of them knew what to say.

'Where's the ambulance, then?' someone asked one of the policemen.

'It's on its way.'

'What do you mean, it's on its way?' the woman kneeling on the ground shouted. 'Ambulance has been on its way for a good fifteen minutes now.'

The policeman looked down at her rather contemptuously. 'It won't be much longer.'

'Policeman nuh care about black people, my dear,' said an old man who had had too much to drink.

A young man pushed forward and put his arm round the old man. 'Time to go home, Uncle.'

The old man smiled enthusiastically at his bemused audience. 'I don't want to go home yet. You see how dem a treat black people so. Now if it was a white man you see how fast—'

'Let's go, Uncle. You're only getting yourself into trouble.' The young man put a firm hand on his uncle's shoulder and they disappeared into the crowd.

The man who was lying on the ground began to moan. The crowd started getting restless again.

'Where's the ambulance, man?'

'Liberty-takers, y'know.'

'Innit tho.'

'Things can't carry on like this, y'know, that's a human being lying there, not a dog.'

The crowd grumbled and rumbled amongst itself for a while, the grumbling and rumbling getting louder. The policemen uttered audible sounds of relief when an ambulance finally swung into the park. In a few minutes the man had been put on a stretcher, carried into the ambulance and was gone.

Janice looked up. The sun was dying down. It looked as though all the excitement had been sucked out of the sky. It was getting cooler too. Chantelle scuffed her trainer against the ground. No one really knew what to do.

The crowd turned to watch a car playing loud reggae pull into the park. It sounded strange to hear ragga now all the sound systems had gone quiet. A young man leaned across to the passenger seat and opened the door.

'Yush, Chantelle.'

'Oh, Tanasha, take your time.'

Chantelle hurried over to the car and kissed the man inside. She looked back to the three girls. 'Are you going over to that rave in Stokey?'

Paula gave the don't-know sign for them and so Chantelle said goodbye. The car moved off, leaving a cloud of toxic fumes for them to breathe.

The all-dayer was done. People were making their way to their next destination. Janice, Shree and Paula began walking back to the car. It was getting breezy.

Shree rubbed her bare shoulders. 'I need to use the loo,' she said.

'Me too,' said Janice.

They turned the corner into Capworth Way.

'Shit,' said Shree. Standing around her new convertible were the beasties they had seen first on the road and again at the all-dayer.

'They must have recognized the car,' Janice said, stopping.

'Keep walking,' hissed Paula. They walked quietly up to their car, passing the black Mercedes and a tall, dreadlocked man who was leaning against it, observing the situation.

'That's right, step this way, girlies.' One of the ugliest men blocked the driver's door. His tone was no longer bantering. His cronies sniggered. One spat on to the bonnet of the Astra.

The girls stopped about a yard from their car.

'Excuse me,' Shree said to the man. 'I'd like to go home.'

'I'll take you home, mistress,' he said.

'Just get away from the car,' said Paula. Although she was scared she didn't show it.

Janice looked up and down the deserted side street.

'That's right, babes. No one's coming to help you.' The men laughed.

The man blocking the driver's door moved away as if to allow Shree past, but when she moved forward he grabbed her arm. 'To tell you the truth, sweetness,' he said quietly, 'me nuh appreciate your manners today. You can't say a civil word to a man. Why you run from us in the park?'

'Because you're ugly,' declared Paula, then she bit her lip. You never knew with these men.

The man still had Shree by the arm. He looked Paula up and down. 'Is we ugly, or is you?' He looked back at his brethren.

'Slap her, Skins,' one of them said quietly.

'No.' Skins looked back at the dreadlocked man leaning against the Mercedes who had just spoken. He let go of Shree's arm but he didn't move out of her way.

Paula was huffing and puffing and tears were coming into Shree's eyes but Janice played it cool. 'Look, right, this morning we weren't blanking you, but my friend had to take her son to the baby-minder. She was paying her and didn't have no time to be chatting to men. This afternoon in the park we didn't want to talk to you because our men were watching us. What do you want us to do?' She looked around at the men confidently, showing no signs of weakness.

'Your men ain't here now, tho',' pointed out one of the group.

'Well, how about if I give you my number?' Janice said, 'Then you can call me and we'll see.'

Almost before she had finished speaking, the same man had darted forward, pen and paper in hand. 'No fake digits now, babylove,' he said as Janice took the pen and paper and wrote down some numbers.

'Let's go,' said the dreadlocked man as he opened the driver's door and got into the Mercedes.

'Ring you 'bout ten tonight, seen?'

'Seen,' said Janice, trying not to laugh as the man scampered off after his friends and jumped into the Mercedes which then sped away. The girls eased sighs of relief. Paula leaned against the car and held her nose, giggling.

21

'Stink!' Shree said, nodding. 'That man's face when you told him he was ugly. One of these days you're gonna kill me, Paula.'

Paula grinned. 'Janice, man, I don't know how you did it.'

'My girl's got style!'

'Oh, it was nothing.'

'What are you chatting about? They could have dragged us into their car in no time.'

'True say you don't mess with them types. Cross them once and next morning, police find you in a canal somewhere."

''Strue.'

Janice, well pleased with her successful negotiation, clambered into the back seat of the Astra. The other two got into the front. Shree started the car and then turned to face the other two. 'Where are we headed?'

'My place,' Janice declared. 'It's nearest.'

Shree drove up through Hackney. Brocklebank Road, Swift Street, Bow Lane. The streets flashed past one after another, dusty and deserted apart from the occasional pub whose regulars sat outside. A group of teenagers appeared from nowhere, darted across the main road and disappeared into the urban landscape. The shops had long since closed along Mare Street and they stood like lifeless cages while the sun hung heavy in a sky brown with heat and dust. A few stragglers from the Hackney Downs all-dayer waited at bus stops.

Paula leaned over and looked in the side-view mirror. She smoothed her hair down and was redoing her lipstick when she stopped suddenly. Slowly, almost against her will, she studied the side-view mirror. Far behind them was a black Mercedes. She let Shree and Janice know the situation. Janice chewed her lip thoughtfully. Shree just muttered curses.

'We can lose them,' Paula stated matter-of-factly. 'Let me drive.'

'What? So you can park us under a bus? When was the last time you drove a car?'

'I've been able to drive longer than you. I've driven my mum's car, Michael's car, I've—'

'Stop fighting, there's no time,' Janice interrupted sharply. 'Shree, pull over and let Paula drive.'

Shree gave Janice a filthy look but pulled over and stopped by the kerb.

'There's no point trying to play the rude girl, Shree. I told you not to park your car in that deserted street,' said Janice.

'Just give me one good reason,' Shree said, as Paula got out and ran around to the other side of the car.

'Paula drives like a madman, you're too careful, you'll never get us out of this mess.'

'But—'

'Hurry up and get out, Shree.'

Shree glared up at Paula before reluctantly unbuckling her seatbelt and opening the car door.

'Calm down,' Janice said, tapping her on the shoulder. 'Paula drives well.'

'She's going to have to,' said Shree as she got out of the car, 'because they're right behind us.'

Janice and Shree braced themselves as Paula accelerated away and jumped the first set of traffic lights. The large Mercedes was stuck behind a bus but as soon as the lights changed it sped after them.

'Paula, turn off the main road, maybe we can lose them.'

'I can't do that yet, Janice, they're too close and too fast. If they catch us down a back street we'll never be able to get away. It's best to stay on the main road for a while because this car's small and can dodge around other cars but their Mercedes is too big for that.'

'At least slow down,' said Shree. 'We'll have the police on our tail in no time.'

Paula overtook a van, nearly causing an accident.

'Yeah, we're gaining. Keep it up, Paula.' Janice patted Paula's shoulder.

Shree looked back. 'They haven't given up,' she said.

'No, but they are dropping further and further behind. You were right about the Mercedes being too big, Paula,' Janice said.

Finally Paula turned off Mare Street and drove along several twisting back streets until they were far from the main road. She looked round at the others, grinning. 'They'll never catch us now,' she said.

Shree sighed and gave a wry smile. 'All right, I'll hand it to you this time, rude girl,' she said.

The others laughed at her shamefaced expression. Paula turned back on to Mare Street and drove up towards where Janice was staying.

chapter
two

Back at Janice's flat, Paula flung herself full length on the plush sofa. The jolt caused a large lampshade on a tall stand beside the sofa to shake dangerously. Janice hurried to steady it. 'Paula, don't mess around. Take your feet off the sofa or take off your trainers.'

Paula ignored Janice and picked up a flowerpot filled with plastic geraniums and threw it across the room at Shree, who caught it. Both of them laughed.

'Paula, don't play with those things. If anything gets broken I'll be the one who has to pay.'

'C'mon tho', Jan,' Shree said, shaking her head, 'china dogs and cats, lace coverings, fake flowers – you need to start getting rid of this stuff.'

'Tell her, Shree,' Paula urged, 'the girl can't understand that all those pictures of Jesus covering the walls won't impress Elroy when he comes round for his romancing.' Paula and Shree burst out laughing once again.

'Damn, you two are so immature. You do this every time you come here,' said Janice. She picked up the potted geraniums which Shree had carelessly tossed on to the floor next to the armchair and carefully put it back on the coffee table in front of the sofa. 'Listen, right, it's not my flat, my aunt's coming back from Jamaica as soon as she's sorted out her sister's children and she's only let me stay here on condition that I take care of her home, not wreck it.'

Paula's eyes twinkled but she straightened her face. 'All right, I'm sorry, Jan,' she said.

'It's not just that, my mum can come and check up on me any time she wants.'

'How come she didn't go to Jamaica? Isn't it her sister as well?' Shree asked.

'No, my mum and Aunt Sarah are cousins and because my mum's been over here for so many years she never really knew Sarah's sister.'

'I see,' said Shree.

Paula kissed her teeth. 'It's just that the place is so cluttered with all these ornaments and everything smells old too. I don't think I could stand it, and your own room is so pretty,' she complained, unlacing her trainers.

'Well, it's better than staying at home where I'm pestered twenty-four hours a day by my parents and that fool, Rio. I'd have done anything to get shot of them.'

'Yeah, and I bet I know why,' Shree said, giving Paula a look that Janice couldn't fail to see.

'Elroy's only a small part of the reason,' she blurted defensively.

'So he *is* sleeping here,' said Paula, as though she knew it all along.

'Only sometimes,' Janice conceded.

'I'd love for your mum to catch you in action,' Paula added.

'Oh, don't say that.'

'Well, we should be able to have at least one party before your aunt gets back, innit, Paula?' Shree said, sitting up.

'Are you ma—'

'Don't be so boring, Jan,' Shree continued, 'all we'd have to do is drop all this rubbish in the bedroom and take down the pictures and the curtains. This room must be well big when it's cleared and we could get Nicole and Chantelle and Sabrina to help and—'

'Stop right there! If you're having that backwards Sabrina in to help, don't include me in the proceedings. That girl is such an irritating bitch.'

'Forget her, Paula, let's get down to the more important details like which boys we're going to invite.'

Janice looked from one to the other in exasperation. They were doing this on purpose, knowing full well that a party was impossible. 'Speaking of parties, where are we going tonight then, girls?' Janice interrupted loudly.

'I'm safe for Shnoela's,' Paula said. So it was decided. If Paula was 'safe' then naturally the other two were.

'I'm first in the bath,' Janice shouted as Shree disappeared into the bathroom.

'Dream on, darling,' yelled Shree over the din of running water. 'It's the early – it's the – the—'

'It's the early bird that catches the worm,' finished Paula, shaking her head.

'Just hurry up, Shree. Mad fool.' Janice took the armchair Shree had abandoned.

Paula viewed her with contempt from the plush sofa. 'Janice, I'm sorry to have to say it, but the way you're living is downright shabby.' She looked around the room, past the climbing plants and the ornate cabinet filled with saucers and glasses and lighted on an archaic stereo covered with crocheted lace net. 'Don't tell me that is still your sound system?'

Janice yawned lazily, curling her legs underneath her. 'Nobody's asking you to listen to it, now are they?'

Paula got up and crossed over to the stereo. She turned it on and fiddled around with the tuning button until she got WNK radio. They were playing swingbeat. Then she left the room to get a nail-file from her bag in the hall. A moment later she was back sitting on the sofa, filing her toe-nails.

'I can't stop thinking about today,' Janice said.

'Yeah, my dancing was wicked.'

'You know what I'm talking about, Paula. That man who got shot. I've never seen so much blood in my life.'

'It's true. I wonder if he's okay.'

'I hope so, but that looked like some serious wound to me, star.'

'I don't know why people can't just enjoy themselves. Certain people always have to make up trouble.'

'Innit. Giving black people a bad name. Did you get a look at his face?'

'Not properly, but I think I've seen him somewhere before.'

'He was one of the men with Derrick at the all-dayer.'

'Oh, yeah, that's right. He was one of the dealers underneath the tree who were eyeing Shree before they realized Derrick was her dad.'

28

'That's it. I wonder what happened, because did you notice that all those men had disappeared?'

'I'm not surprised, there were too many police about.'

'Still, I wonder who shot him?'

'Well, whoever it is, he must be keeping a low profile, 'cause anyhow that man survives, he'll be after someone's blood.'

'Speaking of low profiles, maybe we'd best be careful too, in case we run into those dreadlocked men again.'

'I don't think we will, I'd never seen them before today. That car chase was a close call, though.'

'Only because of your mad driving, rude girl.' Janice and Paula laughed.

'So, how's it going with your man?' Paula said.

'Oh, it's not love. At least I don't love him, I don't even know why because he is really fit and that but let the boy open his mouth and a whole heap of shit comes out. The only things he can hold a conversation on are him and his music and his car and his friends. He's so limited. I know it sounds bad but I don't think I wanna stay with someone who ain't going anywhere. I mean, yeah, Elroy is a lot of fun but there's got to be more to life than music and sex. Sometimes I think that yeah, that's all he wants. Oh, I don't know really.'

'But you're still sleeping with him?'

Janice said nothing.

'Fabian's father might not have been so ready with the dollars, but he always treated me right. I know it's none of my business but if a man don't treat you right it doesn't matter if he's the Prime Minister. There ain't nuthin' to stay for.'

'How can you say that Michael treated you right? He just about abandoned you.'

'I'm not surprised you can't see Michael's finer points. That's what drove him away, everyone putting pressure on him to be a father figure.' Paula returned her attention to her craggy toe-nails.

'You've never liked any of my boyfriends anyway. You always have something horrible to say,' Janice said.

'Well, if you had taken any notice of what I said, you wouldn't be having these problems now.'

'You never criticize Shree's boyfriends and look at how lazy Tyrone is.'

'That's different. Shree's more mature than you because she's doesn't have a mother to take her problems to. She knew Tyrone's faults before she went out with him and accepted them. You go out with someone because you think they're perfect. It doesn't bother me, but when I have to give my opinion, I'm not gonna lie and pretend he's wonderful, I'm gonna tell you what his faults are.'

'I suppose you're still on good terms with Michael?' Janice asked.

'Yeah. He comes round once in a while to see his son and sometimes I bump into him at raves and such. Why?'

'I just wondered. You haven't mentioned him in a while. I'm glad things are still good between you. So many black men nowadays, as soon as they see a nappy, they're gone. You won't see them for dust.'

'Don't knock them, y'know, Janice.'

Paula started filing the nails on her other foot. 'Most times is because they try but the mother don't wanna know. They expect all or nuthin'. Most men seen, they can't give all. They give a little and then when they see it ain't so bad they give a little more. Now with me and Michael, I just went with the flow. I let him love in his own time at first.'

'Yeah,' Janice interrupted, 'and when you figured he'd played enough you made him pay.'

They laughed together, enjoying the joke.

'Yeah,' Paula conceded, 'you know the cue.'

They were both silent for a moment, thinking about their respectives. The phone rang sharply, breaking into their thoughts. Paula, being the nearest, answered it.

'It's for you,' she said, handing the receiver to Janice.

'Hey, baby!'

'Who's that? Elroy?'

'What other man has your number?'

'Eh? Where are you, Elroy? I can hardly hear you.'

'I'm at Sevens down Homerton.'

'Is it good there?' Janice said, sounding uninterested. With Elroy it was always another rave or another concert.

'Actually I'm moving to a next rave. I just phone to see if say you ready.'

'Ready for what?'

'Me coming to pick you up about one. You're coming with me, of course.'

'I'm already going to a rave with Paula and Shree.'

'No, honey, me already tell me friends dem say you're coming so just put on your clothes and—'

'I can't come, Elroy. Maybe tomorrow or some other time. I can't just drop everything to follow you.'

'Janice, who's your man?'

'You are, Elroy.'

'That's right. You're my woman. You belong to me, not your blasted Shree or your damn Paula. Don't disrespect me Janice. Me even tell the deejay say you coming. Just tell your friends that your man is taking you out and you're sorry. It all comes down to who you love, and you love me so.'

'You're a joker, Elroy, but let me tell you something seen? I don't belong to you. You don't own me. Just because you call yourself my man doesn't mean say I have to do every last thing you want. Just understand two things. I'm not coming anywhere wid' you tonight. I don't care about your deejay or your friends or your rave. Love? Don't chat if all you're gonna chat is shit. This don't have nothing to do with love. However, it does have something to do with respect. When it comes to me respecting you and your deejay friends, you've got too much to say, but when it comes to my friends, don't go cussing them down and expect me to allow it. I'm sorry to destroy your plans, Elroy, but I'm going to Shnoela's. You can come and check me there if you feel to.'

Janice paused. There was a click and she was left holding the receiver in her right hand. She replaced it carefully and then looked up at her friends. Shree was standing in the doorway wrapped in a towel. Both she and Paula stared at Janice who stared blankly back.

'Gone too far,' Paula said, beginning to read the inside sleeve of a reggae cassette tape.

'Come, tho', Jan, you didn't have to bawl at the man,' Shree commented as she sat down next to Paula.

Janice kissed her teeth. 'I don't care. What did he ever do for me?' She glared defiantly at her friends but

32

she turned her scrunchie over and over in her hands. 'I don't really feel like going out tonight. You lot go and tell me about it tomorrow.' She wasn't about to cry but she didn't feel too good sameway.

Shree crossed the sitting-room and crashed down next to Janice. Paula crawled across, bringing a cushion from the sofa. They set about comforting her.

'Don't try it with the eye-water business, y'know, Janice.'

'Tomorrow morning my man Elroy will be begging your forgiveness, Janice.'

'Innit, the whole bended knee and gifts type of thing.'

'So what you fretting for?'

Janice smiled.

'Why bother with the raving business, man?' Paula said suddenly.

'But why? What's the time, Jan?' Shree asked, clearly disappointed.

Janice held up one finger.

'Exactly,' said Paula. 'It's already one o'clock and who's dressed?' They looked at each other. Shree was wrapped in a towel, while the other two were still in the clothes they had worn to the all-dayer.

Paula held out her hands to emphasize her point. 'I think we should just have our baths and that and have something to eat and cuss men and done.'

Even Shree smiled, an indication that Paula was winning the argument. Janice nodded enthusiastically.

'Right, then. It's settled.'

Paula settled back in the foam-filled bath and twitched her toes. She closed her eyes and thought of Fabian. She was missing him already. She didn't like to leave him at her mum's but she hadn't had a break for ages. Tomorrow she'd take him out shopping. No, tomorrow was Sunday. She'd take him to the park. Michael drifted into her head. Steady, responsible Michael.

Paula was proud of herself for making such a good choice of father, even if it hadn't worked out in the end. She dwelt for a while on the good days as the steam rose from the bath. She remembered that particular Sunday when it had been hot and sunny and Michael and she had spent the whole day together and then gone back to his house.

His parents hadn't been in, and it had happened. Inevitably, naturally, wonderfully. She had only been sixteen, landed with a baby and an unsupportive mother. She'd gone and pleaded her case to the council who'd fixed her up with a flat and a social worker. Paula had quickly disposed of the interfering woman who claimed to be 'helping', and enjoyed the luxury and freedom of her own flat although it was on a large, run-down Hackney estate. It had been bare at first but her friends and sometimes Michael had helped her to get started and she had bought items of furniture when she could afford it, in time making a home for herself and Fabian. Michael had moved in almost immediately (Paula chose to overlook the fact that he moved out almost as soon as he'd got his own flat), and they'd been a happy family for a while. She got what unemployment and child benefit she could from the DSS. Michael helped out financially when he got decorating work or deejaying work. Paula sank lower into the bath and closed her eyes. Some day she'd find her Prince Charming who adored little boys and they'd have two houses, one in Jamaica and one in London. Oh yes and one in –

'Paula, get your butt out of my bathroom now.'

Paula woke up from her dreaming. She slopped around hurriedly, unplugged the bath and then clambered out. She wondered what had come over her. It wasn't like her to daydream.

The girls, now wearing the night clothes they had brought with them, rummaged around the kitchen, trying to find something to eat. Shree checked out the fridge, Paula searched the cupboards while Janice looked on, amused.

'So tell me, Janice. Is dis how you're living?' Shree held up a dried-out carrot in one hand and a half-full bottle of Diet Coke in the other. Paula emerged from a dusty cupboard and threw her findings on to the sideboard. An extra-large packet of Walker's crisps and a tin of corned beef. They looked at Janice in contempt.

'I swear, you're a disgrace,' said Paula.

Janice, untroubled by the outraged looks of her two starving companions, strode over to her bag, partly hidden by the fridge, and withdrew a packet of easy-cook rice and two ripe avocados. 'Voilà! Dinner will be served,' she announced cheerfully.

Shree munched her corned beef and rice experimentally and then took a long swig of the cola which she spat straight back into her glass. 'Ugh! This stuff's nasty.' She indicated to Paula to taste her own, but Paula declined.

Janice, having finished her meal, decided it was time for some music. She put on one of her ragga tapes.

'Lovin' . . .'

'Lovin' a'dem want.' Paula sang along with Janice.

'Fe true!' Shree's voice linked up with the circuit. Paula got up and began to demonstrate her new style of bogle. Janice tried to follow her steps. She was doing quite well until she tripped over one of Paula's trainers. The doorbell rang, three times in quick succession.

'Who is it?' Shree glanced at the clock on the mantelpiece. 'Uh uh! It's reaching three o'clock!'

Janice ran to the door and looked through the spy-hole. A familiar face peered back at her. She pulled back the bolts and threw open the door in delight.

'Hey, babes,' said Elroy, holding out his arms.

Suddenly Janice was outside in the hallway locked in Elroy's embrace with Elroy whispering how much he loved her and how he hoped things were still sweet between them. Paula and Shree stared shamelessly from the doorway of the sitting-room. They were just as pleased as the two lovers that the argument had been sorted.

After a few minutes Elroy and Janice came in. Elroy hugged Paula and pinched Shree on the cheek. He explained that after his argument with Janice he had made his way to Sevens but missing Janice (at this point Janice humphed loudly in disbelief) he had gone on to Shnoela's.

'Big up five pound me have to pay, only to find that me three fav'rit gals dem nuh in the place.' He looked round appealingly at the girls who giggled, ready to spend their sympathy on one so charming and nice-looking. 'In the end,' Elroy shook his head sighing, 'the need got so bad me just have to jump in me car and come look fe make my peace wid my Janice.' He finished his story, well pleased with himself. He sank back into the sofa, wallowing in the attention.

Elroy's greatest gift, far overstepping his good looks, was his power of speech. Take the toughest, most hardened hag in London, put her in a room with Elroy for five minutes and she would be putty in his hands. He was that good. Janice smiled at him. She knew there would be more arguments in the future, but for now she was just glad to be near him.

In the end it was the midday heat that woke Janice, who stumbled out of the bedroom and disappeared into the bathroom. The flushing of the loo woke Paula who drowsily thumped Shree. 'Wake up, man. It must be late.'

They groaned as they sat up and surveyed the sitting-room. It was a tip: glasses, a can of Guinness, crisps littering the mantelpiece and overflowing on to the makeshift bed the girls had made for themselves on the floor. Janice entered the room and turned on the radio.

'Allow it, Janice.' Paula rubbed her aching and tired head.

'I wanna hear the news and anyway you lot want to be clearing up this mess now.' At this Shree raised half-closed eyes to Janice in sleepy indignation.

'Who's more important to you – us or your bloody weather watch?' This provoked a heated argument between the three as to why the radio should or should not be turned on.

'Now, now, ladies, don't fight.' Three pairs of baleful eyes turned to the doorway where Elroy leaned lazily. All he had on was a towel wrapped around his lower half.

He grinned at them, ignoring the death-looks he was receiving, and winked his eye at Janice knowingly. It had been a good night.

In the end the radio stayed on because no one felt sleepy any more, and Paula went into the bathroom to get washed and dressed. She meant to carry out her intention to take Fabian to the park. Shree set about tidying up the sitting-room while Elroy and Janice disappeared into the kitchen to see if there was anything to eat.

An hour or so later everyone was on their way out of Janice's flat. Weather watch had said it would be another sunny, dry and warm afternoon. Shree was going to give Paula a lift to her mum's and then go back to her own flat and perhaps see if Tyrone's mobile phone was turned on yet. Elroy claimed to be taking Janice out to a surprise destination and although she suspected it was one of his usual haunts she grinned as she locked the front door, concluding that the same self-centredness which had so annoyed her earlier could also be appealing.

Paula threw the ball back to Fabian. She was in a good mood because he was in a good mood. He was in a good mood because she was in a good mood. That's the way it was between them. There were a lot of people in Finsbury Park but Paula had found a nice quiet place where they would not be disturbed. They changed from catching to football. Then Fabian decided he wanted to play hide-and-seek so Paula chased him, laughing, in and out of the trees. In the end they both flopped down on a grassy mound and watched a game of frisbee being played by some young boys.

There was an ice-cream van nearby so Paula started searching in her pockets for some change. She didn't pay attention to Fabian who prattled happily behind her. As she rummaged through her handbag it suddenly struck her that Fabian wasn't talking to her at all. He was talking to somebody else.

'Fabian, who the hell—' She twisted round.

Fabian was having a deep conversation with his father, a tall, light-skinned young man with boyish features.

'Michael, don't scare me like that.'

Michael stretched himself out on the grass next to Paula and kissed her in a friendly way on the cheek. Paula's Sunday was complete. She had the father and she had the son.

'How come you're in the park on your jays? You turning a loner now, Michael?'

'Don't be silly, I'm with a couple of friends. Look.' He pointed to where a group of men were playing football. Paula thought this was odd. They didn't look like Michael's sort of company. Besides, Michael didn't really play football. However, she nodded.

'Daddy, can we play?' Fabian tugged at his father's sleeve impatiently. He ran lopsidedly behind a nearby tree.

'Daddy's got the lurgy, Daddy's got the lurgy.'

Michael ran round after Fabian for a short time and then caught him up in his arms and carried him back to his mother. On the way he studied Paula's face anxiously.

It looked as though she was in a good mood. That would be helpful.

He sat down on the grass next to her with Michael in his lap. 'Paula, can you lend me twenty pounds?'

'Where am I supposed to find twenty pounds, Michael? It's not like you don't know how much money it costs to clothe and feed your son, so why ask?'

Michael was prepared for this. He put on his most charming voice and said some of the things he knew Paula was waiting to hear. He told her how much he had missed her and how he had phoned her on Saturday, only she was out. He hinted that they weren't just friends and he told Paula how Fabian was getting to look more like him every day and how he was going to take Fabian out in the coming week. 'So how about that twenty pound, Paula?'

Before Paula knew it, she had handed over the twenty pounds she had won at the all-dayer. With it went her new sandals and Fabian's new jacket, but she couldn't resist Michael's dangerous charm.

Michael gave her a light peck on the cheek and chucked Fabian on the shoulder and was gone. Paula lay face down on the ground, resting her head on her jacket, and watched half-heartedly as Fabian invented a new way of playing football with an imaginary friend. She did not notice that Michael did not go to join his 'friends' but had run directly towards the main gates.

'I got the money.' Michael swung his arm lightly around a pretty half-caste girl who skinned her teeth at him in delight when she saw the twenty-pound note he was waving in his hand. She looked up through her dark sunglasses at the hill where Paula was watching Fabian. 'What a fool,' she said in a shrill, soulless voice.

She jumped up, trying to seize the note from Michael who waved it high above her head. In the end she pouted and started walking away from Michael. He ran up to her and slapped her bottom.

'Now, now, mistress, no tempers. This is to pay for my cigarettes and my Tennants, y'know.' He leered at her figure. 'But if you treat me right . . .'

They disappeared into the nearby off-licence to spend the money for Paula's sandals and Fabian's jacket on booze and fags.

chapter three

The sun was just beginning to sink below the horizon when a tall, muscular man crossed the road in a north London back street, far from any main road. He heard the sound of a police siren far off in the distance and stopped sharply, sucking in his breath. After making certain that the police car wasn't coming closer he started moving again, only faster. He turned the corner into the Edgerton estate, set in the more industrial area of Hackney Wick, where grey factories loomed in the distance and the East End smog hung low in the sky. The yellow-brick estate consisted of four blocks of flats, each five storeys high, facing one another across a large square lawn which had a neat children's play area with swings and slides in its centre.

As the man passed the play area, a few women eyed him suspiciously. He felt his chin. It was stubbly and rough. He rubbed his head, where his Kangol cap had been. His hair was dirty and uncombed. He needed a bath. He ran up three flights of stairs and walked along the landing, trying to remember which was Pearl's flat. At number seventeen he recognized the curtains. He pressed the bell. No answer. He looked through the letter-box.

'Pearl, Pearl.' He whispered her name hoarsely. 'Are you there?'

'It's no use, dear.'

The man jumped. He turned around to see a short, overweight woman.

'It's no use. She ain't been 'ome for days. Gone on 'oliday. Won't be back for a few weeks. Asked me to keep an eye on 'er flat for 'er. Taken the little 'un as well.'

He cursed.

'Life can't be that bad.' The old woman rubbed her back and watched. He noticed her staring at him and almost laughed. The whole situation was so ridiculous. He sighed heavily. He was a wanted man. The police were already on his back and the gunfight had made things worse. He couldn't go back to his place because they'd be waiting for him.

'Did you hear me, love?'

'Eh?'

'I was just saying, don't we all wish we could go on 'oliday to Jamaica for six weeks?'

'Yeah, yeah. Listen, I'll call roun' when Pearl's back.'

The woman cupped her hands to the window and stared through the curtains. 'She tidied up before she left, just as well. It's 'orrible to come back to a messy 'ouse, isn't it?' She turned around to find the man had gone, and looked out from the landing just in time to see him trudging back out of the Edgerton estate.

*

The washing cycle came to a finish and Shree got up to turn on the dryer. The doorbell rang just as she opened the door of the washing-machine. She made a face at being disturbed but went to see who it was.

'Oh, my God, Daddy, what's happened? You're a mess.'

Derrick looked down shamefacedly at his smeared and torn click suit. He held out his arms. 'I'm sorry to trouble you, baby.'

Derrick was given the hot meal Shree had been making for herself and then he was whisked into a hot, hot bath where he relaxed, letting all the stress and tension pass out of him. When he had shaved and changed into the spare set of clothes he had always left at Shree's for just such an emergency, she plonked herself down firmly on the sofa next to him and took his hand. She could sense something was very wrong.

'Tell me.'

A short time after Shree and her friends had left him at Hackney Downs, Derrick and the other men had got down to business.

The man who controlled the East London drug-dealing scene was known as Terror, big-built with small mean eyes and a lopsided grin that belied the unscrupulous, pitbull nature that was the secret of his success. In the Jamaican shanty-town where he grew up, Terror's role models had been the dons in his neighbourhood, and taking his cue from them he had mugged, murdered and bulldozed his way to one of the highest ranks in the business.

Until recently, Terror had been enjoying the good life. A craving for luxuries had led him into a life of baby-mothers, constant raving and lavish spending. But this decadent lifestyle had loosened his wits. As soon as he made a killing he spent it, his various gold-digging followers speedily cashing in on their realization that he had more money than sense.

Terror could no longer ignore the worsening state of affairs. He was losing his turf and his respect because of careless mistakes that had cost some men long jail sentences and caused fights between rival gangs. Terror saw his kingdom crumbling and knew he needed some-one to stabilize the business. That someone was Derrick. This choice was unexpected. Derrick wasn't one of the top-ranking dealers. He maintained a low-key racket from which he made a good living. He could be trusted with most operations but was generally considered to be on his way out and too old to handle high-profile jobs.

But Terror had been watching Derrick for weeks and had taken note of his natural business sense, the way he was liked and respected by all the men he worked with and above all the fact that Derrick had never been in prison, showing he had made few mistakes. So Terror had approached Derrick with the idea of getting Derrick to take over the running of his organization.

Derrick was not in a good mood that day. True, he'd appeared friendly enough with his daughter and her friends, but that was women. That day he'd already had to deal with street peddlers who tried to shortchange him. Fools. They didn't know say it was a yard' dem was dealing with. Still, a cold knife against their sweating skin and they had soon seen his point of view. But Derrick didn't like it when people tried to take him for a ride, it made him angry. So when Terror came to Derrick with his 'proposition' that Derrick should merge his racket into Terror's and start running the business of a 'bigger man', Derrick had not been amused.

He'd heard about the downroad Terror had been following and guessed his motives. Well, Derrick wasn't about to be used. This business went all possible ways and if Terror couldn't keep up he could just as soon go under, it wasn't Derrick's problem. He knew from experience that Terror was power-hungry with no feelings for anyone else.

Derrick refused Terror's offer point-blank, saying it would never work. He didn't need to give any reasons. When Derrick made up his mind, that was that. But some men only hear what they want to hear and Terror chose not to hear this. For once he had met his match. Derrick hadn't cowered when he'd faced him and this annoyed Terror. He had insisted and in the end tried to threaten Derrick. Derrick had betrayed no outward sign of emotion but he was insulted and angry. Even if Derrick changed his mind, he couldn't go back on his decision as this would lower him in the eyes of his men who now lounged around, looking on in interest. But Terror refused to see anything other than that he was not getting his own way. The veins in his neck began to stand out. He didn't have the gift of tact to soothe or lightning-quick wit with which to ridicule Derrick. His way was violence. Feelings of unease and inferiority slowly gave way to a slow-killing rage.

Derrick, on the other hand, seemed cool and calm. He was perfectly still except for the fact that his right ear twitched. Those of his crew who knew him could see the warning signs. Derrick's men began to slowly, almost unconsciously, position themselves behind him. One of them removed his heavy gold chaps and ear-clips, putting them safely away in the inside pocket of his jacket; another quickly drained the last of his Dragon Stout and gripped the bottle ready in his hand. They could tell something was up, and while to the ignorant observer they seemed still to be a part of the festivities, business was business.

The two men now faced each other, deadlocked. Terror's fists were clenched. No one spoke. Then Terror asked again, for the last time, with deliberate slowness. Derrick did not miss the bullying tone in Terror's words. He refused, for the last time, also with deliberate slowness. Terror, enraged by this refusal, took a step forward and spat savagely, straight in Derrick's face. The next few moments went so slowly that each second was like a minute. The saliva had landed on Derrick's left cheek and he could feel it sliding down his face as if it were red-hot. Trembling with rage, Derrick whipped out his revolver and blasted Terror in the chest. Twice.

The trouble didn't stop there. Terror hadn't come alone. He had brought his half-brother with him and some of his other crew were present. Derrick decided this was no time to make a stand since he knew his men were unarmed. He turned and fled into the woods that fringed the park. Derrick's crew, helpless without weapons, dispersed as soon as they saw him run. Terror's men chased Derrick through the trees and bushes, firing their own guns wildly. But Derrick had always been lucky. In the end he lost them by doubling back through

47

the undergrowth and disappearing into the heart of Hackney.

Derrick didn't sleep. He walked the streets all night as he'd planned what to do. He went to Pearl's flat because she was one of his ex-girlfriends and although they might not be together she would do anything to help him. But Pearl, one of the few people he could trust to keep his whereabouts a secret, had gone away. He didn't want to burden Shree with his problems but there was no one else.

There was silence for a long time in Shree's sitting-room. Shree wasn't shocked because she had known for most of her life how things stood with her father. But something icy-cold ran down her spine when she realized how close she'd come to losing the only person she had. She couldn't remember her mother. She had a few photos of a pretty young woman but she couldn't *remember* her. She tried often; her memories were half-fact, half-fantasy – being swung very high in soft hands, looking down into shining eyes full of laughter. She was quiet for so long that Derrick began to wonder if he had made a mistake in telling her everything. But as he got up to go, Shree put out her hand and held him back. 'What do I have to do?'

They talked for a long time. Derrick was surprised at his daughter's maturity and cool-headedness. Shree was pleased to discover she had a new importance in her father's life. Now she could do something for him. Before Derrick had walked through her front door they had been close. Now they were everything to each other.

Later that evening, under the cover of darkness, Derrick was heading for the open road again but with a difference. He had money in his pockets. He'd slept. He was no longer starving. Refreshed and strengthened, not only by the food and drink given to him but by Shree.

Shree was washing out the grimy bath that her father had left behind but her mind was not on her work. She was thinking about her dad. She knew it was going to be a long time before she saw him again. She lifted the scrap of paper off the floor. 'Bexley' was all it said. Somewhere in Bexley, Derrick was going to hide out, blending in with the scenery. For all Shree knew of Bexley it could have been Australia. Her hand shook slightly. Her father could be murdered or shot or anything and she would be the last person to hear. She felt isolated. She couldn't phone her father because he didn't have a place to stay and he had said a long time would pass before he contacted her. She couldn't go back to his place – he had told her not to – and anyway, it would probably be ransacked by now. And the worst, the very worst thing was that she couldn't tell anyone about the matter, because Derrick had sworn her to secrecy and while she considered Janice and Paula to be as close as sisters, there was family and then there was family. No, Shree had to bear this burden all on her own. The sponge slowly moved around the inside of the bath and despite Shree's resolution not to let the situation get her down, her lower lip trembled as she contemplated all that had just occurred.

*

Elroy's Peugeot sped down the long leafy street where Janice's family lived and parked under an acorn tree near the large semi-detached house.

'Turn down the music, Elroy, my dad could be in,' Janice said. Elroy glanced at the house before turning down the volume. Janice undid her seatbelt and kissed Elroy.

'When am I gonna see my favourite girl again?' he asked.

'When you think of a better "surprise" than the recording studio – as if I couldn't guess.'

'I'm sorry, it was a sly move. Next weekend I'll take you somewhere really smart.'

'Yeah, yeah,' said Janice, shaking her head.

'Are you going to stay at your aunt's place again tonight?' Elroy moved his hand from the clutch to Janice's knee.

'Yes, I am and no, Elroy, you've stayed nearly every night this week and I've had no sleep. Leave it for a few days.' Janice replaced Elroy's hand on the clutch.

'Damn, that's cold.' Elroy pretended to be crushed.

'I'll call you tonight.' Janice kissed him on his forehead before she opened the car door and got out. She ran up the garden path to the double-glazed sliding doors of the porch. From there she waved hard until Elroy drove out of sight.

'How's life, Mum? Those flowers look nice.' Janice's mother was inside the porch, looking down the road in the direction the car had gone. Janice strode past her mother through the open front door and into the house without waiting for a reply. She crossed the hall and peered into a mirror, smoothing her hair and retouching her make-up.

'Janice, who was dat me see driving you here?' Janice's mother was still in the sunny porch, upending a watering can over the rubber plants.

'Just Elroy, why?'

'Him nuh know fe slow down?'

'Calm yourself. He wasn't driving that fast.'

'It looked fast to me. One day, you two is going to crash as me keep saying.'

'You keep saying it but we never do.'

Her mother shook a warning finger. 'One day, chile.'

Rio, Janice's fifteen-year-old brother, came out of the sitting-room. He nodded his greeting to Janice and sat down on the stairs. He had originally been named Orvill, after a distant cousin who had been very successful, but no one had called him this since his first birthday, when Janice, a five-year-old at the time, confused by the tongue-twister, had nicknamed him Rio. The nickname had stuck, and there Rio sat, a boy of medium build and medium ability, looking up at his mother and his sister whom he was not overly pleased to see.

'Evening, Pops.' Janice smiled down indulgently at her father who lay sprawled out on the sofa, his newspaper scattered about his chest, his crumpled socks on the floor next to a glass of Jamaican rum. He raised his spectacles from his forehead at the sound of a voice. When he saw it was Janice, he grinned back and cleared a space next to him on the sofa. He kissed the cheek Janice offered him and slapped her on the shoulder.

'Somet'ing must be wrong fe you to visit us. What's wrong, chile? You need money?'

Janice laughed with him. 'No, Dad, but since you mention it . . .'

'I thought we was never gonna see you again. Just this morning, I said to Rose, now that our daughter has that flat, she's never coming back.'

'Well, I proved you wrong. How is the shop, business good?'

'Not so bad. So what did you come back for?'

'Sunday dinner and some clothes.'

'Young people today don't have no shame. Nuh true?' He said, laughing.

'Not just young people, Pops, look at you. Newspaper all over the place, socks everywhere, I'm surprised at *you*.'

Pops put on his glasses and looked around at the mess he had made. He scratched his head and changed the subject.

While all this was going on, Rio, who had followed Janice into the room, looked on jealously as he leaned against the wall. Janice was like the prodigal son. She could behave as badly as she wanted and stay out late and talk to her parents as rudely as she felt like but the minute she came back everyone lavished attention on her and ignored him. He made an exasperated noise and stomped out of the room and upstairs.

'Rio, come back and shut the door . . . Rio!' Janice's father shouted but the sound of a bedroom door slamming shut showed that Rio was unlikely to return.

'Did I say something wrong?' Janice asked.

Pops stood up and walked to the door, looking towards the stairs. 'Damn pickanny,' he muttered. 'I should run up there an' beat the feistyness out of that bwoy.'

'Stop your noise, Lloyd,' scolded Rose as she passed him in the corridor on her way back from watering the flowers in the porch. 'You know Rio is sulking because he's jealous of all the attention you're giving Janice. The only thing you should be doing is picking up those newspapers, it's nearly dinner-time.'

Lloyd sat back down on the sofa and scratched his head while Janice picked up the papers. 'I don't know why I bother. Everything I say, dat woman jump down my throat.'

Janice laughed, setting the glass of rum on the side table. 'Leave it to Mum, Pops,' she said, before leaving the room. 'She's always right in the end.'

Janice found her mother in the kitchen complaining to herself about her husband. 'Me nuh know how a man so foolish, heey?' She stirred the chicken that was stewing in a large saucepan. Janice found a space on the sideboard and sat herself there, legs dangling down. She watched her mother, small and chubby, efficiently opening a cupboard or putting away a jar of peppers. Sometimes she envied her for her security and her happiness. At other times Janice wondered how her mother coped. An egocentric husband, a troublesome teenage son, and herself. Janice laughed suddenly.

'Ah wha' sweet you?'

Janice had been thinking about Elroy and a sleazy joke he had told her that afternoon. She opened her

53

mouth to tell her mother the joke but then thought better of it, reflecting that it wasn't exactly something mother or her churchy friends would find amusing.

'What's Rio's problem these days?' she asked, gesturing upwards as, from upstairs, the loud sound of heavy hardcore could be heard.

'I don't know, to tell you the truth.' Rose looked a little weary and wiped her brow. 'He's just going from bad to worse. Going down at school, mixing wid all kind of ruffneck. Last week him get suspended from school.'

'Don't lie.'

'You know me never lie, it's the truth.'

'What did he do?'

'Rob some youth at his school of his money.'

'Huh? That doesn't sound like Rio. He's usually quite well-behaved.'

'I ask you. My son, a thief! Anyway, your father did beat him for that but Rio don't cater for anybody these days.'

'Well, it's the holidays now. He should calm down by the time he goes back.'

Rose handed Janice some hard-dough bread to butter and began to take out glasses and plates from one of the cabinets above the sideboard.

'All we can do is trust in God our father. Without Him we would all be lost at sea. Yessir. Sister Nelson always said to me—'

Janice yawned. 'I went to the all-dayer at Hackney Downs on Saturday and somebody got shot,' she said.

'You is always looking for excitement and trouble. I'm sure all the decent people there left long before anybody got shot. I remember the day when young girls used to spend their Saturdays shopping with their mothers, helping to cook the dinner and tidy up the house.'

'Never mind about that, when we were going home, these boys started following us in their car and we were really scared.'

'With some of the clothes you wear, Janice, it doesn't surprise me. I'm sure you was wearing tight shorts or a miniskirt with no tights. I keep telling you that you should cover yourself up, but you don't listen to me. One of these days something bad's gonna happen to you.'

'You worry too much, Mum.'

The smell of food drew the males to the kitchen in next to no time. First Rio came in and sat down at the table, then Pops, rubbing his hands and picking his teeth. It made Janice feel it was just like old times. They all sat around the little table while Pops blessed the meal and Rio made faces at Janice until she nearly choked with laughter.

'So tell me more about what's happening at the shop, Dad?' she said.

'Well, it's still not as good as the golden years, but we having a paint promotion at the moment and that's bringing in plenty buyers. Everyone seems to be staying home this summer and painting their house.'

'Isn't it about time you painted the living-room, Lloyd?' Rose asked sharply.

'It doesn't need any painting, Rose, you is too fussy.'

'It's in a real state. I think you should get to work next weekend.'

'Rose, me back hurt me too much and the shop is wearing me out. When I is not on the counter, I is in the back doing the paperwork.'

'You is just bone-idle. All you do in that shop is gossip with the customers. Never mind, Rio will have to do it.'

'You must be joking,' said Rio. 'I'm a busy man. As if I have time to be running up and down a ladder.'

'You're just like your father. It's only through God's goodness why I never abandoned you two long ago.'

'Mum's right. I'm the only one with sense in this family,' said Janice, smirking at Rio.

'I only hope you're keeping Sarah's flat nice and clean until the lady comes back.'

'Of course I am.'

'Don't let anyone smoke in the flat because you're so careless, you might cause a fire.'

'Janice is a good girl,' said Pops.

'You can just shut up. You've said enough rubbish for today. Janice is too young and flighty to live on her own. I don't know what she gets up to with those friends of hers and that foolish Elroy.'

'Elroy's not fool—'

'That foolish Elroy doesn't know his head from his foot. He's a deejay and we all know what that means. I hope you're not sleeping with him, Janice.'

'Of course not,' said Janice, looking at her plate.

'Well, I will soon find out because I'm going to pay a surprise visit on you sometime this week. I have the spare key so you'd better make sure that flat is in tip-top condition every hour of the day.' Having said her piece, Rose continued eating.

'I was thinking about finding a job,' Janice announced brightly to her family. Rio snorted into his lemonade, her parents just carried on eating as if Janice had never spoken.

'I was thinking about finding a job,' she repeated loudly.

'Oh, that's nice, dear.' Rose's wavering tone did not exactly ring with conviction.

'Yeah, well, don't boost me too much,' Janice said sarcastically.

'Are you serious?' Rio leaned across the table towards her.

'No, you fool, I said it because I thought it would be a good joke.'

'It is.'

Janice reached out and thumped her brother who raised his fists to fight back.

'Rio, don't be so rude. You is not wid your cruff-friends dem now.' Rio subsided. 'Now, Janice, what sort of job is it you 'a search for *this* time?'

'What do you mean, this time?' Janice asked. 'Like you don't think I'm going to do it.'

Rose was frustratingly slow in finishing the food in her mouth because she didn't really want to get into this argument.

'Mum!'

'Don't bother shouting at me, pickanny. Just because you no longer under my roof doesn't mean say you is a big woman yet.'

Janice rolled her eyes at the ceiling. When her mother didn't want to answer a question she always started little arguments. Janice kissed her teeth. She turned to face her father who had been concentrating on his drumsticks. Lloyd had been through these scenes with mother and daughter so often he knew them by heart. So when Janice turned to him for support he decided that silence was the best policy.

'Dad, tell Mum!' No response, just the steady chew, chew on a drumstick.

'Dad!'

'Oh, what? You say something, Janice?' The two eyes turned towards Janice were wide with sleepy innocence.

'Don't try it, Dad. I hate it when you pretend you can't hear me.'

Lloyd scratched his head nervously. He always came off worse in these family tiffs. 'Me nuh kno', dear. If you say you can get a job then you must can get a job, yes?' Lloyd muddled on unwillingly, not really sure of what he was supposed to say and getting the prickly feeling that he wasn't helping the situation. 'Me nuh kno' what you can do from what you can't do. Me nuh see what harm you can do by getting a job from not getting a job. Me nuh—'

'Shut up your mouth, Lloyd, because no sense nuh come outta it.' Lloyd, glad to be able to return to his drumsticks, shut up.

'Janice, your father was trying to say the same thing that I have been trying to tell you ever since you left that school of yours.'

'But I—'

Rose stopped Janice with a wave of her broad hand. 'No, Janice, the trouble with you is that you can't take the talking-to. If you could just forget about your fool-

fool friends for a minute, you would see what me talking about. How many times have you come to me, telling me how you gwan get this job and you gwan try for that job?'

'Only once or twice.' If Janice had the complexion to go red she would have been bright as a beet. Even as she said it she knew it was a lot more.

'But see a my God! Once or twice! What foolishness you a brock 'pon me earhole. A good six or seven, me love.' Janice glared in indignation as her mother clapped her hands, laughing loudly.

'No!'

Rose stood up and began clearing up the dishes, shaking her head, still giggling to herself. 'Once or twice. Heh, hey!'

Back at her aunt's flat, Janice pulled her jumper over her head. It was only ten o'clock but she had decided to go to bed early for once. She put on a Keith Sweat album and went into the bathroom. When she was dressed for bed she went into the bedroom and opened the french doors on to the balcony. Standing outside, she looked across at the houses and flats of the small estate spread out beneath her third-floor flat. The first night she had spent in the flat, she had thought how pretty the window lights had looked, flickering, sometimes switching on, sometimes going out. They were still pretty but they had lost their glow for her. Even though it was quite late, it was still noisy. Janice could hear car doors slamming and voices as one family went into their house. Although she couldn't see the people involved, she could hear a heated argument going on in one of the flats below, while someone above was playing their rock music very loudly. The air still smelled of Sunday dinners, roast chicken, potatoes and fried fish.

Janice climbed into bed and pulled the duvet up around her, patting the empty spot next to her. She wondered if she should bell Elroy or one of her spars. Yawning, Janice decided it would hold. Resting her head on the pillow, she thought back indignantly to her family's reaction to her declaration. She felt upset that no one had believed in her and bigged her up and told her to go for it. Janice had always looked down the tiniest bit on Paula and Shree, although she would never have admitted it, because she was the one who'd come out of school with decent grades, unlike them, and she was the one who came from a good, stable family background. Now she found herself classed with them, not really heading anywhere, interested only in parties and boyfriends.

Janice decided that perhaps this time she would look a little harder for a job. Things couldn't go on as they were. She reached over and switched off the light. Worn out by her exciting but tiring weekend, she drifted off into a dreamless sleep.

chapter
four

Monday morning dawned cold and grey. Nevertheless, Janice had woken with a sense of purpose and bounded out of her bed and into the bathroom. Today was the day she was going to find a job and prove everybody wrong.

She stood outside the Islington Job Centre under her umbrella and took a deep breath. Then she closed the umbrella, pushed open the glass doors and walked in.

It was warm and busy inside. Janice looked around the crowded reception area and the people sitting down stared back at her. Three Indian women chatted loudly in a group. A white woman wearing a faded leather jacket sat with her hands stuffed in her jacket pockets, staring at the floor. Most of the people were men in their late twenties and early thirties. A black man talked in low tones with a fat white man. An older, bald man sitting alone occupied himself by shredding one of the various leaflets scattered on the low tables in front of him. A young man, lounging in a chair near the entrance doors, began trying to catch Janice's eye. Embarrassed, she hurried over to the panels where the jobs were advertised.

Janice had already decided on the kind of job she wanted and so headed straight for the secretarial section. On the way she picked up a few forms and took a pen from her handbag. She was pleasantly surprised by the number of vacancies: receptionist, office junior, secretary. Some of the jobs sounded interesting. Secretaries were wanted by a hotel in Highbury, by a shipping company in the Docklands and by a solicitor's firm in the Angel, but these companies wanted older and more experienced people. Janice wrote down some references and then went to get a ticket from the machine on the wall. Her number was forty-eight. She glanced up at the display box which read twenty-eight – it was going to be a long wait. She was supposed to be at Paula's in half an hour.

She walked over to the reception area to find herself a seat, deliberately avoiding the gaze of the brazen young man sitting opposite. She looked over at the administration assistants. Four of them were at their desks, which faced the reception area in rows. Three were men, two black and one white, and there was one white woman. Janice looked at the leaflets on the table. They were all about unemployment benefit and retraining schemes. She watched a young woman struggling to turn her pram around while looking at the job advertisements. She seemed tired and fed up. Janice felt sorry for her. Two young white women came over and sat down next to Janice.

'This is the third time this month that I've 'ad to come in 'ere, Emma. The waiting's driving me mad,' said one.

'Didn't you find any jobs, then?' asked the other.

'Oh, yeah. I found a few, but I didn't get past the interviews.'

'Lucky you! I haven't found anything yet.'

'Still looking for nursery work?'

'Yeah, I guess.'

'You won't find anything in 'ere. Trust me. It's best to check in the papers.'

'You think so?'

'Yeah. All they 'ave in 'ere is plumbing, decorating and clerical work, unless you're really lucky. What references 'ave you got there?'

'I couldn't find anything. I'm just going to ask one of them for advice.'

'Oh, they won't 'elp you. They'll just make you look again an' then you'll be 'ere all day.'

The doors opened and a middle-aged man came in, shaking his umbrella.

'Look at that man who just come in.'

'What about 'im?'

'Well, what's 'e comin' in 'ere for? He's a bit old to be looking for work.'

'D'ya think so?'

''Course. He looks about fifty an' once you're over forty-five, it's really 'ard to find a job.'

'Which section is he looking at?' The two women looked to see where the man had gone.

'I think it's accountancy.'

'He looks like a City bloke. You don't usually see them in 'ere.'

'I wonder if he's married.'

'Liz, you're terrible.' The women laughed.

'Aw, this queue is really buggin' me. I've gotta get home and tidy up before Nick gets back.'

'It's that woman.'

'Which one?'

'The Indian one, talking to the white man. She's been in that chair for ages.'

'He probably fancies 'er, that's why. They do that a lot in 'ere as well. Spend time with the people they fancy. The woman officers are the worst at that.'

'I know. Look at that woman over there with the baby.'

'So what?'

'I'm glad I'm not in 'er position. Can you imagine lookin' for job with a kid?'

'Well, maybe 'er mum looks after it.'

'My mum always used to say to me, "Emma, never 'ave any kids until you've got a job because I won't be 'ere to look after 'em."'

'I don't know why they do it.'

'It's just stupidity, that's all. Look at that boy, sitting near the doors.'

'The one with the blond 'air?'

'That's the one. What do you think he does?'

'Well, he's quite young an' he's good-looking, looks a bit like the car mechanic in the jeans adverts.'

'No, he's too clean for that. I think he looks like the postman type.'

'He's a pervert, do you see the way he's lookin' at all the legs of all the young girls who come in 'ere?'

'Disgusting. If I ever caught my Nick doing that, I'd slap 'im in the face and then I'd leave 'im.'

''Course.'

'Forty-eight.' When her number was called Janice jumped to her feet and walked over to the free administration officer's desk.

'Hello, how may I help you?'

'Well, I'm Janice Williams. I left school at sixteen and then I did a typing course at college and now I'm looking for a job. I picked out these ones.' Janice laid the forms she had filled out on the desk.

The white man scratched his head. 'How many references do you have there?'

'Oh, I dunno, about eight, I think.'

'Well, that's the thing, you see. We are only supposed to deal with two job references per person in order to keep queues down.'

'I've been waiting ages!'

'Perhaps if we go quickly we can get through them all.' The man tapped away at the computer keyboard on the desk.

'Okay, well, how old are you?'

'Nineteen.'

'Well, your first choice specifies that they want someone aged twenty or over – however, let's move on to their other requirements. How much audio-typing experience do you have?'

Janice chewed her lip, wondering whether she should lie.

The man put his pen down and turned away from the computer screen to face Janice. 'Now, look here, it's one thing to stretch your age but these are real facts. Have you done *any* audio-typing?'

'Yes, but I don't have any experience.'

'Hmm. Okay, let's give them a ring and see what

they think.' The man picked up the phone and dialled a number while Janice bit her finger-nails. When he had finished the conversation and replaced the receiver he wrote on a pad. Then he tore off the sheet of paper and handed it to Janice together with a large form.

'Okay, they aren't too bothered about your age and they would like you to send in your CV as well as this application form when you've filled it out.'

'That's grea—'

'This next one is the office junior position, right?' asked the man. Janice nodded.

The man entered the reference into the computer. 'Too late, there's an asterisk which means that the vacancy has already been filled.'

'Just my luck.'

'Let's move on.' He looked at his watch and then at the queue before picking up the next form. 'This company wants a typing speed of forty words per minute for the receptionist post. Is that going to be a problem?' Janice shook her head. 'Okay, they also want you to have a good telephone manner.'

'Safe, er, I mean that's fine,' said Janice.

The administration officer pretended not to hear this as he tapped the reference into the computer. 'They would prefer somebody with A-levels or at least experience – but don't worry, we'll give them a call and see what can be done.'

He phoned the company. When he had finished talking he looked up at Janice. 'Okay, they don't mind about the A-levels or the experience so long as you can type well and have a nice phone manner. They'll give you an interview tomorrow at eleven if you can make it.

I have to ring back in five minutes to confirm it. That gives us time to go over one more job reference.'

'That's good, isn't it, about the interview?'

'That depends on whether you get the job. I'm afraid this last job has been filled too, it's asterisked.'

'I guess that's what the recession is about,' said Janice.

'That's true. You have to be quick around here as the good jobs go really quickly.'

The man telephoned the company to confirm Janice's interview. 'Okay, here's the firm's address and their phone number. That's the time of the interview and there is a list of things you are required to bring with you.' He ripped off the sheet and handed it to Janice who smiled her thanks. 'Try to be punctual. Do you have a smart skirt or dress?'

'Yes, I think I can manage that,' said Janice.

'Good. Don't wear those headphones around your neck, don't wear trainers and – er – good luck.'

'Thanks a lot.'

'Fifty-two!' Another member of the unemployed stood ready to sit in the chair Janice was vacating. She folded the papers and put them in her handbag before heading for the door. She looked at the clock before leaving. It was a quarter past twelve. She was supposed to have been at Paula's flat thirty minutes ago.

'What do you want a job for anyway?'

Janice looked around at her friends, confused. This wasn't the reaction she had been expecting. She had joined Shree at Paula's flat. The other two had been waiting for her.

'What do you want a job for?' Paula repeated her question.

Janice looked to Shree for support. Shree was pre-occupied with counting out her money. 'I wanted to do something with my life,' Janice replied weakly.

'Answering phones for some company isn't exactly what I call doing something,' Shree pointed out.

'Well, excuse me for thinking you'd be happy for me. I see I came to the wrong place.'

'Your timing's not perfect, Jan, but it's not that. What do you expect us to say?' Paula said, unperturbed.

Everyone was getting bored of the subject so Janice gave up, but she failed to see where she had gone wrong. Her mother moaned that she wasted her time doing nothing of consequence. Today she had done something, and all her friends could do was complain that she had not spent the morning with them.

Janice took a couple of deep breaths, straightened her suit and knocked on the door of the interview room. Think positive, Janice tried to tell herself, but inside a little voice was telling her how humiliated she would be in front of her crew and family if she didn't get the job. She knocked again, this time with more determination.

'Come in.'

She entered a small grey room. Behind a large desk sat a woman who looked tired and unenthusiastic. She smiled unconvincingly at Janice who walked over to the empty chair opposite the desk and sat down.

Janice emerged from the interview depressed. She'd

done badly. Most of the time she hadn't understood what the woman was talking about. She had jumbled her words and looked everywhere but at the woman.

'Thank you for coming. We'll let you know,' the woman had said in a bored voice as Janice had left the room.

'Going down, miss?' Janice nodded dispiritedly to the uniformed lift operator who smiled at her kindly.

'Wait! Hold the lift!' A young man ran through the closing doors into the lift. He nodded his thanks to the lift operator.

'Going down, sir?' the operator enquired.

'Yes, that's right,' the young man replied, putting down his briefcase and leaning back against the mirrored walls of the lift. He was mixed race, handsome and well groomed. His hair, naturally curly, was cut very close to his head. He wore an expensive executive suit and his briefcase was of high-quality leather. He had a confident, intelligent air about him and seemed friendly. At any other time Janice would have been interested but she was fed up and couldn't care less. The man, on the other hand, could. He decided Janice was more sexy than pretty with her slim figure and her smooth, rich, dark skin and heavy eyelashes. Eyeing her tight-fitting suit but seeing no briefcase, he assumed she was new to the company. He coughed, trying to catch her eye. It didn't work. He smiled, but got no smile in return. Piqued, he turned away as the lift descended the last few floors.

'Ground floor!'

Janice walked away from the lift towards the revolving doors. She didn't realize that she was being followed by the handsome young man who couldn't resist this challenge and decided that he just had to know the name of this unfriendly beauty.

'Excuse me, lady!'

Janice turned around.

'You forgot something,' the man said, with a twinkle in his eye.

'I'm sure I have everything,' Janice said, checking for her handbag.

'No, what I mean is you forgot to tell me your name.'

Janice looked at him questioningly and then smiled. 'Janice Williams,' she said.

'Maurice Haccinene Junior.'

They shook hands, the man deciding as he did so that Janice had the most beautiful smile he had ever seen. Taking advantage of the smile, he walked with her across the reception area and through the revolving doors. Once outside the building he pointed to a small but expensive-looking café across the road. As he extended his hand, Janice's eyes caught the sparkle of his white-gold watch.

'May I invite you to lunch with me?'

'Sure,' replied Janice. As she followed him down the steps she decided her depression could be postponed for an hour or two.

During lunch Janice discovered that Maurice was one of the company's high-flying accountants. She also found out that he was well educated, having been to a good university, and she admitted to herself that he was a refreshing change from a certain someone who was always talking about raves or music. Janice in turn told Maurice about her interview for the receptionist job.

'Don't lose hope. This company goes in for equal opportunities quite a lot. Being black won't be such a great obstacle here.'

'So where are you from?'

'I'm English.'

'Oh, no, I mean where are your origins?' explained Janice.

'Well, my father is Nigerian and my mother is English.'

'So you're not exactly English then, are you?'

'That depends upon one's point of view. I've lived here all my life and I've never been to Nigeria so I consider myself to be English.'

'I suppose so, anyway you're an English citizen so, yes, I see.'

'Well, where are your "roots"?' Maurice asked, smiling.

'Oh, I'm Jamaican,' Janice said proudly, even though she had been born in the Royal Free Hospital in Hampstead, London.

Maurice did not look very impressed. 'Oh, right.'

'Do you go raving much?'

'Raving? No, I generally stay away from those places.'

'Oh,' said Janice, unable to hide her disappointment.

'No, see my point of view before you judge me,' he continued. 'I didn't get to my position by constant raving. I'm here because of hard, solid work. If black people could only open their eyes and see how their time could be put to better use, the black nation would be a different one.'

Janice said nothing.

'You're different than the others, Janice. You're looking for a job, doing something with your life. I admire you for that.' He moved his hand across the table, gently placing it over Janice's hand which she immediately removed.

'Which part of London are you from?'

'Well, my parents live in Highbury, near Highbury Fields, but at the moment I'm staying in my aunt's flat in Dalston, while she's in Jamaica – and you?'

'I rent a bachelor pad in Chelsea.'

'That sounds posh.'

'It might sound like that to you but I'm used to it.'

Not knowing what to say, Janice picked up her orange juice and sipped it slowly.

'So what do you do in your free time, Janice, when you're not partying?'

'I hang out with my friends or I spend time with my family.'

'No boyfriend, then?' Janice gave a nervous laugh and shook her head.

'I see. But you don't strike me as the shy wallflower.'

'You didn't strike me as the stay-at-home type either, but I was wrong there.'

'*Touché*,' said Maurice, grinning. Then he glanced at his watch and sighed. 'I'm afraid my lunch break is over, but I'd really like to see you again.'

'Why?'

'You're beautiful and intelligent. Like me.' He laughed. 'Only joking, but I've got a strong feeling you're going to be working here soon anyway. Wouldn't it make sense to have a friend in high-up places?' He smiled engagingly.

'Okay.' Janice wrote down her phone number in his personal organizer and walked to the tube station with her head in the clouds. She was seriously impressed. It was only later when sitting on the tube on her way home that she decided not to enlighten Elroy about her new 'friend'.

chapter five

'Damn!'

The suede shoulder-bag hit the growing heap of bags and wallets and purses on the rug in the centre of the room. Shree scratched her head, wondering where else there was to look. This was the third time she had turned her flat upside-down searching for money. She sat down to contemplate her findings spread out on the side table. A few tattered ten-pound notes and some change. This was all the money she possessed. It had been over three weeks since her dad had disappeared and she hadn't heard anything. Shree bit her lip. She had always taken it for granted that everything was provided for her by her father. Clothes, bills, food, pocket money, her car, had all come from him. The unemployment benefit she collected had been mere petrol money compared to the amounts he had given her.

Something clattered through the letter-box. Shree ran to the door, wondering if it was a letter from her dad. It was a final notice for an unpaid electricity bill. She sighed. It would have to be paid. No more going out for a while. No more new clothes. No more jewellery.

The doorbell sounded. Shree reached out and turned the latch. Tyrone was back.

A young, light-skinned man followed Shree into the sitting-room. He was of average height, very handsome, with his hair curled and styled into a ski-slope. He was dressed casually in baggy trousers and a sweater.

'Oh, come on, Shree. Look, from when you were supposed to be ready? Shree? Shree, don't say you forgot.'

'Have I missed something?'

'Yes, that's right, stupid, the Community Centre having an all-dayer today. We're meeting Aston down there and Wesley and that lot.'

'Good for you. I don't know them. They're all your friends.'

Tyrone shook his head sarcastically. 'What's all this, Shree?' he asked, staring at the pile of bags in the middle of the room. He picked his way around them and dropped on to a chair.

'I was trying to find some money,' Shree replied, sitting down herself and putting her head in her hands. 'I am so broke.' She threw the electricity bill over to Tyrone who glanced at it carelessly before dropping it on to the floor.

'I don't know what I'm going to do.' She looked to Tyrone for an answer.

'Listen, sugar. If I had the money to give you, I would. You're a big girl and you know how things are. I've got clothes to buy and places to go. Now, if I gave all my dollars to you ...' Tyrone leaned back and balanced the chair on two legs. He smiled, thinking about all the things he wanted to spend his 'dollars' on. 'You see, babes?'

Shree didn't say anything. Actually, she didn't see. Tyrone and she had been moving together for the past eight months. He had been staying at her flat for a few days here and there, sharing her bed, eating her food, using her car, borrowing her money too, even though he earned himself an okay wage as a part-time hairdresser. Yet he couldn't even lend her five pounds.

Tyrone, thinking he had played the considerate lover long enough, leaned over and poked Shree in the shoulder. 'Come on, Shree, they'll start cussing me if we turn up too late. Aston's got some wicked beats that I wanna check. Where are the car keys?'

'Over by the window,' Shree said, pointing.

Grabbing the keys off the window-sill, Tyrone strode past Shree and out of the front door, calling over his shoulder, 'Move yourself, woman.'

Tyrone's hobby was deejaying and recording music. He pursued this on his days off and some evenings at Profile Community Centre. The Centre was a large hall at the end of a blind alley off Essex Road. As she stood by the entrance, Shree could hear the faint sound of music and someone, or someones, shouting. Tyrone pushed at the door. It was firmly closed. He banged the knocker loudly, several times. The door opened and Shree and Tyrone walked into a dark, narrow corridor.

'Wha' 'appen, rude bwoy?'

'You safe, Aston? How come the door was locked?' Tyrone and the boy who had opened the door touched fists in greeting. Shree said nothing but smiled shyly. Aston turned to her, anxious to meet the new beauty.

'There's too many people in there. We're having to turn people away. And who's this, star?'

'Mine.' Tyrone put his arm firmly around Shree's waist and met Aston's eyes over her head. A sure sign of ownership.

They entered the hall which was large and circular. The high ceiling was criss-crossed by wooden beams. The place was packed with people who were watching someone Shree couldn't see yet. The music was very loud.

To the right of the entrance was an area sectioned off by long wooden cupboards. These were now being used as seating. A few small kids ran around, in and out of the crowd, playing their own private games. There was a smattering of young parents either attending to their young or watching the performance with interest. The crowd was mostly teenagers, many of whom were standing or balancing on battered chairs. No one paid any attention to the newcomers.

Shree had an intense desire to find out what they were watching. 'Tyrone, let's go into the crowd to see who's performing.'

'You go. I'm going to the decks with Aston to do some deejaying.'

'I'll come and find you there later, then.' Leaving Aston and Tyrone at the hall entrance, she dived into the thickest part of the crowd. Using all her wiles, she at last poked her head out at the front and could see what it was all about.

There was one light-skinned boy, lanky with a

pinched face. He was chatting into a mike. He wore a popular style of click suit and the equally popular trainers. Next to him was a large, dark and not very nice-looking boy about the same age. He was the rapper. They bopped around in front of two large speakers from which their voices boomed across the hall. Having had the misfortune to find herself near one of the speakers, Shree was nearly deafened by the noise, but decided, once her ears had adapted, that she liked it.

As the track finished the hall erupted with loud whoopings, catcalls and general pandemonium. The two boys, not at all surprised by the reception, immediately took advantage of the situation and began handing out T-shirts and flyers and other freebies. Shree moved with the flow. She wanted one of those safe T-shirts. Perspiring, she fought her way towards them, and it was only later, as she flopped down exhausted on a chair, hugging her prized trophy to her chest, that she wondered if it had been worth the struggle.

Tyrone was in his own little world, hidden behind a pair of oversized headphones and two large turntables, happily scratching and mixing his way to deejay heaven. Shree watched him and smiled fondly. Tyrone was just a little boy at heart. As if somehow knowing he was being watched Tyrone raised his head slightly and gave Shree a grin before returning to his beloved beats.

'All right, can we have a lickle stoosh now?' Aston had the mike and was waving his arms around for attention. The hubbub ceased and people once again began clustering around the microphone. 'The evening nuh finish yet. It's free mike now, so any of you feel to make a stand it's your time now.'

Most people looked at each other and laughed at such a ridiculous proposition. A few of them, however, began forming a queue next to the mike. Four boys and one girl. The girl looked very shy and small next to the boys.

The first boy took up the mike. He was tall and large with funky dreads. He was a wicked rapper. After a few verses he handed on the mike and merged into the crowd. The next boy was a rather ugly, wiry young man who had a sort of unwashed, untidy look about him. The first thing that struck Shree as he grabbed the microphone was his disgusting finger-nails. His rapping did not greatly redeem him. His brethren seemed to like it but Shree couldn't understand one word and it sounded like acid music gone wrong.

The girl was the last one on the mike. She was a fairly pretty black girl who seemed to be new in the place. Shree looked around for the girl's crew. She only seemed to have one friend in the crowd – a pretty, slightly older girl who looked partly Asian, partly white, a little black, it was difficult to tell. She looked anxious as her friend nervously took hold of the mike.

When she began rapping, the shy small girl was transformed into a def little performer with tough style and meaningful lyrics. She finished off out of breath but well satisfied with her applause. She gave back the microphone to Aston and melted into a corner of the crowd where her spar congratulated her. She was not allowed to disappear by the boys who came up to ask their names and find out how advanced they were in the rapping business. In conversation with them, the two girls revealed that they were in a group together, wrote their own lyrics and were now looking to make a track.

Their naive optimism made Shree a bit wistful, reminiscing over the days when she, Janice and Paula had cherished their own dreams.

'I see we meet again, precious.'

Shree felt a heavy hand on her shoulder and turned to face a large and earnest dreadlocked man. She flashed back to when they had the nasty encounter with the men in the black Mercedes on the day of the Hackney Downs all-dayer. She returned to the present reluctantly, looking around for a means of escape.

To her surprise the dreadlocked man was smiling, as if admitting that circumstances did lend to the humour somewhat. As he smiled, Shree decided he didn't look nearly so bad, in fact she thought he looked quite pleasant, sort of sweet as his gold teeth winked from behind his smile.

'What can I say?' He held out his hands, weighted down with gold.

'I'm not exactly laughing at you. I'm just remembering that day, the all-dayer, a-and that stupid car chase,' Shree said, covering her mouth with her hand. They both cracked up.

'I'm sorry about me friend dem, foolish like me nuh kno' what.'

'That's right,' Shree agreed, but she was not angry. He pulled up a chair for her and took one for himself. They sat down.

'Anyway, before you disappear again, me call Nero.' He displayed his thick, ropy gold chain which had a broad, smooth link displaying the capitals N-E-R-O.

'Shree,' she said, staring, mesmerized, at the huge gold chain.

'I prefer Precious. Or maybe, Princess.'

Shree looked at the floor. If anyone else had said this to her she would have known exactly how to stem such lyricism, but Nero said it with sincerity as if he really meant it and wasn't just speeching her. She didn't know how to answer.

'Do you know Tyrone?' She pointed to her boyfriend on the other side of the hall.

'Your man?'

'Yes.'

'Me nuh care.' The yardie looked deep into her eyes. When he wanted something he didn't stop because of small, unimportant things like boyfriends, and he had wanted Shree, since the moment he had looked out of the car at the traffic lights, more than he had ever wanted any girl before. Shree felt something of this desire and while it flattered and thrilled, it also frightened her. She had seen too much of what yardies could do.

She changed the subject hurriedly. 'So how you find yourself here?'

'Me reach wid me nephew, Eugene.' He pointed across the room to a pool table where two raggas were involved in a game. The one to whom he referred was very scruffy but quite fit. He looked about fifteen but all the same a cigarette dangled from the corner of his mouth.

'I wasn't doing nuthin' and he wanted to watch dem youths on the mike, so me just come.' He looked around. 'It's not really my scene.'

'I know what you mean, it's not my scene either. It's too busy and there are too many kids running around.'

'True, so why did you come?'

'Well, I promised my boyfriend I'd come.'

'Dat your man a call you now?' Shree turned to where the yardie was pointing. A frenzied Tyrone was jumping up and down, trying to catch Shree's attention.

'Maybe I'll see you around.' Shree stood up.

'Count on it, precious.' Nero gripped her soft small hand with his own big hardened and scarred one. Shree felt unsure and flustered. She smiled and tried to wiggle her hand away but Nero was gripping it too tight. She met his eyes again, this time with a pleading look in hers. Nero laughed and released her hand. He stood up and walked over to the pool table to watch his nephew's game.

'Shree, who was that man?' Tyrone asked as they left the Centre.

'Oh, just someone I know.'

'Oh.' Tyrone left it alone, but he was quiet all the way back to Shree's car.

Shree dropped Tyrone off at the Rocket Club in Holloway where he had to check for a friend or two. Then she decided to call on Paula. As she drove through dusty Holloway, she was surprised by the number of teenagers on the street. Most of them seemed to be heading towards Fairplay, a small but popular amusement arcade on the High Street. It seemed to be packed out with raggas. Shree had moved on from such things but she remembered going there a few times, a year or two ago, and it had been like a home from home for Tyrone. Stuck in heavy traffic on Holloway Road, she watched the comings and goings of the young arcade addicts. A youth who looked familiar bounded out of Fairplay. Shree looked closer. She knew the boy.

She leaned across the passenger seat and wound down the window. 'What ya saying, Rio?'

'Looking good, Shree.' Rio bowled over to the car. Trying to act the bad bwoy, thought Shree.

'I didn't figure on you haunting such places, Rio,' Shree joked.

'Following in my sister's footsteps.' They both chuckled.

'Talking 'bout your sister, do you know how that interview business went?'

'Nah. She hasn't been home. Can't take the shame, I guess.'

'Rio, you should have faith in your sister.'

'No, I'm not knocking her, I'm just joking.' The traffic began to move slowly forward.

'Stay safe, Rio.'

'Later, Shree.' Rio bowled straight back into Fairplay. Shree accelerated and followed the slow line of traffic up to Islington.

People were looking tired as they spilled out from tube stations. The sun had lost its sharp brightness and was hazy and hung heavy and sleepy in the sky, but it was still warm. It was just after seven as Shree turned her car into Paula's untidy estate. The refuse hadn't been collected and rubbish from the overflowing bins was starting to blow around. Some boys were playing football by the garages. Shree parked her car where she would be able to see it from Paula's balcony. She locked it carefully, double-checking the doors.

Paula shifted around on the sofa. She prided herself on being a good listener, but hearing the story of Janice's day for the third time was more than even she could stand.

'So he said you're beautiful and intelligent, just like me, and I thought that was – Paula? Paula, are you listening to me?'

Paula aroused herself from her stupor. 'Oh, what? Oh, yeah, carry on.'

Janice glared at Paula from her chair. 'Anyway, where was I?'

'You said he took out his Rolex and—'

'Don't be stupid, Paula. Weren't you listening to a word I said?'

Paula mimed the word 'No.'

'I was saying that he—'

The doorbell rang. Paula got up from the sofa and hurried to the door.

'Paula, I know I'm your spar but that's as far as it goes,' Shree joked, wondering what she had done to deserve a smothering embrace from her friend. Paula half-closed the door behind her with the air of a conspirator.

'It's Janice. She won't stop talking about some wonderful rich man she's met. She's told me the story three times already. Thank God you're here. She's driving me mad.'

Shree peered over Paula's shoulder towards the front room where Janice sat looking at one of Paula's magazines. Shree raised her eyebrows and Paula responded by raising her own. Exhaling deeply, Paula and Shree went back inside and shut the door.

Shree took off her denim jacket and threw it on the chair she was about to sit in. 'So come on, Jan, what's this I've been hearing about some new material you're dealing with?'

'Oh, for God's sake!' Paula said as she strode out of the room. Seconds later she reappeared, armed with her Walkman and clutching many much-loved tapes to her chest. Smiling sweetly, she settled herself down on the sofa. Fabian, colouring in some pictures while watching the television, giggled. He loved it when Shree, Janice and his mum argued.

'So roll wid it, gal!'

'Well . . .' Janice took a deep breath and told Shree exactly what she had told Paula. Shree listened carefully.

When Janice had finished she looked up, expecting to see Shree as happy and excited as she was. But Shree's expression was worried and serious. 'What about Elroy?'

'That's what I've been trying to point out all day, honey,' Paula said, switching off the Walkman.

'What Elroy doesn't know can't hurt him.'

'Maybe, but when he finds out . . .'

'Listen, right, maybe some things just weren't meant to be. Elroy and me, we just don't think the same any more. Let's just say, before, we did. But then one of us grew up and one stayed back.'

Shree bit her lip. 'Elroy really loves you, y'know.'

'Yeah,' Paula interjected heatedly.

'He'll have forgotten about me in a day or two.'

'You're pure evil,' Paula said seriously. 'You know that's a lie and even so, you're doing Elroy bad.'

'He loves my body, he loves the way – anyway, he doesn't love *me*. He doesn't appreciate the things I need.'

'And what exactly is it that you need?' demanded Paula.

'I need someone who is going to be able to look

after me. Treat me right. I want someone who has a job, who's doing something with their life. I mean, look at Elroy. What does he have going for him? He's always listening to his reggae tunes. He doesn't have time to talk about anything else. In a year's time where is he going to be? In the same place. Maurice's got a car and his own flat, not no high-rise council business.' Janice looked stubbornly at Shree and Paula.

'Is that all you care about, Jan? Money and cars and jobs?' Paula looked at her friend earnestly.

'I wouldn't expect *you* to understand anyway, Paula,' said Janice, looking sulky. Paula jumped up off the sofa, fuming at this last diss, but before she could say anything Shree got there first.

'That's a nasty thing to say, Janice, and I don't know what you meant by it, but it's about time for you to shut up. Yes, Paula may have a kid and yes, she may live in a council flat and be a little hard on the money tip, but that don't give you no cause to chat to her like dat. What's up wid you, girl? You nuh kno' say you're her friend from time and just because you can't take the talking to, you decide to start? Who do you think you are? If you're doing wrong, I have a right to tell you and you are doing wrong. Okay, it looks like you ain't hearing nobody but hear this. Paula may not have some rich man to wine and dine her like you, but the way you're dealing Elroy, it's making us all sick. Paula's got more than you'll ever have, Janice, even if your bups business works out for you, because she's got a heart. Don't treat people like shit, Janice, because they will turn round and do you the same way.'

Janice stared at the ceiling. She knew she had gone

too far but she was beginning to see what Maurice had been driving at. They didn't understand. They didn't mind having no job or money just as long as they got to go raving twice a week. Her lip curled slightly. She looked over her shoulder out of Paula's sitting-room window. Stretched out before her was a series of identical tall blocks, filled with small, cramped flats. She knew that in some of them the lifts didn't work and the windows were smashed. All the inhabitants were the same – small and ignorant and poor. If Paula was right and all she did care about was money and cars and jobs, so be it.

Turning back to her friends, she gave a little sigh. 'I'm sorry, Paula, I didn't mean anything by it and if it sounded bad I take it back. Actually, you've got a point, I suppose. Maybe I am doing Elroy bad and you're probably right that I'm thinking too much about money and that and not enough about the person. Shree's right. You, both of you, have been my friends for ever and I don't want to lose that.'

The last part of this pretty speech was truth. As to the first part, Janice figured that her friends would swallow it. She guessed right. Shree came over and gave her a light hug, then Paula. Janice hugged them back. They were friends again.

'Janice, I have a gut feeling about this one. Elroy is crazy about you, so forget about this man Maurice,' Paula said.

'Yeah, c'mon, Janice. Elroy loves you bad and—'

'Okay, okay,' Janice smiled sourly at her friends. This was the first time she had not been persuaded to follow fashion, the very first time she had taken it upon herself to go against their wishes. 'I'll drop him. Friday when I go to meet him I'll tell him it can't be done,' she lied. 'Come to my yard Saturday at twelve. First thing y'know and I'll tell you everything that went on.'

Paula and Shree were so pleased with her change of heart that they didn't notice the sarcastic tone in her voice or the ever-so-sardonic glint in her eye.

chapter
six

'**Look at** you. We are here, celebrating the fact that you've got the job you wanted, and all you can do is worry about some argument that you've had with a Shree and a Paula who you keep telling me about. Don't bother with them, Janice.' Maurice picked up his glass of white wine and took a sip. 'You don't need them.'

'It's just that sometimes, y'know, they're my best friends, I've known them forever.' Janice said as she looked around the expensive restaurant.

'Janice, is there someone very interesting in the restaurant who I can't see?'

'Oh, no. It's really nice here, that's all.'

'Look, in this life one goes up, or one goes down. There is no standing still. I had a best friend too. We did everything together except work. When it was time for me to do my A-levels he went off with his street crowd. I hated studying, I wanted to follow him wherever he went, parties, fights, clubs, but my parents told me no. I still see him sometimes, still unemployed at twenty-nine, still robbing people, no doubt. Now we don't even say hello.'

Janice gasped. Maurice nodded. 'It's sad, but true. Even if we did talk, we wouldn't have anything in common.'

He grinned at Janice carelessly and ate some more of his pasta. Janice didn't know what to say, so she remained silent, wondering what Elroy was doing. Making a new track at his cousin's studio, helping out at the Community Centre, maybe calling on some of his brethren.

'Janice, Janice?'

'Er, yes, what is it?'

'Janice, haven't you been listening? I said, what would you like for dessert?'

Janice grabbed the menu and began trying to decipher the Italian.

'Oh, um, I'll have, er, pistachio ice-cream.'

It was the only thing she could recognize. She felt really bad, thinking about Elroy when Maurice was taking her to dinner to congratulate her on getting the job as receptionist.

'Don't worry about your old friends. You have a new job and a new life. I'll introduce you to all of my friends.' Maurice covered Janice's hand with his own. This time Janice let him and met his eyes. Over ice-cream Maurice told her about his friends, the skiing holidays, the barbecues and the fast cars.

Maurice put the key in the ignition of his Saab, then turned to help Janice who was struggling to fix her seatbelt. This action brought him so close to her that he could see the lace curving around her breasts underneath her blouse. He gently raised Janice's face to his. 'Where would you like to go?' he asked suggestively. No mistaking the look in his eyes, thought Janice. What should she do? She hadn't known him long, but she had protection. What could she lose? He was fit, well-off, nice. She blotted out Elroy and Shree and Paula, she could style it out with them.

She smiled encouragingly. 'Wherever you'd like to take me,' she whispered.

Maurice loosened his tie.

'Now, if I was an evil-minded person . . .' They both laughed, dispelling some of the tension they were both feeling, and Maurice started the car.

Janice woke up the next morning with a guilty feeling. She lifted her head from the billowy pillows and looked at the hump next to her. For a minute she wondered who it could be, then she remembered how Maurice had driven her to the smart building where he rented a flat. He had been very considerate and had given her the time she needed to get comfortable in the new surroundings.

It had all been very romantic and passionate. He had kissed her slowly, tenderly but firmly and caressed the sides of her face, slowly letting his hand slide down from her cheek to her neck, down her back to her waist. As Smokey Robinson's moving songs had filled the room, Janice and Maurice had been creating smoke of their own.

But now . . . Janice checked that Maurice was sleeping and then hurried into the bathroom to put her clothes on. She looked at his watch. It was eleven o'clock.

She had to get back to her flat as quickly as possible. When she had dressed, she returned to the bedroom and nudged Maurice. 'I have to go.'

'What's wrong?' Maurice asked as he rubbed his eyes sleepily.

'Nothing, only my friends are coming to see me and I have to get home.'

'All right, well phone me when you get there.'

Janice kissed him on the forehead and was gone. Maurice smiled to himself, grunted contentedly and went back to sleep.

'Where is she, Paula?' Shree sank down on to the hard concrete floor outside Janice's flat. She looked at the expensive watch which had been a birthday present from her dad.

'It's coming up to one o'clock and we've been here since just after twelve. I'm a bit worried.'

'Pshaw.' Paula was not in a good mood. She had had to get up early in order to drop Fabian at her mother's. 'Where do you *think* she is, Shree? Isn't it obvious?'

'No. She wouldn't play us out like that, Paula. C'mon, man. She's been our best spar since day one. She said she was gonna drop him. Janice don't lie.' Shree undid her sandal straps and eased her feet out of the delicate high-heeled suede sandals. 'She better come soon, though, my feet are burning up.'

Paula glanced at Shree's red and blistered toes. 'Why did you buy those sandals, then?'

Shree glanced up at her sheepishly. 'I needed some to go with my black chiffon dress ages ago, remember?'

'No. I remember you moaning about your financial troubles, though.'

'This was the last pair of shoes that I bought before my, er, money problems.'

'Well, that was clever.'

'I wish I hadn't bought them. I'm broke now. I had to sell some of the bangles my dad gave me when I was a kid, just to pay my bills.'

'If your dad finds out he'll kill you, man.'

'I know.'

'How come he doesn't give you money no more?'

'I'll tell you another time.'

'I don't blame him, though. You're a shopaholic.'

'Forget you, man. You wouldn't understand. You don't have my natural shock-out flair.' Shree waved aside Paula's criticism good-naturedly.

Janice raced up the stairs to the third floor and turned the corner on to her landing. At that instant she wished she could just melt back into the wall, but it was too late. There was nowhere to hide.

Shree scrambled up off the floor. She stood by Paula's side. Janice was shaken by the anger in their stares. She knew it wasn't just the waiting, it was the suspicion lurking at the back of Shree's eyes and the blatant anger blazing in Paula's. She stopped a few feet in front of her friends.

'So?' Paula eyed Janice's hastily buttoned blouse and her laddered tights.

'Don't start, Paula.'

'No, Janice, don't try your big-woman act with us. It doesn't come across.' Paula folded her arms and looked squarely at Janice. 'Now, are you going to tell us

93

where you spent the night or do we have to take three guesses?'

'It's none of your business.'

'It is our fucking business when you keep us waiting on your doorstep like this.'

'Like Janice is talking to some stranger in the road, y'know,' put in Shree.

'Don't be coming feisty again either,' Paula added. 'Whose business is it if not ours? Maurice's?'

A neighbour opened the front door to her flat. 'Excuse me, but you lot are causing a whole heap of noise in my house.'

'Sorry, Denise,' Janice apologized to the woman.

'Look at your hair and clothes, don't try telling us you went to bed early and left your house to visit a relative at eight o'clock this morning, Janice, 'cause you look a mess. We were so worried, I rang you all night and Shree rang you all morning. You should have told us you was going to screw Maurice and then we wouldn't have bothered.'

Janice, who had been unlocking her front door, turned around indignantly. 'I didn't spend the night with Maurice.'

'Fuck you!' Paula said as she followed Janice into the flat. 'You lied to us, Janice, you're nothing but a—'

'Leave her, Paula,' Shree said. 'She's made her own decisions. She ain't listening to no one.'

'That's right.' Janice flung her handbag into a chair. Everything fell out, including a packet of condoms. She glared defensively at her friends. 'This is my business. If I thought it had anything to do with either of you I would have said, but as it goes, it doesn't. I'm sick and tired of you assuming that I'm going to do exactly as you do. Everything I want to do nowadays, you've always got some reason why it can't be done. Whatever I do, regardless of whether it's right in your eyes, or wrong, just remember that I don't have to answer shit to no one.'

'Oh yes you do.' All three turned towards the doorway. Elroy was standing there. He surveyed the room coldly, taking in the handbag and its scattered contents. He wore a dangerous smile and there was an unfamiliar glint in his eyes. He nodded stiffly to Shree and Paula while throwing Janice a bitter look. Catching its full impact, Janice suddenly dried up.

Shree and Paula understood. They left the flat silently, shutting the front door behind them. By the time they had reached the lifts they could hear the sounds of raised voices. Shree half-turned to go back but Paula shook her head.

'What the fuck is going on with you, Janice?'

'Go home, Elroy.' Janice turned on the radio but Elroy leaped forward and wrenched out the plug.

'I'll go when this is sorted. Who is he?'

'Who is who?'

'I heard your argument, you bitch. Shree and Paula are right.'

'I don't know what you're talking about.'

'Don't handle me like a fool, Janice, who is he?'

'Why? Are you going to bust him up or get your posse or grab your gun, Elroy?' Elroy winced. 'You're a fool, Elroy, you're such a fool!'

Elroy's hand struck Janice's cheek. Janice gave a small scream and fled to the corner of the room. Elroy stared at his hand, deeply shocked. He had never hit a woman in his life, never even thought about it. It was hard for Elroy to accept how close he was to losing Janice, the girl he had spent the last year next to, longer than with any girl. It was also hard for him to admit he cared for anyone or anything, to put aside the bad bwoy image that was him. Cool, dangerous, gallis, hard, these were words that described Elroy. But now he discovered that there was something else too. Underneath all that roughness there was a soft heart that belonged to Janice, and the irony of it was that now, after all this time, when he offered it to her, it wasn't wanted.

'What's happening to us, Janice?' Elroy sank down limply on the sofa and put his head in his hands. Still in the corner of the room, Janice also sank down to the floor and hugging her knees with her hands, pressed her head against the wall. Elroy looked at her, but it was hard to tell what she was feeling.

'Some things just weren't meant to be.' Her voice was barely a whisper and it was icy-cold.

'Is it money? I've hard that he's rich. I didn't figure you for taking after a bups, Janice.'

'This is what I mean, Elroy. Your attitude. You're so wrapped up in your raves and your music and your friends that you can't see that I'm sick of it! I'm sick of hearing about raves and music and record deals that never happen. I hate your friends. I'm sick of you, Elroy. I want something else.'

'So I've noticed.' Janice looked up to see Elroy staring at the packet of condoms lying amongst the other strewn contents of her bag.

'Don't be so immature, Elroy, this has nothing to do with sex.'

'So this new one. What's so different about him?'

'He's a real man.'

'Didn't we have fun?'

'There's more to life than having fun, Elroy. I want someone I can talk to, someone who understands me. I want to be treated right.'

'Didn't I treat you right? Weren't you happy?'

Janice looked up again for a moment as if searching for something in Elroy she had never seen before. But then she looked down again. 'All good things come to an end,' she said.

Elroy moved over and knelt next to Janice. He tried to take her hands in his. Janice looked up in surprise. There were tears in Elroy's eyes. 'I love you, Janice. I love you so much.' He tried to take her in his arms but she fought him off and turned away.

Elroy stood up with quiet dignity and straightened his jacket. 'We had some good times, Janice.'

She heard his slow footsteps disappear down the passage and the click of the front door. When she decided he was too far away to hear her, she ran into the bedroom and threw herself on the bed. 'Elroy,' she wailed. Now she believed what her friends had been telling her all this time. Elroy did really love her and had she the chance to do it all again she would never have slept with Maurice. Now it was too late and all wrong. She missed Elroy already, his touch, his smile. The tears poured down her cheeks. She would have given anything to have had Shree and Paula there to comfort her and pat her on her shoulder and promise that things weren't as bad as she thought and that any minute now Elroy would come running back through the door. But Janice had driven away her friends, just as she had driven away Elroy.

Eventually her tears ceased, although every now and then a lump came up into her throat and she sobbed. As she dried her eyes on the edge of her duvet, her eyes lighted on the little framed picture on her dresser, of her and Elroy. They looked so happy together.

She smiled sadly. 'Yeah, we had some good times.'

It was another beautiful day. A light breeze, a cloudless blue sky, a brilliant sun. A little too bright, Shree thought as she left her flat dressed in a mauve minidress. She had to go by bus today because Tyrone had borrowed her car, so after checking in her handbag for money she turned left towards the main road.

The bus was hot and stuffy. Shree rarely took the bus, but out of habit she went upstairs to the back seat and sat down in the corner, looking out of the window.

A woman came and sat down next to her. 'Excuse me, dear, do you have the time?'

Shree turned and smiled at the woman. 'Yeah, it's almost eleven.'

'Thank you, thank you, thank you,' said the woman. After a moment she began to fidget around nervously. 'Excuse me dear, does this bus go to Finsbury Park station?' She asked before giving a high-pitched laugh.

'Yeah, it does.'

'He-he, that's good. That's real good. He-he.'

Shree squeezed as close to the side of the bus as she

could but the woman wouldn't leave her alone. 'Can I try on your sunglasses?' She leaned towards Shree who pressed back against the seat. The woman's breath stank of alcohol. 'Pleeese.' She reached out a scrawny hand to pluck the dark glasses off Shree's head but Shree covered them firmly with her own.

'No!' she snapped.

'Now, now, there's no need to get angry.' The woman lost interest in Shree's dark glasses and began playing with strands of her hair and laughing to herself. After a few minutes she got up from her seat, walked up the aisle and sat down beside a middle-aged businessman. 'I can get any man I want,' she declared happily to the man, who tried to ignore her.

The bus stopped and Shree ran down the stairs and stepped off into the sunlight. She could still hear the woman's high-pitched voice from the street. She giggled, shaking her head, then she turned and walked through the main gates of the park.

'Shreeeeee!' Paula and Fabian ran up. 'Sorry we're late.'

Shree glanced at her watch. 'You're not. It's only five past and you did say to come at eleven.' She held out her arms to Fabian, who went for his hug. Shree loved kids and especially Fabian, who although quiet and timid with those he didn't know, was really lovable and good-natured. Paula had done well.

The three of them walked through the park, looking for a place to sit down and chat. They joked around for a while and when they ran out of jokes they talked about each other's boyfriends and other problems. Fabian, worn out by a game of tag with an invisible friend, fell asleep in his mother's arms. Conversation drifted for a short while and then petered out to silence. At length it was Shree who took the initiative. Rolling on to her stomach and facing Paula, she said, 'What are we going to do about Janice?'

Paula looked down at her sleeping son and stroked his hair. 'What can we do? Leave her, man, she doesn't want us to distress her.'

''S'true, but I can't help wondering what went on with her and Elroy.'

'They must have broken up, innit?' Shree flicked a few strands of grass at Paula who gave her a rude stare and then threw them back.

'Not necessarily,' said Shree. 'Maybe Janice saw the light, and that Elroy really loves her and—'

'Wake up, gal. How do you see Janice seeing the light? Don't be forgetting where she was coming from yesterday morning.'

'Maurice.' They said it in unison, glumly. Shree began making a daisy-chain.

'Is he that nice?' she asked Paula.

'Shree, I know you're a really sweet person and all that, but can't you see? It's the money. Janice is after a bups, woman to woman.'

'Naah. Janice has never been like that, if she was like that why did she go out with Elroy for so long?'

'That's different.'

'How?'

'Janice was just a lickle thing when she met Elroy. Remember how impressed she was with his gold and his car and his deejay friends?'

'Yeah, she thought she had caught the ultimate rude boy,' Shree agreed.

'Exactly. Janice doesn't come from that sort of thing,' Paula grinned at Shree. 'Not like me and you, eh, rude girl? I suppose it was really exciting for her to be running with a fast crowd.'

'So . . .?'

'Janice is the type of girl who always has to be impressed. She's a dreamer. Everything has to seem wonderful to her and perfect. You get me?'

'Yeah.' Shree stretched out the finished part of her long daisy-chain in the grass. 'Time fe her to wake up and find out her reality.'

'That's it, just when she's realizing that Elroy's life isn't so wonderful and that the man's got his faults—'

'—along comes Maurice.'

'And pow! Girl's got the lurve fever.' They laughed. Fabian stirred restlessly and Paula put a finger to her lips. 'Stop. I don't want this one waking on me till I'm ready to leave this park.'

'But you're too right,' Shree continued, 'Janice is all taken up with the older man, the designer suits, the gold watch.'

'Not just any old gold, star. Twenty-four carats!'

'Last time I heard it was fifty!'

'Big up!' Fabian showed signs of waking up again as the girls stifled their giggles. Shree rolled over, squashing her daisy-chain and hugging her sides.

'But seriously, Paula, do you think it's gonna last?'

'Who knows? But I won't give it more than two months.'

'Do you think he loves her?'

'I don't want to sound bad, but I doubt it. He's taken her out, but has he given her anything?'

'It's early days, man.'

'I'm not going to wish evil 'pon her but it just don't feel right. Y'know what I'm saying?'

'Yeah.'

'The vibes just aren't there.'

'What do you think Elroy's going to do, batter him?'

'Don't be silly. Elroy's going to go out like a man.'

'Are you sure, tho'? He nuff cares for Janice.'

'I know that, but look at it good. What can Elroy do? It's up to Janice, isn't it?'

'Forget Elroy. What are we gonna do?' Shree and Paula looked at each other. Both of them wanted to do the same thing, but Shree didn't feel like doing it without Paula, and Paula, having made her stand, was finding it hard to climb down.

Paula watched some ants scurrying around on the ground. 'She doesn't need us any more, Shree.'

'She'll always need us, Paula.'

'But look at what she's done to Elroy. Doesn't that mean anything?'

'Doesn't her friendship mean more?'

There was a long silence.

'I suppose it doesn't matter who she's dealing with,' Paula conceded softly. 'I mean, a friend's a friend, no matter what.'

'That's right,' Shree said happily. 'So let's go and—'

Paula held up her hand for silence. Her tone was hard. 'Don't be so fast, Shree. She did us bad that morning. If she cared about our friendship she wouldn't have treated us like that. I'm not about to go running to her like some fool. I'm not begging her friendship. She's got my number, she knows where I live. If she wants a friend she can come and find me.'

'But—'

'No, she was trying it yesterday. Who did she think she was talking to? She fed us enough lies the other day about how she was going to drop him and the rest. Janice thinks she's just too damn smart for the rest of us, and no, Shree, I haven't forgotten all what she said about how *I* wouldn't understand. Well, I understand this, y'hear. Janice don't need no friends, she don't need advice or support or someone to hang out with now she's found her loverman. The sad thing is—'

'But—'

'No, hear me out, Shree. The sad thing is that as soon as she breaks up with him and he's blanking her on the street and such, see how fast she's looking friendship then. I know Janice like I know Fabian, and so do you. Shree, you're too soft. I know how you stay. You'll always be the one to give in or make the peace but I'm not going to let you go running back to that Janice till she changes her ways. You know I'm right. She doesn't deserve friendship, that one,' Paula finished emphatically.

There wasn't anything else to say, so Shree said nothing. She delicately arranged the crushed daisy-chain on Fabian's head. Paula woke her son and they walked down from their hilly mound towards the gate.

'Where are you going?' Shree asked Paula as they got to the bus stop.

'We,' Paula had a twinkle in her eye, 'are going to see Janice, of course.'

Shree stared at Paula in surprise. 'Seriously?'

Paula shuffled her feet shyly. 'Well, a friend's a friend and all that.'

Despite the inviting weather, Janice was sitting in bed with a pile of tissues next to her, feeling very sorry for herself. She had got over her initial sadness about Elroy, that was now a dull pain, but what really hurt her was the absence of her friends. Janice was suffering from loneliness. The flat was a reflection of her mood, dark and gloomy and showing signs of distress: glasses and half-drunk cups of hot chocolate surrounded her.

The doorbell rang. Janice went to the front door, wondering who it could be. She opened the door and—

'How are you girl?'

'Are you all right, dahling?'

'Hi, Janice.'

Shree, Paula and Fabian rushed into her flat as if nothing had ever happened. Janice stood dumbstruck, still holding the door-handle, watching them make themselves at home.

'Janice, a wha' gwan in dis flat?'

'You're going from bad to worse. You're my spar and that, but bwoy, you need to sort this place out!'

'Janice, please can I have crisps?'

Janice smiled slowly. She closed the front door and went into the kitchen to find Fabian some crisps.

About two hours later, when Shree and Paula had long since gone, Janice lay on her sofa and savoured the afternoon. They had fussed over her, tidied up her flat, done her hair, helped her choose what to wear, promised that no man would ever break up their friendship, and after making her something to eat and chatting about everything but men, had said goodbye, leaving her feeling much happier than she had in a long time.

Not really knowing what to do with herself, Janice was still lying on the sofa when the doorbell rang again. Thinking it must be her friends returning because they had forgotten something, it was a shock to see Maurice standing on her doorstep holding a large bunch of flowers.

'Maurice!'

Well satisfied with her reaction, Maurice stepped forward, planted a kiss on Janice's cheek and pushed the flowers into her arms. 'I hope you like them,' he said quietly.

'They're lovely, thank you.' Janice leaned over and kissed Maurice and then stood back to allow him into her flat. 'Come in, I'm sorry it's so messy but my friends came round and—'

'Believe me Janice, I did not come here to see your flat, I came to see you.' Maurice perched on the edge of the sofa. He looked larger than life in a crisp white polo shirt with a preppy sweater tied around his shoulders.

'Today is Sunday. You were supposed to telephone me on Saturday, Janice, remember?'

Janice's hands flew to her face. 'Oh no, it really slipped my mind.'

'I see I'm not that memorable.'

'No, no, of course—'

Maurice smiled. 'It isn't important. At least it gave me an excuse to try out your address. I hope you have nothing planned for the rest of the afternoon.'

Janice shook her head. 'Good, because I'm taking you somewhere nice.' Maurice got up and handed Janice her handbag. 'Are you ready?'

'Do I look all right?'

'You look great. I love the way you've done your hair.'

They made their way out of the flat and down to the car.

'Well, you know, this estate isn't too bad,' Maurice said.

'You're just saying that. I saw the way you were looking at the graffiti on the walls.'

'No, no, really. Apart from the odd spot of vandalism it's quite clean, and it's small, which is a good thing. The houses opposite the blocks are rather neat with their front gardens and flowers. Much better than some of the crime-ridden high-rise blocks I saw driving through Hackney.'

'Mmm.' Janice was relieved when they reached his Saab. 'Where are we going?' she asked.

Maurice took his Ray-bans out of the glove compartment and put them on. 'Oh, they're having a match at the tennis club where I'm a member. I thought perhaps you'd like to go and meet a few of my friends.'

Janice didn't feel like watching a tennis match but she smiled as if she thought it was a wonderful idea.

'No, I prefer Gstaad. St Moritz is best at Easter.'

'Well, I still say that St Moritz is the nicest place to ski at Christmas.'

Janice suppressed a yawn. She was bored. After spending almost an hour watching a men's doubles, they had gone up to the bar where they had joined some of Maurice's friends 'from old school days'. Maurice had ordered them all Perriers and ever since she had been hearing about holidays and cars and politics.

'What do you think, Janice?' A pretty blonde woman looked expectantly at her. Janice suddenly realized everyone was waiting for her answer. Maurice smiled encouragingly.

'Well?'

'I really wouldn't know, I'm afraid. I haven't been there.'

'Really? You haven't been to St Moritz?"

Janice opened her mouth to reply but the conversation had moved on, this time to whether the Seychelles was still the place to go during the summer months. Janice looked at Maurice. He was enjoying himself, in the thick of the discussion.

'So did you enjoy yourself?' Maurice asked as he turned the car out of the car park into the main road.

'Well, it was interesting.'

'I knew you'd like it. Donald is such good company. He always has a joke at hand.' Maurice laughed. Janice couldn't remember Donald but she was sure that none of Maurice's friends provoked laughter.

'Yes, Janice,' Maurice continued, 'I think, as you obviously do, that entertainment like opera and sports like skiing are for everybody, black and white. I wish more black people would follow your example.' He pointed to a group of raggas who were joking by the kerb outside a McDonald's. 'It is disappointing to see that they can find nothing more fulfilling to do than hang around on street corners.'

He swung into her estate. 'Would you like me to—'

'I'll see you later, Maurice.' Janice avoided his eyes as she kissed him on the cheek. Then she quickly got out of the car. 'Thanks for a great afternoon,' she said as she shut the door and hurried towards the stairs.

In her flat Janice turned on her radio. WNK blared out its ragga. She absorbed the music thankfully. It felt good to get back to something she knew. St Moritz, skiing, tennis were not things she could identify with. She was impressed – the posh white friends, the mani-cured tennis lawns, it had definitely sunk in; but it didn't mean the same things to her that it did to Maurice. She tried to picture Elroy in that tennis club. It made her laugh. When she had changed into some leggings and a T-shirt, she decided to phone Paula and share the day's events with her, now that they were friends again.

'What's up?'

'Hi, Paula, it's me, Janice.'

'Tyrone, put back my tape, you damn thief – oh, y'all right, Janice?'

'Yeah. Who's at your place? Sounds like enough people.'

'Yeah. Shree came round and so did Michael and Tyrone and Asher and Chantelle and a couple of other people.'

'Oh, I see. You're practically holding a rave in your house but don't bother asking me to come or anything like that.'

'Oh, don't talk rubbish. We belled you enough times but you weren't in. We even phoned your parents' house 'cause we thought you might be there. We guessed in the end that you was out with Maurice. Where did you go?'

'Nowhere very interesting.'

On the sofa in Paula's sitting room Shree pricked up her ears. 'Is that Janice?'

Paula nodded and Shree came across the room and took the phone. 'Why don't you come round?'

'No, I don't think I should.'

'Why?'

'Well, I've got to go to work tomorrow morning and I shouldn't be up too late.'

'Well, I'll drop you home.'

'I shouldn't.'

'Well, if you're sure, no one's forcing you.'

'Okay, I'll come, see you in around half an hour.'

'Safe, later on, Janice.'

'Is she coming, then?' Paula asked.

'What do you think?' Shree said, going back to her seat.

Twenty minutes later Janice arrived. Everyone said hello. Tyrone passed her a Babycham from a six-pack. Chantelle and Sabrina made space for her on the floor around the television. They were watching a video of some reggae show in Jamaica.

'Eh-eh, mark them go-go girls, tho',' said Sabrina. Asher, her boyfriend, came and looked sceptically over her shoulder.

'Nastiness, boy. Hey, Tanasha, what would you do if you saw your girl doing something like that?' Asher pointed to the picture of a woman in a bikini, whining in a cleared space by herself.

'Slap her,' said Tanasha.

'Now, now, don't be teaching my son bad ways.' Michael hugged Fabian close to him with one hand and playfully boxed Tanasha on the chin with the other.

Everyone laughed. Janice opened her Babycham, soaking up the happy atmosphere.

'I heard you and Elroy split,' whispered Sabrina. Janice nodded.

'Who finished who?'

Janice looked indignantly at Sabrina, a girl with a mouth like a radio station. 'Actually,' she said, 'we both came to the same decision, that it was time to move on.' And with that she clamped her lips together and Sabrina got the message.

'No, *ma petite*,' Tyrone arrogantly addressed Shree. 'None can test me when it comes to blackjack. I'm the undisputed, undefeated—'

'Fool!' Chantelle, Sabrina and Janice collapsed, laughing.

'Listen, yeah,' Tyrone said. 'No one can beat me at this game. You don't know. You've never played a real expert before. Playing you, it wouldn't be fair. It would be just like playing my granny.'

The girls had cleared a space on the floor and laid out a pack of playing cards before Tyrone finished his sentence. There were four teams. Chantelle and Janice, Tyrone on his own, Tanasha and Michael and Asher and Paula. Sabrina and Shree watched and made sure everyone kept to the rules. Each pair put 10 pence into the centre of the space.

Tyrone shook his head sadly. 'I can't do it to you. There's a recession going on, it would be like taking food from the mouths of the starving.'

'Just deal and done.'

Tyrone sighed and dealt. He won the first two games but then Asher and Paula had a winning streak.

'I'm on a roll!' Paula announced as she added another 10 pence to the growing heap by her side. Chantelle and Janice looked ruefully at their cards, then at each other. They put their last 10 pences into the middle. When the game was over everyone stretched out on the carpet.

'Admit it, Tyrone man. You got blasted, good and proper.'

Tyrone shrugged his shoulders. 'You win some, you lose some, and I ain't complaining,' he said, pointing to his substantial winnings.

The mood had waned. It was about three o'clock in the morning and everyone was tired. Shree stood up and brushed off her leggings. She hauled Tyrone up by the arm. 'Janice, if you want that lift, now's the time.'

Janice got up quickly. 'Yeah, another week, another working day. It's a working woman you see before you.'

''Bye, Fabian, 'bye, Paula, see ya.' Shree, Tyrone and Janice left the flat and went down to the car park. In the car Tyrone put in a ragga tape, despite the unfriendly hour, while Janice and Shree sort of dozed in their seats. At her estate, Janice got out of the car and waved goodbye to Shree and Tyrone. She ran up the stairs and let herself into her flat. She quickly changed into her nightclothes, but as she drew the curtains she stopped for a moment and looked out of the window at the clear night sky.

'Hanging around on street corners, indeed! Maurice, you don't know what you're missing!'

chapter
seven

Several weeks passed. July faded into August. Nothing much changed . . .

'Tyrone . . .' Tyrone, move yourself, man!' Shree kneaded her fingers into Tyrone's back until he squirmed and eventually, after much grumbling and cursing, sat up.

'C'mon, Shree. Leave it alone. A man's had no sleep all weekend and you're waking me up all early hours and t'ing.'

'A man will have *nowhere* to sleep if a man doesn't listen, star.' Tyrone cursed, but he didn't continue the argument. 'What's the problem now, Shree?'

Shree threw a heap of bills at him. Tyrone picked up one or two but soon lost interest and brushed them off the side of the bed. 'So? Bills are bills, ain't they?'

'That's right, Tyrone. Electricity bills, gas bills, *phone* bills.' She emphasized the word 'phone'.

Tyrone shook his head vigorously. 'Don't be framing me. You know I'm a mobile man.' He gestured with his arm. 'I'm here. I'm there. I'm all over the place. Why would I use your phone if I've got my Cellnet at the ready?'

Shree kissed her teeth and looked away. 'It's not cover-up time, Tyrone. You know how much you use my phone to call up this brudder or that brudder. You know how much you wear out my electric to play your damn tapes and you're always here, so you should share my heating bills too.'

Tyrone folded his arms and looked hurt. 'You're hyping this, Shree. You're putting me in a corner. It's your phone, it's your electric, it's your gas. If you thought I was using too much you should have told me, innit? That's sense, but you never said a word so it must have been cool. Maybe they sent you the wrong gas bill or—'

'Don't be foolish, Tyrone. Don't talk stupidness in me earhole about wrong gas bill or my phone. It takes two to run up bills this high, Tyrone, and it takes two to pay them. You're the one with the job. Are you going to help me out or not?' Shree snapped.

Tyrone started throwing his arms about again. 'Hold up, Shree, I'd know if I was using your things out. I'm not stupid, y'know. But – but – look, I'm not a bills type of person. I'm not even a dollars type of person. I don't think in figures or units or dis type of thing.' He waved one of the bills in the air. 'I mean, if it was serious like, of course I'd – but it's not all that. You're kicking up fuss about little things that don't matter – don't be bawling me down with eye-water now, Shree . . .'

Shree gave an exasperated yell, walked out of the bedroom and slammed the door behind her.

'Cha, man! Women!' Tyrone shouted but gave no

further thought to Shree's 'little things' as he snuggled back down in the warm bed to get a few more hours sleep.

Shree reached up and slid back the doors of her bathroom cabinet. She took down a packet of Nurofen. She had not been feeling well lately. She took out the last two pills and swallowed them. As she slid back the mirrored cabinet doors she caught sight of her face. The worry spots were creeping back on to her forehead. Her skin was dry, her hair was splitting and her afro was growing back because the relaxer hadn't been touched up in a long while. Tyrone's snores floated into the bathroom. Shree pursed her lips. Some things were going to have to change around here, soon.

She had never expected much from Tyrone. They had an easygoing relationship and Shree had been satisfied with her man. But lately she'd been feeling a sense of burden. Coping with the absence of her father and the difficulties of real independence hadn't been easy, and as far as she could see, Tyrone was more a hindrance than a help. It wasn't something that had bothered her before, when life had been carefree and she'd had her father to draw support from. When he'd gone she'd looked to Tyrone to fill that gap, but she had looked in vain. She'd given it time but Tyrone hadn't yet realized he was expected to help with bills and food and the rent. Shree felt as if she was slowly sinking.

Already dressed, she decided to slip out and visit Paula. She didn't feel like seeing Tyrone stretched out in her bed, so she didn't go back into the bedroom. She took her bag and keys and made her way to the front door. She started the car engine. Then she stroked the black leather steering-wheel. If things went from bad to worse she might soon be parted from her much loved motor.

Paula was dressing Fabian when Shree arrived. 'How come you're here so early?'

Shree pressed a hand to her forehead. 'You don't want to start me off, Paula, believe me.' She followed Paula into her bedroom where Fabian smiled his hello.

'Marital problems again?' Paula asked over her shoulder.

'Tyrone's driving me mad, and less of the marital if you please. I ain't an old woman yet.' Shree grinned and pinched Fabian on the cheek.

'What's he done?' Paula asked.

'Oh, I don't know. He's really stressing me out.' Shree kicked off her shoes and sat with her legs crossed on Paula's bed.

'Shree, where are we going today?' Fabian asked as he mimicked Shree's cross-legged style on the bed.

'I don't really know, baby, ask Mummy.'

'Fabian, you know you're going to nursery, so why ask Shree?'

'Don't you want to go to nursery?' Shree asked Fabian, who shook his head solemnly.

Paula laughed. 'Don't believe a word of it. Fabian loves his nursery more than his home. When I come to pick him up he starts screaming and hiding from me.' Fabian giggled as Paula began lacing up his trainers.

'I see you bought those little Huaraches after all.

They look really sweet.' Shree picked up one of Fabian's trainers and examined it.

'It was a choice between the Fila or the Huaraches and I decided the Fila were a bit dated.' Paula looked across at her own kicked-out Avias lying in a corner by her wardrobe. 'I need some trainers for myself, never mind my son, but the things cost so much, it's ridiculous. I can't afford to pay thirty pounds for a pair of trainers.'

'It's all right for those with the money,' Shree sighed.

Paula looked up in surprise, 'That's a change of attitude for you, Shree.'

'Yeah, well, we all have our hardships, don't we?'

'Something's wrong, isn't it?' Shree shrugged her shoulders and was quiet.

Paula decided to leave it for the time being. 'Janice has gone to work by now hasn't she?'

Shree looked at her watch. 'Must be.'

The nursery was at the back of a local school. It consisted of several large rooms where the toddlers ate, slept and played. Fabian raced up the steps to the double doors. A plump nursery worker leaned down and picked him up.

'Where's Mummy, dear? Oh, hello, Paula. For a minute there, I thought Fabian had dropped out of the sky.'

Paula and Shree, just reaching the double doors, laughed. 'Hi, Leila, I'm sorry we're a bit late today but Fabian was really playing up so everything took twice as long.'

'It's all right, you're not the last.'

They went into the nursery. Kids were running

around everywhere. Fabian darted into a crowd of small boys and girls who were playing war games. A small, cute girl with pigtails skipped up to them.

'Leila.' The little girl slyly tugged on her apron.

Feeling the tug, Leila looked down. 'Are you all right, Priya?' she asked in her soft, undulating voice.

Priya drew closer. 'Can you read me a story?' From behind her back she produced a large book with a dog on the front cover.

'What's the magic word?'

'Pleeese!'

'Good girl.' As Leila took Priya by the hand she mouthed goodbye to Paula and Shree. Then she led Priya towards the reading area where she was soon surrounded by a cluster of children who also wanted to hear the story of 'Spot the Dog'.

Paula did up her seatbelt. 'Tell me what's the matter, Shree,' she urged. 'I know something's not right.'

Shree didn't start the engine but looked out of the side window at the passing cars. Paula put a hand on Shree's shoulder. 'I think I know what's wrong.' Shree turned and looked at Paula sharply. 'Don't look at me like that, Shree, you always keep your problems to yourself and it's wrong. You know I'm not going to tell anyone your secrets. I'm your friend and friends should share the bad times as well as the good times. True?'

'What exactly do you know?'

'W-well, I don't know everything of course, but I do know about your father.' Paula looked across to see Shree's reaction. There was pain in Shree's eyes.

'How do you know?' she whispered.

'Janice and I remembered that the man who was shot was with your dad at the all-dayer, when he gave us the money, and we sort of guessed the rest. I mean, it was in the papers, about the shooting and the drugs thing. When you didn't mention your father or suggest that we all go and see him like you usually do, me and Janice kind of worked it out. It wasn't hard. Ohh, Shree baby—'

Shree had started crying softly, trying to hide her tears from Paula. 'I'm not crying.'

'Yeah, right, and I'm Michael Jackson.'

'I just miss my dad a bit, that's all. It's stupid, really.'

'I understand.'

'Do you? I thought you'd just think I was being a brat, 'cause you don't know your dad and you don't get on with your mum and you don't complain.'

'Doesn't mean I don't care.'

'Yeah, I know, but you never show it.'

'That's because I've got my baby.'

'It's true. You have Fabian and Michael. Janice has Maurice and all her family. I've got nobody. Tyrone doesn't count.'

Paula reached over and hugged Shree.

'It would be different if I knew where he was, if he was safe or anything.' She sniffed into Paula's shoulder. 'He's been gone for over six weeks and I haven't even had a postcard. I can't go back to his flat because he said the police would be there or maybe Terror's men or something like that and I can't ask any of his friends because he said not to deal with them.' She was calming down. 'I don't have a penny, Paula. You don't know how bad things are. I'm falling behind with the rent, I've got all my bills to pay, I've even been cutting down on food. I haven't been to the hairdresser's for ages, I feel like I'm losing my hold.'

Paula patted her on the shoulder. 'Tyrone's not helping, is he?'

'I don't want him for his money, Paula—'

'But he's not helping.'

'Tyrone tries in his own way—'

'But he's not helping, is he?'

'Perhaps he doesn't really realize how things are. He'll come round, I'm sure of it.'

'Don't let a man run t'ings in your life, Shree. Hear me good now, if Tyrone's not helping where help is needed, then obviously you don't need him.' Paula spoke firmly.

'Tyrone's been there for me in the past,' Shree said, looking down at her hands.

'In the past when you didn't need him. It's not the same thing. Listen to me, Shree, I know men.'

'Yes, but you're still craven for Michael and he's not doing much for you either.'

'Is Michael living with me? Is he using my phone? Is he eating my food? Maybe Michael hasn't been giving me money lately, I'm not denying it, but he doesn't drain me, Shree. Tyrone's draining you. Can't you see it? Shree, I love Tyrone, he's a joker and he's quite sweet, but I love you more. You're my best friend. If Tyrone don't earn his keep, kick him out.'

Shree chewed her lip.

'Well?' Paula demanded bossily.

'I'll sleep on it,' Shree promised. She started the

engine, turned the car into the road and began driving back.

'Where are we headed?' Paula asked.

'My place,' said Shree.

As she turned down a side street Paula looked at her curiously. 'This isn't the way to your flat, Shree, and you know it. The Two Towers are dead ahead?'

Shree stopped the car, turned off the engine and looked at the tall grey blocks of flats at the end of the road where they had parked. Paula looked at her excitedly. 'I thought you said that your dad told you not to go to his flat?'

'He did. I don't really know why I came. I just wanted to look at it. We'll go now.' She restarted the car.

'Don't be stupid. We're here now. You know you want to look, so what are you trying to style it for?' Paula undid her seatbelt. 'Turn off the engine and let's go.'

Shree looked at her in horror. 'No, Paula. We can't. My dad must have had good reasons. There could be people watching the flat. It's not worth it.' But Paula already had one foot out the door.

'Come on, Shree. If you're that worried about people seeing us we can go through the car park. Anyway, it's almost two months since Derrick left. No one will still be watching his flat.'

'I guess you're right.' Shree got out of the car and locked the doors before following Paula in the direction of the car park.

The Two Towers' car park was situated underneath the two tall blocks of flats. It was a huge cavern, with space enough for hundreds of cars. Yet few cars were ever there at any one time. After sunset, when the lights failed to work as they sometimes did, it was dark and silent. During the day, whatever the weather was like outside, the car park maintained a dull grey half-light. It was through this gloomy car park that Shree and Paula now walked.

'Suppose you had to spend the night down here,' Shree said.

Paula rubbed her shoulders. 'That's not very likely, Shree, but it's damn creepy.'

'My dad used to tell me about people who got into trouble down here. Nobody ever heard them scream because the walls are too thick.

'Thanks, Shree, I feel much happier now.'

Shree stopped. 'What's up?' Paula asked.

'I'm just trying to remember which exit we're looking for. I don't usually come through the car park. Dad is always telling me to avoid it.'

Paula looked around. 'Well, just hurry up about it.'

'Getting scared, Paula?'

'You're not looking too brave yourself,' Paula retorted.

'We came in from there so I think this is the one.' Shree pointed to a stairway to her left. They hurried towards the stairway and soon found themselves in the second tower.

'Now what was there to be afraid of?' Shree asked.

Paula laughed. 'I know you're an idiot, Shree, but don't push it.'

The lifts weren't working so they had to walk up the

ten flights of stairs. They literally crawled their way up the last flight and by the time they reached flat 105 they were half-dead. Shree scuffled around in her bag.

'Don't even try telling me you don't have your keys, Shree,' Paula warned. 'I will fling you back down the stairs so fast.'

Shree just looked worried. 'I don't have them, Paula. Seriously.' Paula advanced on her.

'Only joking!' Shree quickly dangled the keys in front of her friend. She looked apprehensively at the numerous locks on the door and then at Paula. 'Shall we?'

'Yes.'

As the two girls disappeared into the flat and shut the door behind them, one of the doors opposite slowly opened. Two pairs of eyes gleamed wickedly. The waiting had paid off. A mobile phone was picked up.

'Terror,' a coarse voice rasped, 'de gal 'a come.'

'Time fe action, me cousin. Don't do anyt'ing till me reach. That rasclat Derrick gwan see wha' gwan fe people when dem test Terror.' There was a click and the line went dead.

Shree opened the windows in the sitting-room. 'It smells terrible but otherwise everything's still here.'

Turning around, Shree surveyed the small flat. The stereo system with its two loudspeakers, the television and video, a pair of ironed trousers hung over the back of the leather sofa as if someone was intending to go to a dance.

'Ughh!'

Shree ran into the kitchen where Paula was looking at an open pot in the stove. It had contained cornmeal porridge once, but it had dried and turned mouldy and stank. Shree looked in the fridge.

'How come the electric's still running?' Paula asked.

Shree went to the cupboard in the hallway and looked at the electric meter. 'It hasn't been that long, has it?'

'Oh yeah, I forgot.' Paula went back into the sitting-room and sank into one of the leather armchairs. Shree went into the bedroom. It was neat and tidy. Polished shoes in a corner. A few pictures were arranged on the chest of drawers. Shree's grandparents who had died before Shree was born, Derrick and Shree's mother and Shree as a baby. Shree took the first two photos out of their frames and stuffed them in one of the breast-pockets of her denim shirt. Since her dad wasn't there, he wouldn't miss them. She looked through all the drawers, underneath all the underwear and socks.

'Looking for money?' Paula asked.

'I might as well. I need it more than he does.' Shree took one of the drawers out and handed it to Paula to look through. They came up with nothing. Paula and Shree pushed the drawers back in.

'Didn't your dad tell you where he put his dollars?'

Shree shook her head regretfully. 'No, and I never thought to ask him.' She looked under the bed. Nothing. She lifted the mattress. Nothing.

'Maybe he had a bank account?' Paula suggested.

Shree shook her head. 'Yeah, he did, but he was careful not to keep much money in there because of what he, er, did.'

She flopped on to the bed and rested her head on the pillow. As she did so she caught sight of a hidden drawer underneath the small table by the bed. 'Yo, Paula, this must be it.

The two girls turned the table over and examined the drawer. Shree tried pulling the small knob but it was locked.

'Shree, there must be a small knife or something in the kitchen?'

Shree ran into the kitchen and was back a moment later. 'Here, use this.'

Paula took the knife from Shree and prised open the drawer. As it gave way the girls looked eagerly for the money but there was nothing inside but a few letters.

'Well, there's nothing in here.'

'I'm not blind, Paula, I can see that,' snapped Shree.

'Do you want to leave these letters in here?'

'No, I'd best keep them safe now we've broken the lock.' Paula handed the letters to Shree who carelessly shoved them into her empty shirt pocket.

'There won't be any money in there,' called Shree as Paula opened the wardrobe doors.

'Who said I was looking for money? Your dad's got the livin' amount of silk suits, Shree.' Paula fingered the crisp shirts and soft filmy jackets. Shree walked over to the window and looked across at the other tower.

'Hey, what's this? Help me get this on to the bed,' Paula said as she dragged a black metal box out of the wardrobe. The two girls lifted it on to the bed. They looked at it and then at each other.

'It's a safe. This must be where all Dad's money is,' Shree said excitedly.

'How are you going to open it, though? Do you know the combination?'

'Of course not. Damn,' Shree groaned. 'That's that, then.' She reached down to pick up the photographs that had fallen out of her shirt pocket when she had helped to lift the metal box. As she picked up the photographs Paula leapt up and pointed.

'Shree, there's a number on the back of one of the photos.'

'But the number could mean anything, Paula.' Even so, she tried the combination. For a minute nothing happened and Shree was just about to dismiss the number when there was a small click and the lock pulled back. Shree opened the door and looked inside. 'Waaa!'

'Selasse!' Shree scooped the contents out on to the bed. There were bundles and bundles of twenty-pound and fifty-pound notes. 'There must be a million pounds here,' Paula said, staring at the notes.

'Oh, don't be so silly, let's count it.'

'Two thousand and counting.' Paula was counting the fifty-pound notes.

'One thousand and counting.' Shree was counting the twenty-pound notes. When they had finished, they added up their totals.

'Well, it's only about four thousand pounds,' Paula said.

'There has to be more than that, Paula.' Shree looked around the room. 'My dad had enough money.'

'Well, I don't think it's in this place. Are you going to take it all?'

'Yeah, at least it will pay my present bills. Here, take a couple of hundred for yourself.'

'Are you sure? It's not exactly your money, is it?'

'Just take it.' Shree shoved some fifty-pound notes into Paula's hand.

'Thanks,' Paula said, pleased. Shree dragged a sports bag down from the top of the wardrobe. They stuffed the money into it.

'What are you going to do with those?' Paula pointed to two small guns which were still in the safe.

Shree chewed her lip. 'I think we should leave them in the safe, lock it and put it back in the wardrobe.'

Once they had replaced the safe in the wardrobe, Shree took the sports bag and went into the sitting-room. Paula followed.

'I'm thirsty. Do you want a drink too?' Paula nodded, and while Shree was in the kitchen she turned on the stereo system. 'Your dad's got some wicked tapes,' she called from the sitting-room.

'Yeah, I know, I get all mine from him.'

'How's things getting on with your mum then, Paula?'

'All right, I suppose. We have our arguments and that, but I don't know, we're still talking.'

'Oh,' Shree said as she carried in their drinks and sat down in the armchair next to Paula.

After a couple of munutes she got up and started to pace around the room. Paula tried to ignore her but this soon became impossible. 'What's wrong wid you, man? Your stomping is driving me mad.'

Shree sat down again and twisted her hands over and over. Paula looked at her curiously, as if something had just occurred to her. 'If you want to go, Shree, why don't you just come out with it?'

Shree needed no further encouragement. Putting their glasses in the kitchen sink, she made for the front door, unlocked the chains and went outside. She stood in the corridor, waiting for Paula. It occurred to her that she was waiting a long time. She pushed open the door with her foot.

'Paula, move your—'

'Aren't you forgetting something?' Paula waved the sports bag in front of her.

'Oh, er, thanks.' As they left the flat they saw a mechanic coming out of one of the lifts with his toolbox.

'Is it working now?' Paula asked.

The mechanic nodded. 'Yes, I've just tested it, runs like a dream.'

'Wicked,' Shree said going inside. 'I didn't feel like walking down all those stairs.'

The two girls walked into the car park, then stopped in confusion. 'Why didn't you make a note of which exit we came in from?' grumbled Paula.

Shree looked around the gloomy car park. 'I think it must be over there somewhere.' She pointed to the other side of the car park. 'We came down in the lift this time. Don't forget we went up by the stairs before. The lift brings us down on the other side of the flats.' She began to walk across the car park.

Paula rubbed her bare arms. She was cold in her sleeveless chiffon shirt. As they reached the middle of the car park, she laughed.

'What was that for?' Shree said surprised. 'Scared, are we?' They both laughed. The noise echoed off the walls of the empty car park, sounding eerie. Paula bent down to do up the laces of one of her trainers. Hearing more laughter, she said, 'Stop, Shree, the joke's over.' But the laughter went on. 'Stop laughing, Shree,' Paula said again.

'I'm not laughing,' Shree replied.

'Then who is?'

A shadow shifted.

'Shree. You nuh know me?'

A man stepped forward and lifted up his shirt to reveal a bandaged chest. 'Me t'ink say you must know me now.'

'Terror,' Shree whispered. As two more men emerged from the shadows the girls began edging towards an exit.

'I thought he was—'

'You thought I was dead? Fi real?' Terror laughed again. He stepped closer. 'Terror hard fe dead. Shoot me two, three, four times. Man of steel.' Terror touched fists with one of his brethren.

The two girls were backed up against a wall. The three men had been whispering among themselves but now they broke off and stared at the girls. One ran his eyes over Shree's curvy body. There was no mistaking the intent in his face. Shree wished she could disappear into the cold concrete wall behind her. Terror took out a long knife from his jacket. The girls watched as it caught a few rays of light, glinting strangely.

'Why are you doing this?' Paula shouted.

Terror pulled his jacket open to show his bandages again. 'Nobody, but nobody, does this to me and gets away with it. I lost my men, I lost my respect, I lost my power. No, it's time fe someone else to lose something.'

'But that was *my* dad, that's got nothing to do with her,' Shree said, pointing at Paula.

'Derrick must have known seh, dat if him bring war 'pon me, then me gwan bring war 'pon him. That includes him and his.'

'But we haven't done anything to y—'

'Listen.' Terror held up his hands. 'It's like this. I don't care about you or the other gal. When Derrick sees what happens to those who cross me, he'll learn a lesson. You don't!' Terror stamped his foot violently. 'You don't shame Terror, and not feel pain.'

Paula and Shree looked at each other. 'I'm sorry Paula,' Shree said, crying. Paula searched for her friend's hand and gripped it tightly. The men were coming closer. Then, just as Paula was about to scream, a car full of people swung into the car park, loud music blaring. Terror motioned to his men who ducked behind a small van so they would not be seen. The car came to a stop nearby and the young people inside spilled out. They stood around for several minutes, joking and laughing, before heading towards an exit. As the sounds of their voices died away, Terror and his brothers emerged from behind the van.

'Dem gaan!!' Terror kicked a tyre of the van in anger. The other two men began searching around the cars and then ran outside the car park to look for the girls, but Shree and Paula had slipped quietly out of the car park with the young people while Terror and his men were crouching behind the van.

Driving back towards Hackney, Shree was very quiet.

'What's up, Shree?' Paula asked.

Shree turned to her, tears in her eyes. 'I'm sorry, Paula. You're my best friend, because of me and my troubles you nearly got hurt. Those men might have done anything to you and it would have all been my fault.' She turned away again. 'I'm just so sorry.'

Paula was quiet for a minute. 'I'm not angry, Shree. In a way I'm sorry for you because with you it's more personal, so don't worry. You're like a sister to me. If you went back right now I'd go with you.'

'Seriously?'

''Course.'

'What's happening now?' Paula looked at the time on the car radio.

'Well, it's coming up to three o'clock, so I guess we'd better go straight to the nursery to pick up Fabian.'

'We were there ages.' Paula nodded in agreement.

'We got there about eleven. We've spent the last four hours in—'

'Oh, no!'

Paula looked at Shree in surprise. She was groaning and clutching her head. 'What's wrong?'

'The sports bag! We must have left it in the car park.' Shree looked at Paula in dismay.

'Don't be silly.' Paula reached under her seat and pulled out the bag. 'You don't think I was leaving it for those men to 'tief, do you?' She opened it, looked inside, then zipped it back up. 'It's all there.'

Shree laughed. 'Trust you, Paula.'

chapter
eight

'**Thank goodness** it's Friday. I can forget about Portman and Portman until Monday.'

Janice smiled at Maurice who was concentrating on the road. 'There's a modern version of *Midsummer Night's Dream* at the Barbican. I rang them this afternoon and they still have tickets left.'

'I didn't think you were interested in Shakespeare.'

Janice laughed. 'I wasn't interested in a lot of things until I met you.'

Maurice grinned. 'Are you saying you're not the Janice I met?'

'You can say that again. I used to do the stupidest things, gell my baby-hairs, spray my curls gold and wear these terrible plimsolls covered with gold studs.'

'And then I took you shopping and you never looked back, right?'

Janice leaned over and kissed Maurice on the cheek. 'Yes, it's true, and you haven't just changed my dress sense either. So, how about *Midsummer Night's Dream*?'

'Actually, I've heard that this modernized version is not very well acted.'

'Okay, there is an opera on at the Coliseum. Mozart, I think.'

'That sounds quite good, if we can get the tickets. You go home, change and call me when you're ready and I'll come and pick you up. If I cannot get tickets we can go to a movie or try a new restaurant.'

Just then Maurice's mobile phone rang. He turned aside and spoke quietly into the receiver. The conversation was brief.

'Who was that?' Janice asked as he put the phone back on the dashboard.

'Oh, er, just a colleague.'

'It sounded like a woman.'

'Really? Well, er, it was.' Maurice smiled. 'There are female accountants, you know.'

'So what did she want?'

'Hmm, well, it's my fault, I forgot that we were supposed to work on a project this evening. It is important.'

'Is it going to take all night?'

'No. However, I'll probably be tired afterwards, so . . .'

'No opera?'

'I'm afraid not.'

'Maurice, this past week, we've hardly spent any time together.'

'I know, but it's out of my hands. I'll make it up to you, promise. Listen, tomorrow you can come round to my flat and we will open a bottle of champagne, how does that sound?'

Janice smiled up at him and kissed him on the cheek.

'I knew you'd be pleased,' Maurice said.

'I'm sorry, Maurice, but I'm busy for the rest of the weekend. In fact, I'll just get out here and catch the bus home. We don't want to make you late for your appointment, do we?'

Maurice pulled over to the pavement. 'Perhaps it would be better,' he muttered as Janice got out of the car. She watched him drive away and then caught a bus which would take her down to Shree's place.

Walking along the landing to Shree's flat, Janice could hear shouting. As she reached the flat, the door flew open and Tyrone ran out, quickly followed by a mug which crashed against the opposite wall. Tyrone dashed past Janice and headed for the stairs. Shree appeared, holding another mug.

'Move out of the way, Jan!' she ordered as she prepared to hurl the mug after the fast-disappearing figure of Tyrone.

'Give it up, Shree. What's he done now?' Janice said, laughing. Shree shut the front door after her with a slam.

'Damn fool,' she complained. 'He only took my car to carry his crusty friends to some One-Love concert, y'know.'

'But you always lend Tyrone your car, Shree, so what are you getting so worked up about?'

'But it's such a liberty-take. The boy doesn't ask, my car probably stinks to the high heavens of smoke and sweat and drink and anything else dem bring along.'

'Come on, Tyrone's not that bad.'

Shree ripped open a packet of biscuits and stuffed one into her mouth. 'I know, but it's just – do you want one? – it's just that he takes everything I have for granted and he has no respect at all.'

Janice nodded and jumped up on to the sideboard. 'I know what you mean,' she said.

Shree looked at her in surprise. 'I thought your Maurice could do no wrong.'

'Oh, don't be silly. I'm talking about Elroy of course,' Janice huffed.

'But I think that Elroy did have respect for you.'

'No, he didn't – anyway, not like Maurice has respect for me.'

'How does Maurice have respect for you?'

'He takes me out to nice places, he talks about nice things. Do you know what I mean?'

Shree nodded because she knew it was expected of her.

'Elroy just doesn't know how to handle a woman, that's probably why he hasn't found another girlfriend yet. I don't even know why I wasted my time on that boy.'

'You're probably right, Jan. You're better off with Maurice.' Shree sprang up from her chair. 'Oh, no. I've got to get my suit out of the dry cleaners, what's the time?'

Janice looked at her watch. 'Twenty-five minutes past seven. What suit?'

Shree grabbed her wallet and ran to the front door. 'Come on, Janice. It's the suit for Tricia's wedding tomorrow. That stupid Tyrone made me forget totally. I have to get it out today before the shop closes.'

They ran out of the flat and got to the dry cleaners just as the woman who ran the shop was turning the 'open' sign over to 'closed'. Luckily, she knew and liked Shree so she opened the door for them and Shree got her suit. Outside the shop they leaned against the wall, holding their sides, panting and laughing. They walked slowly back to Shree's flat.

'I was surprised to get an invite to Tricia's wedding, you know, even if we were good friends, because I haven't seen her for ages,' Janice said as they crossed the main road.

'Yes, but you really were friendly, so it's not that much of a shock.'

'It's going to be a massive wedding, if we're going and most of our year at school and then all her family.'

'It's true. I think it's really sweet that she's marrying Darren, you know. They've been together forever.'

'That may be, but I could never commit myself like that at my age,' Janice said.

'Nineteen may be young but it's her decision, girl. If she thinks she can make it work I'd tell her to go for it.'

'Yeah, well, you was always the sentimental one.'

'If I'm naturally sensitive, tender, good-natured, peaceable and loving, then who am I to complain? Would you like to grab a pizza and come back to my place?'

'No, thanks, I should be getting home. I'm tired and I've been in these clothes all day. See you tomorrow.' Janice waved goodbye to Shree and crossed the road to catch a bus.

Janice was sitting up in bed reading a fashion magazine. She glanced at the clock on the bedside table. It was ten o'clock. Maurice should have finished working by now.

Janice got out of bed and went into the sitting-room to the telephone. She dialled his number. The answer-phone switched on. Not bothering to leave a message, Janice replaced the receiver and went back to bed. She wondered what Maurice was up to.

'Come now, people. We're going to be late.'

'Shree hasn't done my hair yet.'

'Fabian! Come here now! Damn pickanny!' Paula quickly did up Fabian's braces while he sniffed and gave her dark looks, then she picked up his shoes, put them on his little feet and laced them up. She stood back to see the results of her effort.

'See, you look real handsome now.'

Fabian folded his arms. 'Noooo.'

Paula kissed her teeth dismissively and took his jacket out of the wardrobe. 'Trouble with kids is that when they are ugly they always want to look nice. When they are handsome they do every last thing in their power to look ugly.'

'Shree!' Janice shouted. Shree was still doing her make-up in the bathroom. 'You're gonna make us miss the church bit . . .'

'You're such an old woman, Janice. It's only one o'clock. The wedding doesn't start till three. I've got plenty of time to do your hair.' Shree walked out of the bathroom and pointed at Janice's dress. 'It's all right for you, Jan, you arrived already dressed up. Don't forget that I've had to change here.'

'You don't exactly look like a witch yourself, Shree.'

'Yes I know, but everyone from college is going to

be there and I don't intend for them to go home saying how I looked like any haystack. Come on.' They went into the sitting-room and Janice sat down on the chair. 'Now, how do you want your hair done?'

'Exactly the same as how Paula did yours, half up in a knot and half down with the ends curled underneath.'

'No, Janice. Just for once, can we please not look the same?' pleaded Shree.

'But that's how I usually have *my* hair when we go out. Nothing else suits me because my face is so long.'

'Well, let's strike a deal. I'll do your hair differently but if you don't like it, I'll do it again.'

'I suppose that's fair.'

'Then shut up.' Shree centre-parted Janice's hair and wrapped it back into a sleek French pleat. She pinned the back down neatly and then took a lock out from the front on either side of the parting and curled it to frame Janice's face. 'There, it's done and you'd better like it because I'm not touching your hair again today!'

'It looks really nice, Shree, don't worry,' Janice said, but Shree had gone back to the bathroom to finish her make-up.

'Do you think my dress looks all right?' Janice asked Paula who was doing her make-up in the bedroom.

'Janice, I remember telling you the dress was wicked when you walked through the door, so why must I tell you again?'

'You don't think the halter-neck looks cheap, then? Or too low?'

'No.'

'Maurice bought it for me. He says the sparkling green contrasts with my ebony skin. What do you think?'

'I think you're annoying, now go away.'

'It's so boring, waiting for you lot.'

'If I were you, Janice, I'd go and check your make-up again, there's something wrong.'

Janice pushed Paula out of the way and scrutinized her face in the mirror. 'What is it? Is my lipstick fading? Is my blusher too much? Is my nose peeling?'

'Yes, all of those and one eye looks bigger than the other. Go and ask Shree.'

Janice hurried out of the bedroom and Paula was able to concentrate on her make-up once more.

Eventually they were all finally ready.

'Just watch your step today now.' Janice wagged a finger at Paula. 'Shree told me there was nothing wrong with my face, but a lot will be wrong with yours if you continue to upset me. Besides,' and now she smiled, 'we are going to a House of God. It's not good to lie.'

Paula grinned. 'Wait till the flash comes on before you press the button, Janice.'

Paula was wearing a long, navy-blue, velvety side-split skirt with a matching patterned jacket to go with her son's navy-blue suit. Shree was wearing a classic black dress with gold braid and red stones on the sleeves.

'*Ebony* magazine, here we come,' remarked Janice.

'Yes, but please tell Shree that if she intends to look that good, not to come running to me for protection when she gets mobbed by all the men.'

'Don't talk stupidness, Paula. Most of the men there will be taken, anyway,' said Shree.

'As if that ever stopped men,' said Janice. 'Stop moving around, Fabian, and say "Cheese".'

There was a small explosion of light and the picture was taken. The three girls grabbed their handbags and left the flat with the little boy.

The church was large and traditional, built of grey stone with wooden beams criss-crossing the high triangular roof. Sunlight filtered through the stained-glass windows.

As the organ rang out the Wedding March everybody stood, and Tricia Lauren glided through the church entrance on her father's arm.

'Aaaah, she looks so sweet,' Shree whispered to Paula, who was holding Fabian so he could get a better view.

Tricia was wearing a simple, classic white wedding dress, her face was covered by a white chiffon veil and the long train that trailed behind her was held at the end by one of five bridesmaids. Her forehead was framed by a coronet of maroon and white roses which matched those in her bouquet. She was not exactly a pretty girl, but there was an aura of innocence about her as she reached the altar where her young husband to be and the best man were standing.

As they looked on, the three girls had different thoughts. Janice was thinking of Maurice and how she was going to have a much bigger and more expensive wedding than Tricia's which wasn't as big as she had expected it to be. Shree was looking on and fantasizing that she was the one gliding down the aisle on her father's arm, only she wasn't certain that the man standing by the altar would be Tyrone. Paula stroked Fabian's head thoughtfully. She was reminiscing about the good times with Michael.

'Do you, Darren Marshall, take Tricia Lauren to be your lawfully wedded wife, to have and to hold till death do you part?'

'I do.'

'Do you, Tricia Lauren, take Darren Marshall to be your lawfully wedded husband, to have and to hold till death do you part?'

'I do.'

'Then by the authority vested in me I hereby pronounce you man and wife.'

Darren took the ring from his best man and slipped it on to Tricia's finger.

'You may kiss the bride,' said the vicar.

Darren lifted the veil and kissed Tricia.

Once the service had ended, family and friends streamed out of the church and joined the newly-weds on the lawn outside for the wedding photos.

The reception was held in the nearby church hall which had been decorated with flowers, ribbons and balloons. The hall was full of round tables, each of which had been covered with a pretty white tablecloth and adorned with a small flower arrangement and name cards. On the stage at the end of the hall was one long table reserved for immediate family. Also on the stage was the four-tier wedding cake.

A West Indian catering company was in charge of everything and had prepared a magnificent cold buffet which was spread out on a series of tables running all along one side of the hall. There was fried fish, Caribbean bread, fried dumplings, fried chicken, rice and peas, curried goat, patties, calalloo, plantain, quiche slices, sandwiches, cheese and pineapple chunks on cocktail sticks and assorted salads. The hot food which would be available in the evening was being cooked in the large rectory kitchen. Drinks were being served from a table at one end of the buffet. Jamaican rum and whisky were flowing in abundance.

'Thanks for coming.' Tricia smiled shyly at Shree, Paula and Janice who had walked over to congratulate her. Shree winked away a tear. 'You look so lovely, Trish. I'm jealous.' Tricia sighed happily and looked around the reception hall. 'I just hope everyone else is, the amount of money this is costing.' She saw her mother beckoning to her from the stage. 'I have to go now, see ya.'

Everyone found their places at the tables. Shree, Paula and Janice were seated at a table together. Michael, Tyrone, Tanasha and Elroy were also seated together but so far they hadn't turned up.

'Let's go and get our food, I'm starving,' urged Shree. The others agreed and walked over to join the queue for the buffet.

'So much fried chicken, Shree?' Janice asked, nudging Paula.

'Shut up,' said Shree guiltily. 'I'd call this happy occasion a reason to pig out.'

Janice took pineapple chunks, salad and a few cucumber sandwiches.

'Janice, are you dieting *again*?' Paula asked.

'Maurice doesn't like fat women, so I'm not touching fried food.'

'And if Maurice didn't like black women, I suppose you'd bleach your skin,' Paula said sarcastically.

'You can hardly talk! Michael's got *you* wrapped around his little finger.'

'Okay, kids, that's enough bitchiness for today,' Shree said, shaking her head at them. 'Janice, it's up to you if you feel like starving yourself, but I'm having as much fried chicken and spicy fish as I please.'

'I'm saving myself for the hot food,' Paula said as they made their way back to their table.

'Well, you'll be waiting a long time. They won't bring it out until about nine, long after the dancing's started,' Janice said smugly.

Once everyone had sat down to eat, the master of ceremonies stood up and the speeches began. Fabian fell asleep in his chair as Tricia's uncle droned on about how he hoped Darren and Tricia would live humbly and honestly. Darren mumbled something about loving Tricia till 'death parts them'. The speech was touching, but although Tricia squirmed with pleasure and pride, most girls from her year were beginning to understand what it was they had never seen in Darren. After the best man had made some really embarrassing jokes, Tricia's twelve-year-old brother stood up and read out his speech while Tricia buried her head in embarrassment.

Finally, when all the speeches were over, the wedding cake was cut. Then, as people finished eating, all the tables except the one being used for the bar were taken out of the hall and the floor was swept. Once the hall was cleared, the band took up its position on the stage and started up, and the bride and groom took to the dance-floor. Tricia and Darren were young, so it was more like a rave than a wedding.

Paula nudged Janice and Shree and pointed to the doorway. 'Oh, so it's now they decide to show their faces.' Tyrone, Michael, Tanasha, Elroy and the rest of their crew had just trooped into the hall.

'Oh, the shame of it,' Shree complained. 'Mans can't even turn up for the respectable part.'

'It's so out of order,' Paula agreed.

Although a few eyebrows were raised as the boys immediately went to the kitchen and began filling their plates with food, their presence gave the reception a bit of life.

'Hey, Paula, you don't know how to say hello any more.' Tanasha chucked Paula on her shoulder with the hand that wasn't weighed down with fried chicken and rice.

Paula smiled and indicated the overladen plate. 'Well, I could see you had *other* things on your mind.'

Michael slapped Tanasha around the head as he passed them on his way to the bar. 'I see you're getting finished again, my brother.' The boys jostled around Janice, Shree and Paula, making jokes and asking them what piece of foolishness Darren thought he was trying by getting himself tied up so early. Tyrone stuck out his chest. 'Not me, man.' He touched fists with Tanasha. 'I got sense.'

Shree fixed him with one of her looks. 'More sense than money,' she said. Another slap was handed out by Michael.

'Touchdown,' Elroy joked. 'Now, stop playing with

the girls, Tyrone. The booze is free and I'm off to refill.'
They moved off to the bar.

As Janice danced with an old school-friend she thought about how strange it felt to hear Elroy's voice again. When he'd come in with his crew, he'd said hello and that meant at least they were friends. Janice felt a kind of warm glow because they were talking again. She hoped she hadn't encouraged him too much because she didn't intend to go out with him again. Still, she could flirt with him. Suppose he tried it on her and begged her for her forgiveness? Janice imagined the scene. Elroy pleading with her to go out with him. Threatening to batter Maurice. Offering to marry her. She looked over her partner's shoulder to where Elroy was leaning against the wall chatting to Fabian. He was looking so kriss, Janice almost felt proud of him. As if he felt her watching him, he looked over at her. Janice smiled warmly. Elroy didn't exactly smile back, but she was sure she saw a twinkle in his eye before she spun away.

'Ahem, ahem.' Tricia's father went up on the stage, leading his daughter by the hand. 'It's about time for my daughter to throw the bouquet, so if all you ladies, young and old' – he smiled fondly as his eight-year-old grandniece ran forward to take up a good position – 'you never know.' All the females shuffled towards the stage, laughing amongst themselves. Janice, Shree and Paula jostled each other as they made their way forward.

'Hey, watch Janice's eyes, Paula. They're going misty.'

'Don't talk stupidness, Shree,' Janice said. 'It's only a bit of fun.'

'Yeah, Shree, I agree with Janice. Anyway, when was

the last time Janice won anything? She's the unluckiest girl I know.'

Tricia stood in the middle of the stage and slowly turned her back on her fellow sisters. Whoosh! Thunk!

'Who's got it? Who's got it?' Everyone began jumping around to see if one of their friends had the bouquet. Janice, unprepared for its weight, staggered back a yard or two as the bouquet hit her chest. She bumped into someone who held her arms to steady her. 'Oh, sorry,' she said, before she was whisked away by her friends so that everyone could see who had won Tricia's bouquet of roses.

Not long after, Janice found herself standing next to Elroy. They looked at each other and smiled, embarrassed, and then looked away again at the people dancing. The band was playing a fast reggae tune. Janice tapped her foot impatiently. Finally, Elroy got the message. 'Dance?'

They had only been dancing a few seconds when the music changed. This time it was a slow, suggestive song. Janice moved closer to Elroy who hesitantly put his arm round her. She rested her head on his chest. She could smell all the familiar smells.

She looked up. 'I'm sorry about—'

'It's in the past, Janice. Don't worry.' Elroy kissed her lightly on the forehead.

'Elroy, I—' Janice was about to pour her heart out, tell Elroy how much she still loved him, when all of a sudden he stiffened and roughly pushed her away. She looked up and saw that he was looking towards the hall entrance. She followed his gaze. A very pretty girl was standing in the doorway, shyly looking around for someone. She was about the same age as Janice, with fair skin and long hair that fell down past her shoulders in soft curls. She looked sophisticated in a purple dress with a scalloped neckline and high heels. Janice looked from Elroy to the girl. Elroy patted her on the shoulder as a means of apology. 'See ya, Jan,' he said and was gone. Standing alone on the dance-floor, in the middle of a slow song, Janice felt humiliated. She looked around for Shree or Paula, but Shree was dancing with Tyrone and Paula was dancing with Michael.

As Janice navigated past the locked bodies she felt angry and hurt. For her the evening had suddenly lost its glow. How could she have been so foolish as blatantly to throw herself at Elroy? And everyone must have known that he had a new girlfriend. What a joke she must seem. Elroy was now dancing with the girl to another slow song. Janice's eyes involuntarily followed them around the dance-floor. If the girl had been a dried-out nobody Janice wouldn't have minded. She would have been able to gloat and feel superior. But she knew she was the one who had paled into insignificance beside the new girl's stunning looks. For a brief moment Elroy's eyes met Janice's. His expression was searching. The look she returned was hard as nails.

For Janice the song seemed to last forever. When her friends finally came back she quietly asked Shree if she could drive her home. Shree agreed and also offered to take Fabian back to her own place and babysit him overnight so that Paula could stay at the wedding. Paula jumped at the offer. Shree and Janice went to kiss Tricia and Darren goodbye. As they left the hall, Janice glanced at Elroy. He was whining passionately. The girl's head was on Elroy's shoulder and Elroy was whispering something in her ear.

'Thanks a lot, Shree, I'll come around at about ten or eleven tomorrow with some clothes for Fabian.'

'Yeah, safe, Paula. 'Bye.'

Shree opened the door to find Janice and Paula on her doorstep.

'How come you're both here at the same time?' she asked as they followed her into the sitting-room.

'Well, we saw each other walking up from the bus stop,' said Paula. 'Where's my baby?'

'He's been watching a video,' said Shree. 'Here he comes now.'

Fabian came racing along the hallway and ran into Paula's arms. She hugged him. 'Did you behave yourself last night?' she asked.

'Yes, an' now I'm watching *He-man*.'

'All right, well you go back and finish your video then and I'll come in a minute.'

'Okay.' Fabian ran back to the sitting-room.

'Where's Tyrone?' asked Janice.

'As soon as he knew you two were coming he disappeared quicktime. I think he's gone to his mum's house,' Shree said, laughing as she walked towards the sitting-room.

'I wish Elroy would go to the ends of the earth and never come back,' said Janice.

'Men, who needs them?' declared Shree as she emptied her magic box of hair essentials on to the table.

'Agreed,' said Janice.

'Agreed,' said Paula to the others' surprise.

'What's brought on this change of heart, woman? And don't tell me it's nothing to do with Saint Michael.'

'Yeah.' Janice nodded.

Paula smiled wryly. 'Well, start on Janice's hair, Shree, while you hear me out.'

Janice sat on a chair and Shree, standing behind her, parted her hair into two sections, so as to make it easier to style. Paula gave Fabian a quick look. He was engrossed in the *He-man* video and wasn't listening. She lay down on the sofa and told them what had happened.

'Well, after you lot left the reception, I danced some more and then I had some drinks.'

'How many?' asked Shree, looking worried.

'Four or five, I forget. Then most of Michael's friends left, so we went too and Michael didn't have any cab fare, so I said he could share my cab and walk home when he got to my place.'

'Don't tell us any more, we can guess,' said Janice.

'Shut up, Jan. Go on, Paula.'

'He was only supposed to stay for five minutes but when I woke up this morning he was still there.'

'How could you be so stupid, Paula?' said Janice.

'Even then I was still happy about it because I thought maybe it was the start of new things and I cooked him breakfast, but when he woke up, he didn't want to know. He just muttered something about an appointment and got dressed and ran out of the flat.'

'Uh uh. I didn't think he was like that, you know?' tutted Shree.

'He didn't even touch the food,' Paula said sadly.

'That's not nice – ow, Shree, this ain't steel wool you be combing. Remember that, all right?'

'Sorry, Jan.'

'I guess it was my fault really,' Paula sighed, playing with some hair bobbles, 'I let him take advantage.'

'From what I'm hearing it wasn't your decision to let him or not,' Shree remarked firmly.

'Yeah, that was a dirty thing to do. He just assumed that because of Fabian being away he could do anything with you.'

'You've got a right to be angry.'

'You think so?' Paula asked hopefully.

''Course, if we say so then you do.'

Paula smiled. 'What are you trying to do to Janice's hair, Shree?' she asked, changing the subject.

'The way you said that, Paula, it's like you're worried for me,' Janice said anxiously, trying to feel her hair.

'Janice, you're messing up the style, man. If you do that again I'm gonna bop you over the knuckles with this comb. Just wait.'

'But what are all those knobs in her hair for?' asked Paula. 'It's not just you who has to walk street with her, y'know, it's me too.'

Shree chuckled as she began unrolling some of the bumps in Janice's hair. 'They're not staying there, you chief. I put them there to make my job easier.' She picked up some massive gold, shiny bobbles. 'I'm going to put two bunches at the front tied with these.' She pointed to some black and gold ringlets laid out on the table. 'Oh, yeah, and I bought these gold butterflies from Old Miss Loretta's stall in Brixton market the other day, and some diamond stones that you can just thread through the hair. She showed me how to do it. It's gonna look wicked.'

'Shree, all I want is a nice sensible style. Don't experiment. Stick to what you know, please,' Janice pleaded.

'Maurice's ideas on style do not impress us,' Shree snapped in annoyance.

'It's true. The way that coconut has had you pushing your platforms and your damn straight jeans down our throats has not made me like him any the more.'

Janice jerked her head out of Shree's hands in indignation. 'Maurice is not a coconut. He's very in touch with his blackness. Besides, he *is* half white.'

'Yeah, he knows *that*. He just doesn't know he's half black,' Paula continued sarcastically.

'You're just slamming him because he doesn't go to all-dayers or clubs or Dalston to buy his *patties*,' Janice retorted, leaning back as Shree pulled the brush through her hair.

'Yes, well, it doesn't help.'

'You don't have to be black to do those things,' said Janice, 'and you don't have to do those things to be black. Compared to most of the *in-touch* black men you know, Maurice is a role model.'

'He shouldn't be,' said Shree. 'Maurice doesn't like black people.' She tapped Janice's head with the comb. 'Hear me out before you start defending *that* one. He *doesn't* like black people. He acts like white people. You're the only black person I've seen him with. He goes around with white people. He goes to West End wine bars and exclusive sports clubs.'

'The ones that will let him in.'

'I'll bet he doesn't know any black history and yet knows who all the Queen's cousins are. In fact, I'm surprised Maurice is going out with you. You're not exactly his type now, are you? It *must* be love.'

'Shree, what have you done to my head?' Janice shrieked, looking in a hand-mirror.

'I think it looks wicked,' said Paula.

Janice chewed her lip. 'Maybe if we take out the diamond stones and the gold baubles and just make one pony-tail.'

'Janice, there is no way that you are going to ruin that hairstyle. It's taken me ages to do and I had to buy so many of those gold baubles, just for you.'

'Shree is right, Janice. Stop trying to be what Maurice wants. It looks ten times better than those boring ways you've done your hair ever since you started hanging out with that fool.'

'It's just that it won't come across with what I'm wearing,' Janice moaned, looking down at her platforms and smart, straight black trousers.

'That's the least of your worries, Jan. You're with *us* now. *We* are black.'

Shree pulled Janice into her bedroom. She went to the large double wardrobe and flung open the panelled doors.

'Now let me – mmm, no, not that. Maybe – I know.' Janice sifted through the pile of clothes that Shree was throwing out of the wardrobe on to the bed.

'This is you!' Shree announced triumphantly, holding up a glittering sequined top and leggings suit. It was gold, silver, pink and blue. It had diamond dollar signs on it and 'Dem nuh wicked like me' in gold beads across the chest.

Janice looked horrified. 'No, Shree, I cannot wear that.'

'What do you mean?' Shree asked innocently.

'Which part of "NO" don't you understand, Shree? No, no, no!'

'There's nothing wrong with it, Jan. It looks good.'

'Then how come I've never seen *you* in it?' Janice demanded suspiciously. Shree opened her eyes very wide. 'It's too big for me, Janice. You know how tiny I am.'

In the end it was Paula who decided the matter. Sauntering into the room to see what they were up to, the first thing she caught sight of was the glittering creation in Janice's reluctant arms. 'Now that is beautiful,' she said.

Shree folded her arms and looked at Janice. 'You see? Now put it on.'

Janice was certainly catching the stares in the walk from the tube station up to Brockwell Park. Her self-consciousness was wearing off and she began to enjoy the attention.

'Aren't you cold, Janice?' Paula asked, bending down to zip up Fabian's jacket. Janice shook her head.

Shree smiled. 'I don't see how you could be with all those men beggin' to keep you warm.' She gave Paula a nudge. Janice looked at the ground and didn't deny it.

They turned into the side gates of the park, a large circular area which gently sloped upwards into a hill.

Around the edges of the park were trees and bushes which separated it from the neat houses beyond. At this all-dayer there was a huge stage instead of various sound systems and this had been built at the bottom of the hill so that the setting served as an open-air concert hall with people able to see more easily by going further up the hill and looking down. As the girls neared the stage they saw it was surrounded by masses of people. Not just ragga or yardie types either. Someone was singing on the stage. Shree jumped up to see who it was.

'It's quite good,' Janice said, moving her head to the thumping beats.

'I can't see,' Fabian complained.

'Okay, then, let's go up there and look around,' Paula suggested, pointing higher up the hill to where there were some stalls.

'Hey, let's just stay till the end of the song,' Janice said.

When the song ended they walked up the hill towards the stalls.

'Look, there's my uncle's pattie waggon,' Paula exclaimed. She hurried to a stall with an open-air stove, which was selling Caribbean food. An overweight and overworked man was selling patties as fast as his co-worker was taking them out of the oven.

'They must taste good,' Shree said, nodding towards the queue that wended its way to the stall. The girls joined the queue.

'Y'all right Paula? How the lickle one dere?' Paula's uncle waved a greasy palm at Fabian.

'I see business is booming, Uncle Francis,' Paula said, smiling.

'None can resist de true Jamaican style a cooking,' Francis replied, beaming. They all laughed.

'Me hungry,' Fabian announced.

'Fabian, don't be so fast,' Paula scolded.

'Blouse an' skirt. Paula, see how you let me jus' a ramble hon and the poor t'ing jus' a cry out from starvation!' Paula smiled as her uncle handed out patties all round. 'Just say hello to ya mudder fram me. Say she have a phone. She can ring her cousin Francis anytime.' Paula said she would and then they moved on.

Shree bought Fabian a small silver whistle from a group of rastafarians who were peddling carnival paraphernalia, before moving back to the stage where the familiar sounds of Buju B were being played. There were a lot of people there and the girls couldn't see much from their position.

'Me want see! Me want see!' Fabian tugged at his mum's shirt, then at Shree's skirt, then at Janice's arm. He was ignored on all sides. Following the throng, the girls started dancing and were getting into it when suddenly the music stopped and everyone moaned. A man with long thick dreadlocks came on the mike and held up his hands for peace, ignoring shouts from several feisty people to shut up and just 'run de rhythm'.

'Is a you fault this so don't curse the sound people. Beca' me nuh know why unno can't take care a your own.'

'Dis time,' humphed the man. 'A child called Fabian, lost his mother, who call Paula. Paula, your son is waiting for you backstage. Please come an' get him. Just remember, if we did not have him, who would? Is good to enjoy yourself and dat type a t'ing but unno must look after your children. Dem no replace, seen?' He put the mike

154

back on its stand and disappeared and the music resounded from the speakers once more.

As the man spoke, Janice and Shree had turned to face Paula who looked about her wildly as if she couldn't quite believe it. 'I don't think there is another Fabian with a mother called Paula,' said Janice. Paula looked at them through her fingers.

Shree tapped her on the shoulder. 'Hadn't we better go and get him then?'

Fabian was playing with a security guard's sunglasses and looked up disappointedly when his mother and her friends came running round the corner of the stage.

'Don't you ever do that to me again, Fabian,' Paula hissed as she hauled the boy down the steps at the back of the stage. Fabian grinned up at her disarmingly.

'Don't be too hard on the baby, Paula, he doesn't understand about murderers and psychopaths,' Janice advised.

'I'm too glad to see him safe to be angry, to tell you the truth, and I feel guilty because it's my fault.' She bought Fabian an ice-cream to show him they were still friends.

'Oh, this is getting boring now.'

'Yeah, each act they bring on stage is starting to sound the same.'

'It's beginning to rain too, let's go.' For Shree, Janice and Paula, this particular all-dayer was over. They walked out of the park and jumped on a bus to Brixton station where they could get the tube back to Hackney.

chapter
nine

'**Don't even** think to come feisty with me,' said Donna heatedly.

'Yes, well, the way you carry on fresh with other people's men gives me good reason,' replied Chantelle.

Shree and Paula looked at each other while Donna and Chantelle pursued their petty argument. The four of them had been down to the Sight and Sound Technical College to get a catalogue of the autumn training courses and they had been making their way home when an argument about Tanasha had flared up out of nowhere.

'The whole of Hackney knows you for what you are,' continued Chantelle. 'My God, if you only knew what they are saying about you, you would die of shame.'

As they waited at the traffic lights, Donna faced up to Chantelle.

'Which people?' she asked.

'It doesn't matter which people, what matters is what's being said,' Chantelle answered, beginning to walk away. Donna pulled her back by her arm.

'Hey, let go of my arm, if I don't wanna stand here chatting rubbish wid you that's up to me.'

Donna let go of her arm. 'I don't know who you think you are, you little—'

'Little what? Don't even begin something you know you can't defend, Chantelle. Little what? Don't make me have to call you by your name in front of Shree and Paula.' Shree and Paula shuffled their feet and looked away.

'You nasty bitch, you couldn't call me jack-shit before I would just slap you in your face. You and them greasy people you move wid ain't in no position to call me anything. Who are you to talk to me? You think you're so nice, all you do is big up twenty-four-seven, but you ain't got nothing I want.' Donna put her hands on her hips nonchalantly and kissed her teeth loudly. Then she started walking away.

'Just keep your legs closed when you're around *my* Tanasha, low-life, he don't want you.'

Donna stopped, then spun round, fists clenched, raised and ready. People were beginning to stare. Donna had long since stopped pretending she wasn't really bothered. Her voice was very loud when she wanted it to be and now it was harsh too.

'You're so craven for that man that maybe there are a few things you just don't see. He is so ugly I don't see how you make him out to be some sex symbol. He's mashed and you're the only woman who sees anything in him. I wouldn't touch him with rubber gloves on, you don't know what skin diseases he's cultivating. Oh yeah, speaking of diseases, don't treat Tanasha like he's some angel. He's sleeping with half of Hackney and you know it. You better get yourself checked out, Chantelle, because with the life he's been leading he's probably got everything under the sun. No decent girl would ever go with that piece of nastiness because he's been everywhere.'

'Just like you,' muttered Chantelle.

Donna put her fist up close to the side of Chantelle's face. 'I ain't afraid to fight you, you filthy tramp. You can't even cuss me to my face. Go on, cuss me to my face, cuss me to my face.' Chantelle put her mouth really close to Donna's ear and shouted as loud as she could. Donna immediately punched Chantelle who tottered back in surprise before she lunged after Donna, shouting all manner of death threats. Shree started to try to make peace but they shouted at her to stay out of it and Paula quickly pulled her back out of the fray.

Donna grabbed hold of one of Chantelle's massive gold heart-hoop earrings and yanked it hard until blood started to drip from Chantelle's ear. But that was the last time she had the advantage. Chantelle, mad with pain and rage, held Donna's head in a lock and started raining lightning-quick blows in her face and on her head. Donna struggled like a wild animal but she was no match for Chantelle. Shree and Paula were stunned by the pace of the fight, but now they leaped forward to break things up before Donna got killed or somebody called the police. It took a while to disentangle them.

'And look at you,' Paula said in disgust. Chantelle's damaged ear was bleeding heavily and her delicate sandal straps were ripped beyond repair. She glared fiercely at Donna who was in a much more pitiful condition with several long and deep scratches down one side of her face. Her left eye was bruised and closing fast, while her upper lip was swollen and split. Donna sank down into a heap on the pavement and began crying softly.

Paula decided it was best to get these two casualties to a flat to clean them up.

'My place or yours, Shree?'

'Mine's closer but Tyrone's probably still asleep.'

'Well, that's out. He'll think it's all a joke and be telling everyone,' Paula said.

'S' true. Anyway, you've got all those plasters and creams for Fabian at your place and we're definitely gonna need them.'

'Owwww!'

'Stop moaning right now, Donna,' Paula said, haphazardly applying antiseptic cream. 'You open your mouth just once and you are going to find yourself on the main road with your face like that. This is all your big idea, so just shut up now while you are still on the right side of the door.'

Donna bit her lip, but the tears welled up all the same.

On the other side of the room, Shree was handing out the same treatment to Chantelle.

'Look what that bitch did to my ear.' Shree just carried on looking for a plaster.

'Shree, are you listening to me?'

'Quite frankly, no.'

Chantelle glared at her. 'I know all of you are backing Donna. You must be – ah!'

'Oh, sorry! Didn't I say it would hurt?' Shree gave an innocent little laugh.

When Donna and Chantelle were patched up, Paula and Shree tried to get some sense out of them.

'What the hell were you two fighting over? Me and Paula are just minding our own business and two minutes later we have to separate you before you beat the shit out of each other, me nuh right, Paula?'

Chantelle and Donna looked at the floor.

'Okay, so Chantelle first,' commanded Paula. 'Tell us what happened.'

'We were at Trenz, y'know, the full crew was there and you want to see the way *that* – ' Chantelle threw Donna a vengeful look – 'was clocking Tanasha. Then she begged him to dance and she was all pushing herself on him and then taking him into corners and whispering things in his ear. I wouldn't mind, yeah, but that left me having to talk to her date. You've met that bean-head Shane. You don't get any sense out of him because he's always smoking something unnatural. I suppose that was all she did but it was enough. It bring me down as well, 'cause all the other girls are telling me about how bad she's carrying on and is it true that she's my best friend? I don't mind defending her and I did, but it just can't go on this way. It's making me look stupid.'

'All right, and now it's your turn, Donna.'

Donna, who had been kissing her teeth, began her own tirade. 'Chantelle's neurotic, it must be that time of the month or some such problem. She should trust me because I've been her best friend for long enough and I've already stated the reasons why I don't want Tanasha. For a start, I wasn't "clocking" Tanasha. I just smiled to say hello and that's it. I did ask him to dance, it's true, but not because I wanted any physical business. The boy

I came with was dancing with some other girl and I didn't want to stand alone since Chantelle was at the bar, so I just asked him to dance. What's wrong with that? By the way, Chantelle, you should know better than to listen to spiteful, nasty little beasts like Sireeta Marsh. All she knows how to do is make trouble, that's why she's always on her own.'

'Well, all that can be said from all of this,' said Shree, 'is that Donna stay extra-far away from Tanasha from now on just to show people that it's nothing, and Chantelle just forget about all of this business.'

'After all, you are best friends, right?' Paula asked, but got no response. 'So don't be fighting over a man of all things. That's the lowest. If you have to fight, fight because of your own personal, serious problems, not because some girl's getting more attention from him than you. Don't be broadcasting this either. Especially you, Donna, because we know what you're like. If Tanasha hears about this it's gonna boost him no end and trust me, that boy's head is big enough.'

'Someone I really haven't seen in a long time is Alisha Dean,' said Shree. 'She's you lot's friend, ain't she? How's she doing these days, then?'

'She's doing all right. She was one of the assistants at the Afro Hair and Beauty exhibition this year,' Chantelle said, shrugging.

'Oh, did you go?' asked Shree.

'I guess so.'

'Who did you go with?'

'Um, Donna.'

'So?' urged Shree. 'What happened?'

'Well, everyone was getting their hair done free so I

decided to get my hair done too. Anyway, this man did my hair, and boy, was he kriss.'

'Was he what?' Donna entered the conversation. 'He was a dog.'

'He was kriss,' insisted Chantelle.

'Yes, well, with your taste in men he probably looked that way, but to people who know, he was a dog.'

'Just consider for a moment who among us wears the glasses, and then rest your gums, Donna.'

'I may wear the glasses, darling, but it's obvious who needs them.' Shree and Paula looked at each other bemused.

'Well, I'm sorry to break the happy mood,' said Paula, standing up, 'but it's time for me to pick up my son from nursery.'

Everyone got up. 'Yeah, I'd better go and organize my household too,' said Shree. 'What are you doing tonight, Paula?'

'Oh, I won't be in. I'm going to see my mum.'

Donna looked up in surprise. 'I thought you two fought like cat and dog,' she said tactlessly. Paula gave her a very dirty look before she went into the bedroom to get her bag.

'Oh, is you.' Paula's mother left the front door ajar and went back into her sitting-room. Paula and Fabian shuffled in uncertainly, mumbling their hellos. Fabian inserted his hand into Paula's big palm and kept it there.

'So what is it you want, Paula?' her mother asked, stretching herself out on the sofa. She used the remote control to turn up the volume of the television. 'Me nuh have no money fe give you.'

'You know I don't want your money. I just came to say hello and for you to see Fabian.'

'Hello. I've seen Fabian, he's looking the same as usual, is that all you came round for?'

Paula bit her lip. She sat down in one of the armchairs and watched the television. Her mother ignored her.

'I saw Uncle Francis at Brockwell Park a few days ago.'

'Oh.'

'He was asking how you were.'

'Oh.'

'I was sur—'

'Sssssh! Can't you see I'm watching this?' When the sitcom finished, Paula's mother got up and went into the kitchen to make herself a cup of tea. The doorbell rang. Paula looked up in surprise. Her mother went to the door.

'Hello, Lucille.'

'How you keeping, Enid?'

'Well, you know, me have a spot of chill and me very tired these days what with work and everything. Come in and sit down.'

'And who is this?' asked Lucille.

'Dat my grandson.'

'You too young to be a grandmother, Enid.'

'And my daughter too young to be a mother.' She gave Paula a dirty look. Paula smiled uncertainly at her mother's friend who smiled back warmly.

'You want a cup of tea or a drink or any'ting, Lucille dear?' Enid cooed.

'Yes, please.'

'Come into the kitchen then and we can have a little chat.' Paula heard Lucille ask her mother if perhaps Fabian and Paula wouldn't like something to drink too but she heard her mother tell her friend that Paula and Fabian had drunk almost everything in the house and weren't hungry.

Paula got up and strode into the kitchen. 'Fabian is hungry, Mum, what can I give him to eat?'

Enid sighed and sipped her tea. 'There's nothing to eat, me thought the sensible thing would a been to feed him before you leave your flat.'

'He is nearly starving. I have to give him something,' Paula said as she walked over to the fridge. Inside were some rashers of bacon and some baked beans in a bowl. She took them out.

Enid stood up and barred Paula's way to the cooker. 'Now, what is it you t'ink you doing?'

'I'm going to make Fabian some dinner.'

Enid took the bacon and put it back in the fridge. 'Not with my bacon. That's for my breakfast tomorrow before I go to work.'

'What else is there?'

'Your son is not my problem, Paula. I'm done with you and yours. No one told you to go and sleep with a man and get pregnant. Not even yardie lickle Shree have baby but you must a run go mess up your life. You see my situation. Your father run, gone lef' we. You want to know where him is? Him one of dem drunkard people now. See him dere outside a road all hours and your baby father is de same way. Trust me 'pon dat. You're no good, Paula. I can say dese t'ings in front of Lucille because she already know how you stay. You just a run from one blues night to de other. You don't work. You in your council flat and you t'ink life is good but ten years from now, you still gwan be in that council flat and life won't seem so fresh. You see dis house. Me still working to pay fe it. It nuh come easy to me but I was never lazy. Not like your father, and you just like him. Live like an animal.' Enid spoke in a low, mean voice. 'I suppose what I'm trying to say is that I try so hard to teach you by my example but you so hard of hearing, you go and be worse. Well, you might be hitting rock bottom but don't come pile your problems 'pon my shoulders. Me nuh have no food fe give you. Me sorry.' She shrugged her shoulders and picked up her cup of tea.

'I-is him hungry?' Lucille asked Paula, looking at the doorway where Fabian was now standing. Paula said nothing. Lucille rummaged around in her handbag.

'Give him these mints, then.' She held out a half-finished packet of Polos. Fabian innocently moved towards the outstretched hand but Paula pulled him backwards sharply. 'We don't need nothing from you!' she spat as she grabbed up her son and marched out of the house.

'And so, you know, I just felt my blood boiling up inside me. That fridge was so full it could hardly stand up but she wouldn't even give Fabian a crust of bread and her friend had to offer her *mints*.'

Janice put her arm around Paula, who had finally, at her friend's flat, broken down into hot tears.

'I'm sorry to bother you with my problems, Janice, but I hate to see her treating my son exactly how she treated me and I just had to talk to someone about it.'

'I know your mother has always been mean like that.'

'I mean, some people love their children, like your parents,' Paula sniffed.

'I know this sounds cold, but if she treats you like that then why do you keep going to see her?'

'I don't know. I keep hoping that one day she'll soften and accept me and Fabian. It's stupid but sometimes I think that this will be the day, but of course it never is.'

'I think that you should stop going to visit her. I'm sorry to say this, Paula, but I've seen the way she's treated you since day one and she's a horrible woman.'

'She's all the family I've got.'

'No, you're all the family she's got. She's the one that's going to miss out. You've got us, girl! Aren't me an' Shree your family too?'

Paula smiled. ''Course. I'm sorry.' She smiled and hugged Janice.

Fabian came running in from the kitchen where he had been eating fish fingers and chips. Paula quickly turned away and dried her eyes. Looking around the sitting-room, she saw a smart dress laid out on the back of a chair. On the floor next to the chair was a pair of polished shoes.

'Are you going somewhere, Janice?'

166

Janice shrugged her shoulders. 'I'm going to go to my mum's with Maurice later.'

'Oh. All right, I'll go in a minute.'

Janice started to object but Paula got up and put on her jacket. 'No, it's all right. I don't want you to miss this. It sounds serious.'

Janice laughed happily. 'Well, it's nearly the end of August. It's been almost two months, and well, my mum's just begging to see him.'

'Yeah, I bet she is, *after* you told her about the Armani suits and the high-powered job.'

'I can't lie. It's the truth.'

'Looks like another wedding will be happening soon.'

'Now that, I doubt.'

Janice was finishing her hair when the doorbell rang. She ran to open the front door. Maurice was standing there, wearing an extra smart suit and a bow-tie.

'Very smart indeed, my mum's going to—'

'Janice, I can't come.'

'But . . .'

'I have to go to the tennis club tonight. They're having a special function. It's business.'

'But Maurice, we're supposed to be going to my mother's, remember? For dinner?'

Maurice smoothed the front of his jacket. 'Listen, sweetheart. It just came up and it is very important.'

'Sure, just like all the appointments with the female accountant.'

'I'm sure your mother's, uh, home-cooking will, um, wait.'

'No, Maurice. My mother's "home-cooking" took ages to prepare. She's really looking forward to you coming. We have to go.' Maurice didn't answer but looked at his highly polished shoes.

'You can go early if you must.'

'Oh, very well,' said Maurice with visible reluctance. 'But I can't stay for long.'

'Fine,' Janice snapped as she went to get her coat.

As they walked up the neatly kept drive, Janice's mother rushed out to meet them. Beaming from ear to ear, Rose noted the expensive suit and the car, then she took in Maurice's good looks.

'Oh, Maurice, you didn't need to get all dressed up like this just for our little dinner,' she simpered as she ushered them into the hall.

'Well, I always knew the way to a girl's heart was through her mother's.' Maurice smiled at Janice.

'Janice, show Maurice into the sitting-room and then come and help me carry some things into the dining-room. Lloyd, offer Maurice a drink.'

Janice's family seemed to have gone all out. Pops was dressed in a neatly pressed white shirt, some smart trousers and a short-sleeved jumper, while Rio, the surprise of the evening, was in a suit.

Rio followed Maurice into the sitting-room. 'But is it the artical Rolex?'

'I don't know about the *artical* Rolex, Rio, but it's the real thing, yes,' Maurice said.

'What about the Saab? It's a turbo, isn't it?'

'That's right. Are you interested in cars?'

'You bet. I've got pictures of sports cars on my bedroom wall. I'm going to have a Porsche when I'm older.'

'Oh, I've had one of those but I sold it. They're fast cars but who needs a fast car in London? Besides, they're far too low. I like big cars.'

'Yeah, I know what you mean,' said Rio enthusiastically.

'Would you like a glass of wine, Maurice?' Lloyd asked, pouring himself a glass.

'No thanks, I'm driving.'

'That never stopped our dad,' Rio commented.

Lloyd glared at Rio. 'Do you go to church, Maurice?' he asked.

'No, I'm too cynical and find Christianity too dogmatic.'

'There's nutting wrong wid going to church.'

'Quite.'

There was a pause while Lloyd wondered what to say next.

'So, what line of business are you in, Mr Williams?'

'I own a building materials store in Leyton. It sells wood, wallpaper, paint, that kind of thing.'

'How is business?'

'It does all right,' Lloyd said.

'I can see. You live in a very nice area. When did you buy this house?'

'Shortly before Rio came along.'

'It will be worth a lot more now. Property values in Highbury and Islington have soared.'

'Maybe.' Lloyd looked relieved when Janice came into the room a moment later.

'I hope nobody has been giving my Maurice a hard time. Mum says if you'd all like to come into the dining-room, dinner will be served in a minute.' Janice pulled Maurice up from his seat and squeezed his arm as they walked to the dining-room. Lloyd watched the way Janice smiled at Maurice with shining eyes. He noticed Maurice glance at his watch.

'More gravy, Maurice dear?' Maurice smiled his no to the gravy but took some more of the rice.

'I'm so happy that you and my Janice are together. You're so right for her.' The corners of Maurice's mouth twitched as Rose pressed his hand confidently. 'I have heard that you have a wonderful job, Maurice.' She leaned eagerly across the table.

'I wouldn't call it wonderful, but it is a living, I suppose.'

'Maurice is really rich,' Janice announced.

'My Janice has changed so much since she started going out with you. She used to look so scruffy and go around with ignorant people.'

'No I didn't.'

'Be quiet, Janice. But Maurice, Janice told us how you used your influence to help her get her job.'

'Well, they do say it's not what you know but who,' Maurice said, smiling.

'I knew enough,' said Janice.

'That's not what they were saying at reception when I got back from lunch,' Maurice said, laughing. Rose and Rio laughed too but Janice looked annoyed.

'Tell us more about your job, Maurice,' Rose said encouragingly. 'Rio is thinking of becoming an accountant too, aren't you, Rio?'

'Er, yeah,' Rio agreed, nudging Janice.

'Well, it's quite boring. I've been working for Portman and Portman for almost two years. My job is to keep an eye on the people doing the accounts and all the financial paperwork. I also help make sure our cash is being invested wisely and monitor all expenses. I'm number two to the Finance Director.'

'So what do you like to do in your spare time Maurice?' Lloyd asked. 'If you weren't here meeting us, what would you be doing on a fine Saturday evening like this?'

'Anything to do with sports. Meeting similarly-minded people, playing a game of tennis, I'm a sports fanatic. I adore tennis, it's the love of my life along with golf.'

'Yes, Janice loves those sports as well,' Rose lied.

'No football then?' Lloyd asked.

'Dear me, no, I prefer games where the spectators aren't hooligans.'

'I enjoy watching football matches,' Lloyd said.

'Maurice, you've eaten that chicken very quickly, try the fish. I made it especially because you were coming. It's Janice's favourite,' urged Rose.

Maurice wiped his mouth with his napkin and pushed back his chair. He gave the table a sheepish-looking smile.

'Some other time, I'm afraid. This must look absolutely terrible but I have another engagement I must attend to this evening. *Très important*, as they say. Thank you for a charming dinner, it has been a pleasure meeting you.'

Janice's mouth dropped in horror. Maurice stood up and straightened his suit. He kissed a confused Rose's hand and shook a silent Lloyd's. He kissed a furious Janice on the cheek. 'I'll see myself out,' he said as he sauntered out of the dining-room, leaving an embarrassed Janice, a flustered mother, a quietly disapproving father and a surprised brother sitting around the table. They heard the front door close and the sound of the Saab being started.

'I wonder if I overcooked the chicken, you know?'

'The chicken was delicious, Mum,' Janice said wearily.

'Yes, but the gravy was too thick, you know?'

'The gravy was fine, Mum.'

'There must have been something wrong with the cooking, I—'

'There was nothing wrong with the cooking.'

'Janice, you're definitely stepping up with Maurice. He's got one kriss pair of wheels. That's the sort of car that I'm going to get, I'm not getting a Porsche any more and did you catch that Rolex? Wow.' Rio babbled on. Lloyd got up and walked out of the dining-room into the sitting-room and closed the door behind him.

Rio loosened his tie. 'Mum, I'm going out tonight with my crew.'

Rose looked up. 'No, Rio, I think the family should be together tonight.'

Rio got up. 'Sorry, no can do, people are waiting on

me. Some other time, eh?' He ran upstairs to get changed.

Rose sighed and got up to start gathering up the dishes and plates. Janice helped clear the table and was then shooed away by her mother. She went into the sitting-room and curled up inside a big comfy armchair while her father watched the news. He was silent and in the end Janice couldn't stand it any more.

'How come you're the only one who didn't have anything to say about Maurice's disappearance, Pops?'

'It's all up to you, Janice. I can't make your decisions for you but I don't think Maurice is any good. I know he's got a lot of money and a good job but even though I want the best for my girl, money isn't everything. I'd rather see you happy with a builder than miserable with a banker. Maurice is all smiles and airs and graces but he don't have no real manners. Janice, I saw the way he is when he thinks no one is watching him and he doesn't have any heart. No real feelings.'

'But he's ten times better than Elroy,' Janice said defiantly.

There was no response from Lloyd.

'I said that he's better than Elroy.' But Lloyd didn't answer. He simply picked up his glass of wine and went upstairs to lie down. Alone in the room, Janice was trying to tell herself that Maurice was not the person her dad had described. Janice had been overwhelmed by the effort and love her mother had thrown into their meal and it had touched her. But it had not touched Maurice. He couldn't care less and that had disappointed her more than anything that he'd ever done to her.

Rose came into the sitting-room after finishing the dishes and told her to ignore her father and that she thought Maurice was lovely, but Janice wasn't really listening to her. She was thinking of Elroy and how she still cared.

Meanwhile, at Shree's place, there was more stormy weather going on.

'No, Tyrone, I don't feel like going.'

'But Shree, I can't turn down a brethren, you know how it is.'

Shree was lying on her bed. 'You can go alone, you know.'

'Eh? A man can't be turning up at a dance without his girl. It don't look right. Besides, Marcell wants to see you, he ain't seen you before.'

'Take him a photo.'

'No, Shree, you must come.'

Shree sat up. 'Can't you stay home just this once?'

'It's a mate's dance and thing. We won't have to pay to get in and it's our sound playing there so I know it's gonna be wicked.'

'Yeah, but I won't know anyone there and you're going to run off with your friends and leave me and I don't have a thing to wear.'

'You've got plenty of clothes and you will know people there. I think Tanasha's girl is gonna be there.'

'I don't want to go to no packed-out blues dance in New Cross. It's too far. It's gonna take ages to get there and I'm not in the mood.'

'It doesn't matter how long it takes. You'll be in the

car, I'll drive and you'll feel in the mood when you get there.'

'But you're going to get drunk and I don't want to have to drive home.'

'Just for you, I won't touch any drink, so you won't have to drive back.'

'I don't know.'

'Come on, Shree, I'm meeting you halfway.'

In the end she gave in. 'What am I supposed to wear?' She went to her wardrobe and took out the first dress her hand touched. A plain black one. She couldn't be bothered to dress up. She shook her hair loose and then put the dress on. She looked in the mirror. The dress was all right.

Unfortunately, Tyrone didn't see it that way. He took her by the shoulders and propelled her back into the bedroom. 'Take it off, Shree. You're not wearing rags to a dance that I'm going to be at too.' Shree looked at Tyrone indignantly.

'I just want my woman to stand out, that's all, so that people can see how beautiful you are.' He looked in the wardrobe and pulled out some red sequinned leggings and a red sequinned halter-neck bra-top. He looked in her jewellery box and took out her large rose earrings, her Gucci link chain and four of her gold bangles. Shree took the clothes and the jewellery reluctantly.

'We both look very good,' Tyrone said as they passed the mirror on the way out of the flat. Light-skinned Tyrone with his meltdown good looks, his ski-slope and a grey-blue silk suit and the thick chaps that Shree had bought him for his birthday contrasted with Shree's very dark coffee-coloured skin. Her hair was loose and tonged into curls at the sides, her bright red ensemble was mellowed a little by a black chiffon jacket and the gold bangles that jangled noisily on her wrists.

The dance, as Shree suspected it would be, was deep in the heart of south London's New Cross in a small terraced house. Inside it was very dark but Shree could see there were a lot of yardie girls of whom she knew only a few.

'Come on and meet my friends.' Tyrone propelled Shree to one side of the room where a great many rude boys were propped up against the wall, nodding their heads to the slow reggae beat. They came to inspect Shree eagerly enough and even when they found out she was Tyrone's woman they were for the main part undisturbed, so in that respect there was no shortage of bodies to chat to that evening.

The ragga girls eyed Shree and her gold. 'How could that lickle something come down here with all that gold on and she don't know nobody,' one hardened female muttered.

'I wouldn't touch her for nuthin' if I was you,' another whispered in passing.

'Why? She ain't too much.'

'She's Derrick's youth, from Hackney.'

'And who's Derrick?'

'You know him. He's the one who shot Terror.'

'Oh.' There might be many Derricks, but there was only one Terror. So Shree was eyed with veiled envy and blatant awe by most of the girls there and left to her own devices.

'You never got those in no shop, Shree.' Chantelle said, referring to Shree's earrings. Each was a large rose made of sheets of very finely rolled gold studded with tiny red stones.

Shree shook her head. 'No. My dad got them made and brought over from Jamaica.'

Chantelle sighed. She really did try to aspire to Shree's level of krissness but she never quite made it. Shree always had the most jewellery, the wickedest clothes, the fittest men. Chantelle slavishly studied changing fashions and all her money went on clothes. She denied herself food so she could look glitterous in her catsuits. She would gladly spend the whole day doing her hair for a rave in the evening, but no matter how hard she tried or how much time she spent, she never quite earned the stamp of an untouchable. Life was unfair, she reflected. And then there was Shree's fragility. The aura that followed her everywhere and just made people want to protect her. A few of the less blessed girls truly believed that if they went to sleep one day and woke up as Shree, they would not be disappointed with the reincarnation.

Shree felt someone pull her backwards gently but firmly into the centre of the room. She whipped round to cuss the man about his feistyness and found herself staring at Nero's large frame. He didn't say anything or smile. He just pulled Shree closer to him. Normally she would make a man ask properly for a dance but her tongue was tied and she couldn't move. She didn't even dare to lift her head to see if Tyrone was watching. He would be furious.

'You come wid your English man?' Nero asked softly.

Shree nodded. 'H-how come you're here?'

Nero just smiled. They moved together to the slow beat. Nero did not try to whine with her. He didn't push himself up against her like men usually did. He kept his distance and Shree felt a bit peeved that he wasn't eager for her like all the other men were. He didn't eye her body or make suggestive remarks. He just held her. Unconsciously Shree moved closer and pressed her body against his. She didn't even realize she was doing it but Nero stepped back instantly and laughed his deep laugh warningly. 'I thought you said you came wid your man.'

Shree looked at him sideways, flirtatiously. 'Never trust a woman,' she whispered and disappeared into the crowd. Nero let her go. The lady could play it cool all she wanted but Nero had been able to feel her pulse while they had danced and it had been much faster and harder than it was supposed to be. Things had gone well.

'Shree, I was looking for you,' Tyrone complained. Shree smiled but said nothing.

'So where were you?' he persisted as he held her around the waist.

'Oh, just talking to some girls in the corridor.'

'Are you sure you wasn't dancing with some man?'

'You're all the man I need, Tyrone, and you know that.'

'Really?'

Shree was irritated by Tyrone's foolish smile. He was so easily pleased it was pathetic. She detached his arms and went to the kitchen to get herself a drink and to get away from the deafening and smoky atmosphere.

'No, girl-child, is all right. For you the drink costs nothing.' Shree thanked the smooth-talking man serving the drinks and took her peach Canei back into the room where people were dancing. Tyrone was sharing out some weed with his brethren in a corner and Chantelle was dancing with some man. Shree looked about for Nero. She saw him drinking a beer, chatting to some man. They made eye-contact. Shree smiled. She crossed the room and joined them. The two men abruptly ended their conversation and the other man moved off.

'So how come you're not dancing with any other women here?'

'I'm waiting for the right song and the right girl.'

'What do you mean by the right girl? There are plenty of pretty girls here.'

'It's got nothing to do with looks. The right girl knows how to move her hips and when she walks every man looks. She has a smile like diamonds on water and her voice is soft and sweet. Not all coarse like enough of the women here and smelling of stale cigarette.'

Shree said nothing. She looked around the crowded room.

'Maybe that girl is the one you're looking for, then,' she suggested, inclining her head towards a corner of the room where a girl was dancing by herself. Nero shook his head. 'Well, what about that one in the yellow catsuit?' Again Nero shook his head. 'The one with the go—'

Nero put one finger on her lips as if Shree were a

child babbling on foolishly. 'None of them. When I get her, I'll let you know who the right girl is.' This time it was Nero who melted into the crowd, leaving Shree standing by the speakers.

'Dangerous games, Shree,' murmured Chantelle as she passed by. Reminded of her obligations, Shree immediately looked around for Tyrone. He was standing on the opposite side of the room looking after the yardie as if he thought he knew him from somewhere but couldn't quite place it. Shree smiled, but Tyrone did not smile back.

'Why are you going so early?' Chantelle asked as Tyrone practically dragged Shree out of the party. Shree just looked at Tyrone sulkily.

'I have a hard day tomorrow, Chantelle,' Tyrone explained. 'I'm on the morning shift at the record shop in Mare Street.'

'Oh, it's like that, Tyrone. I never figured you as a business-before-pleasure man,' Chantelle joked.

'I have to go and say goodbye to someone,' Shree said to Tyrone, but he simply gripped her arm even harder and walked towards the door.

'Tyrone, what's the matter with you?' Shree snapped. He let go of her arm as they got to the car. 'I should have listened to you, Shree, I think we both need more quiet nights at home.'

chapter
ten

'Summer goes by so fast you're looking forward to the next one before it's even finished,' Janice said, sitting on the edge of Paula's bed. Paula was ironing some of Fabian's clothes.

'It's true. It's carnival tomorrow and then it will be September. Autumn and we'll all be taking out our winter coats.'

'Buying our fur boots,' said Shree.

'Looking for Christmas presents. Speaking of which,' Janice took out some rubbish from her pocket, 'let me give you yours now.' The others laughed.

'Yes, you know to put them back in your pocket, rude girl,' Paula joked.

'No, but it's true. After the carnival, there's going to be nothing.'

'I have to look for a part-time job,' said Paula.

'So do I,' said Shree, but not very enthusiastically. 'Or maybe I'll do one of the courses listed in the Sight and Sound Technical College catalogue we were looking at.'

'So are you sticking to your receptionist job, then, Janice?'

'Yeah. It's bringing in some money and soon they might send me to night classes once a week to get some decent secretarial skills. Then I could get a better position and be paid more.'

'How come you still need to work when Maurice has got all that money?' Paula asked, smiling. Janice said nothing.

'How's it going with Maurice?' asked Shree.

'It's *not*, really.'

'When did you last see him?'

'The night that you went to that party in New Cross.'

'What? That was over a week ago! Doesn't he phone you?'

'Occasionally,' Janice lied. 'I phone too, but he's really busy and he never has time to go out. He's been working on a project with another accountant at nights. It's really been eating up his free time. It's going to earn him a lot of money though.'

'Elroy's getting on well these days,' Paula said.

'Yeah. I heard that he's deejaying everywhere now. At all the good nightclubs and he's got something on with one of these radio stations too. Tyrone says he's into the big bucks,' said Shree.

'He works hard at what he does, you have to admit,' Paula said. Janice just shrugged.

'I've heard that he's really crazy about this new girlfriend too. I think her name is Mona or Mina. Anyway, he buys her all these little presents and takes her out everywhere.'

'What is the point of telling me this, Paula?' Janice interrupted impatiently.

'I just thought you might want to know how your ex-man is getting on.'

'Well, now I know, so just spare me the details, okay?'

'So what are we wearing to the carnival this year, Shree?'

'Well, I've thought about what each of us has and our budgets and everything and I think we should all wear the lace and gold suits.'

'You mean the one where I wear the black and gold and Janice wears the white and gold and you wear the red and gold?' Paula asked. Shree nodded.

'But we've worn those before.'

'But we've never worn them at the same time and Janice has never worn hers.'

'With good reason,' Janice retorted.

'Look. I'm working on effect here. Trust me, do I ever do us wrong?'

'It's all right for you two, but I have the worst colours, and why does Shree have to be the one to stand out?' Janice moaned.

'You chose to buy the white and gold. But you can always wear the red and gold if you want,' offered Shree.

'No, it's all right. Never let it be said that *I* was the one to break up the happy mood.' Janice looked at the clock. 'Oh no! Now I'm late.'

The other two looked at her. 'Late for what?' asked Shree.

'I have to get home. It's a family dinner, you know. See you tomorrow.'

'Nine o'clock at Paula's. Don't even *think* of being late,' Shree called after the disappearing Janice.

First thing in the morning Shree staggered into Paula's flat carrying a huge box.

'What's in there?' Paula asked curiously as she shut the door behind Shree.

'Every hair-piece, every weave, every bead, every comb, all the oils, gels, ribbons, lace and sequins that I own,' Shree gasped as she dropped the box down on the kitchen table. 'And where the hell is Janice?' She put one hand on her hip. 'Me tell her not to be late.'

Paula rubbed the sleep from her eyes. ''Llow it, Shree. It's way too early. Give her a bit of time. It's still night.'

'No, Paula, it's nine o'clock and we have to do each other's hair and get dressed and take Fabian round to Janice's mum's and—'

'Calm down. It won't take us that long to get ready.' Shree walked over to the telephone and dialled Janice's number.

'H-hello.'

'No, Janice. No hello or who's there or goodnight. Get your butt down here this minute.'

'Yes, yes, I'm coming, I'm coming, I just—'

'Stop coming and come. Get out of bed. Take off your nightie and put on your clothes. Leave your flat, turn right at the main road – no, no, I'll come and get you. That way I can be sure you're going to turn up.'

'No, no, it's all right, Shree, I'll just slip on—'

'I'll be there in five seconds, so be ready.'

'You see what I have to put up with, Paula?' Shree said as she returned with a glowering Janice following behind.

'Keep the noise down, I don't want Fabian to wake up just yet,' Paula said.

'I need something to wake me up,' Janice said as she disappeared into Paula's kitchen.

Paula always did Shree's hair, Shree did Janice's and Janice did Paula's. Since Paula and Janice were still a bit sleepy, Shree did Janice's hair first of all, sewing in a small weave to give her a side fringe and taking the rest of her hair back in a pony-tail with a hair-piece attached. Then Paula did Shree's hair in the same style although as her hair was already long there was no need for any hair-pieces.

Janice was trying to do Paula's and at the same time listen to Shree's lectures on boys, clothes and most frequently Paula's hair. Shree herself was ironing out their dresses in the middle of the room while supervising everything. Paula was contemplating aloud that she might not wear the gold suit but her black dress with the matching jacket or the red trousers and T-shirt instead.

'But we all have to look the *same*,' wailed Shree. 'That's the whole point of the gold dresses.'

'The point is that we don't look the same,' Paula stated with maddening practicality. 'I'm a size fourteen and you're a size four. That's the point.'

Shree dismissed her with a wave of the hand. 'I didn't bring half my house so you can turn around and moan that we don't look the same. Trust me, by the time I've finished with us, we *will*! Janice! You're doing Paula's hair all wrong. You need to weave the straight piece into the right side of her head, not the left. Wake up! We've got to get dressed soon.'

Janice drew in her breath and counted to ten. Then she undid the weave to re-sew it on the *right* side. Shree, after a long hard look to make sure Janice was doing the hair right this time, returned her attention to ironing the dresses.

The telephone rang. Paula half got up to answer it, but Shree shooed her back and went to pick it up herself. It was Michael. Shree handed the phone to Paula.

'Hello?'

'What ya saying, babes?'

'Oh. It's you.'

'What do you mean, "Oh, it's you"? Trying to make out you aren't overjoyed to hear my voice.'

'So what's up these days, Michael?'

Janice and Shree looked at each other and groaned. Paula had told them how the next time she talked to Michael she was going to cuss him into the ground and let him know what was what, but it was the same old story. She just couldn't resist him.

'Oh, I've been out with my boys as usual. Doing a little business, going to a few raves. Nothing special.'

'So how come you're in such high spirits this morning?'

'I'm always in high spirits when I'm talking to you, darling.'

Paula giggled. 'Don't flirt, Michael. I'm not your woman any more.'

'But I will always be your man and you know it. I'm the original gallis, admit it.'

'Sorry, did you say something? This line is really bad,' Paula laughed.

'So what are you doing today? Where's my son?'

'Fabian's still asleep and we're going to the carnival today. Are you going?'

'I can't say yet. I might pass through, catch a few of my spars and that.'

'Paula, I need to do the other side of your head,' hissed Janice.

'Look, Michael, I have to go now. I'll bell you tomorrow, yeah?'

'Safe, Paula. I see you haven't got time to say hello any more.'

'No, it's not that. You know that's not true,' Paula laughed.

'All right, I see how you stay. See ya.'

Paula put the phone down and walked back to the chair.

'For a start, Paula, you don't go skinning teeth with him when you know how he likes to take liberties,' Janice said heatedly.

'Yeah. You let him walk all over you,' Shree added.

'No I don't.'

'I don't know what it is with you and him,' Janice said, shaking her head. 'But from now on please leave me well out of it.'

'Me too,' said Shree. 'Now turn around and let Janice finish your hair.'

'What will Chantelle and Donna be wearing?' Paula asked.

'Oh, ruffled denim shorts and bra-tops to match.'

'Sounds nice.'

'Yes, it is. I was going to buy a suit for myself, but you know, money is kind of lacking.'

'What happened to all that money you got from your dad's flat?' Paula asked. 'Shree! Don't tell me you spent it all?'

'No, not all of it but there isn't a lot left. After I paid my bills and put down on the rent and had new tyres put on my car and bought a few clothes—'

'A few clothes?'

'W-ell.'

'Shree, when will you realize that there is more to life than looking good?' Paula shook her head. Shree just shrugged. 'What are you going to do if you see Terror at the carnival?' Paula asked anxiously.

'It's true,' Janice said. 'From what you've told me about him it sounds like he could do some damage.'

'I don't think he'll be there. Seriously, I know the way these people think and they don't go to these carnival things. Too many police around for them to feel safe. He might go to a rave, but trust me, we won't see him there.'

'Aren't we raving at Shenola's tonight?' Janice asked.

'Yes,' confirmed Paula.

'Who else is raving there?' Janice asked again.

'Oh, Tyrone got a stack of free tickets from Elroy so I guess it will be the usual crew.' Janice grimaced.

'Now, now, Jan, don't be bitchy. Mona is such a nice person and you shouldn't begrudge her Elroy. You're being jealous like my Tyrone.' Janice looked up.

'Chantelle did tell me that he was carrying on stupid at that rave down New Cross.'

'What was it about?' asked Paula. Shree considered for a minute and then told them about Nero.

'Urrgh!! You mean to say that Nero is one of those pieces of nastiness who gave us all that trouble at Hackney Downs?'

Shree had left out that part. Now Janice sat up, jerking the comb out of Paula's head.

'Errgg, they was damn ugly and bad-mannered beyond reason. Shree, don't tell me you've taken a liking to one of them.'

'H-he's sweet.'

Janice and Paula looked at each other and laughed. 'Sweet my foot. Those men looked like pitbulls.'

'Pitbulls' backsides.'

'Dogs, anyway.'

'Wild beasts.'

'That's too kind. They didn't look like anything natural.' Shree tried to laugh it off but when that didn't work she pouted. 'I like him.' Janice and Paula looked at each other and then looked away.

'Well, what's happening with Tyrone?' Janice asked.

'I don't know. We're still okay. I'm not going to drop him, but there's something about Nero that interests me.'

'Well, you don't sound very sure about what you want,' said Paula.

'You can't drop Tyrone for this Nero, Shree. Tyrone is so kriss and this Nero is blatantly one of the ugliest men I've seen all summer.'

'Janice has a point,' said Paula.

'Looks aren't everything.'

When Paula's hair was finished she woke up Fabian to get him ready. He shuffled in dozily, dragging his toy trumpet with him. He submitted to being kissed and cuddled by his mother's friends and then sat down on the sofa. Paula went into the kitchen and made him some toast and brought it in on a tray so he could eat it in the sitting-room.

'Pass me the phone, Shree,' Janice ordered.

Paula looked up from the ironing-board where she was ironing Fabian's shirt. 'Janice, don't run up my phone bill with those mobile numbers again.'

Janice ignored her and dialled Maurice's home digits. 'It's the answering-machine again,' she said crossly.

'So maybe he's out?' Shree suggested.

'He's not out, he isn't picking up the phone, just like last night,' Janice said.

'Perhaps he doesn't want to speak to you again . . . only joking,' Paula added hastily, catching Janice's stricken expression.

'I'm sure it's not that. It's just that he's never in when I call his flat, or at least I always get his answering-machine and I've left so many messages but he never ever calls back and I know it's because he's very busy—'

'He shouldn't be too busy to chat to you,' Shree said.

'Don't start thinking that you're not worth the time of day. If he ain't giving you that then there's something wrong with him!' Paula agreed vehemently.

'I think you should go round there as soon as

possible. If things are going wrong you need to sort it out.'

'I know, but I don't want to go alone.'

'I'll go with you,' offered Paula and Shree at once.

'On second thoughts, I think I would be better off on my own. Otherwise he would know that I'm suspicious and that would only make things worse.'

Conversation dwindled as Paula disappeared into the bathroom with Fabian and Janice and Shree changed into their dresses.

Finally, after the most painstaking procedure of the year, the three young women were ready. They surveyed their reflections in Paula's wide dressing-table mirror.

'Uh uh, we *do* look exactly the same,' said Janice in the white gold.

'You see. Take note. Shree makes no mistake,' said the proud lady herself in the red and gold.

Fabian, who had a bandana around his head, squeezed himself between them to look in the mirror. 'Mummy, do I look like a rude boy?' he asked innocently, trying to pull the bandana from over his eyes.

Paula smiled. 'No, baby, you look like a sweet boy.'

Fabian folded his arms and stamped his foot. 'I don't want to be a sweet boy, I want to be a rude boy.'

Shree leaned over and whispered in his ear. 'Rude boys are fools. Sweet boys get all the girls.'

'Do they?' asked Fabian.

Shree nodded solemnly. He contemplated for a while and then tugged at his mother's black and gold dress. 'Mummy, I don't want to be a rude boy any more, I'm want to be a sweet boy now because they get all the girls.' Paula laughed.

'Well, do we have everything?' Janice asked for the third time before closing the door behind them.

'Yes,' Paula said, patting her baby bag. 'It's so nice of your mum to offer to have Fabian for the day.'

'Oh, it's nothing,' Janice assured her as they left the flat. 'My mum is devoted to Fabian. She was just waiting for an excuse to take him away from you. She loves kids.'

'Brr, I hope it warms up later,' Paula said, shivering in the passenger seat of Shree's car.

'I'm just praying that it doesn't rain,' Shree said as she started the car.

'Morning, Rose,' chorused Shree and Paula as Rose opened her front door.

Rose smiled. 'Good morning. My, aren't we looking pretty today?' She ushered them into the hall and shut the door. 'But won't you be cold in those little dresses you have on? It's quite breezy out there.'

'No pain, no gain,' Shree said.

'All his nightclothes are in the bag and his toothbrush and things and here's a little food that I packed for him, y'know, crisps, some fruits—'

'Paula, you didn't have to trouble yourself with the food.'

'No. I don't want to put any burdens on you. I'm just so grateful that you're looking after him. It's so nice of you.'

'Oh, I know what you young girls are like. Don't worry about Fabian. Go and enjoy yourselves. I wouldn't want those gorgeous dresses to go to waste.'

The girls giggled bashfully. As Rose shooed them

towards the door, Fabian's bottom lip began to extrude and tremble. 'Go on, goodbye. Me and Fabian have lots to do today. We'll drop down the carnival later and see the processions or something, so we might see you there.' Rose scooped up Fabian before he could feel sad and gave him a kiss on the cheek. 'You want to play in the garden?' she asked. Fabian nodded vigorously. Paula laughed and kissed him goodbye.

'How are we going to get there from here?' Janice asked as they walked towards the car.

'Oh, Tyrone's told me the way and it's very easy, almost straight. We go down to Pentonville Road, along Euston Road and Marylebone Road, then into Sussex Gardens to Bayswater and that takes us into Notting Hill Gate and Holland Park if we can get that far,' said Shree. 'It's going to be a long drive.'

Despite the heavy traffic leading up to the carnival, the girls were enjoying themselves. 'Some people have no shame,' Paula said as a rastafarian crawled past them in an old Datsun Cherry with no roof. Janice nudged Shree, making the car swerve towards the pavement.

'Janice, do you want to kill us?' yelled Shree.

'Calm down, nothing happened,' Janice said, giggling.

'Hey, coca-cola shapes, do you need a lover-man?'

All the girls turned their heads simultaneously to see a black, kriss convertible, several cars behind them, full of really fit, well-groomed men. The one who had called to them was standing up on the back seat, holding out his arms. Tall, dark and very handsome, the gold in his teeth glinted happily at them from his sweet smile. The girls started giggling and shooting coy looks and being very suggestive as the traffic moved at a snail's pace. When they reached the traffic lights the man who had called out got out of his motor and walked towards them. The lights changed before he got too close and Shree put her foot down on the accelerator. The man stood in the road for a minute in mock anger and then dashed back to his own car.

'The first nice man I've seen today,' Janice said, and her friends nodded.

'Dark boys are so much krisser than light-skinned boys, don't you think?' Paula said thoughtfully.

'You're only saying that because you're light-skinned. Light-skinned girls always go for dark-skinned boys and vice versa,' said Shree.

'No, Paula's right. Dark-skinned boys have that certain something, that extra finesse—'

'Like Wesley Snipes.'

'Yes, that cool, very smooth complexion—'

'Much sexier,' said Paula.

'They're also much more in touch with who they are.'

'Like hell they are! A dark-skinned man is ten times more likely to go for very light skin or half-caste than a man with light skin. Darker-skinned men don't appreciate their black women!' Shree said indignantly.

'The traffic is *very* heavy, Shree, don't you think?'

'Yes Janice, the traffic is very heavy and whose fault is that? Next time, when I say to come at nine o'clock, you damn well find yourself there at eight-thirty.' Shree grumbled while Janice fiddled around with the radio and Paula read an old copy of *The Voice* which she found in the corner of the back seat. Finally Shree had had enough. She turned down the first side street she came to and parked the car.

'There's just too much traffic, it will be quicker if we walk it. There are probably about ten floats in front, holding up the traffic.' The others got out, they needed to stretch their legs anyway. Shree put up the roof and locked the doors.

Now that they were walking, there seemed to be more congestion on the pavement than on the road. However, they were quite near to the carnival and could hear the music.

'The houses around here are really nice,' said Paula.

'Yeah, they must have about five floors,' said Shree.

'Who do you think lives in houses like these?'

'Millionaires and movie stars probably.'

'Imagine if I lived in a house like that.'

'Keep dreaming, Paula. The only one of us who could get that chance is Janice, if she sticks to her Maurice.'

'That's not very certain though, is it?' said Paula. Janice smiled but didn't say anything.

They followed the masses down a street and were there. A float was some way in front, playing calypso and soca. People were hanging out of the windows of the houses that lined the streets.

Paula pointed up to a balcony. 'Look at that woman up there in her bikini.'

Shree and Janice looked. 'Foolish woman.'

'She's too magar to be showing off her body like that anyway.'

'When she drops down off that roof, I'll be here laughing.'

The three moved on. It was a sunny and warm afternoon with a light breeze. Just perfect for carnival. Everywhere you looked you could see handsome males and people enjoying life. There was so much colour. A profusion of pink and blue, green and yellow, purple and gold, everything clashed yet blended perfectly. It was intoxicating and exciting. A lot of girls dressed as Caribbean fruits danced past in single file, supervised by their dance teachers who tried to look inconspicuous as leafy green trees. Shree took a picture.

'Yes, it's all very nice, Shree, but don't waste out the film,' said the unsentimental Paula.

They followed the procession down to the end of the road and then let it go. Shree was thirsty so they looked around for some sort of shop where she could buy something to drink.

'What is you want?' The Indian man poked his head out of the window of his shop. Bodyguards moved around outside as well as inside, security was tighter than tight. Once Shree had paid for her drink they walked on to where there was a hip-hop sound system. They stayed for a while as the music was good and all the young people were doing their hip-hop dancing. Shree clambered up on to a small platform by the side of the sound system where some other girls were dancing and began to bust her stuff. 'Watch her go,' Paula remarked to Janice.

Several old ladies were moving through the crowd, collecting money for some charity. Janice felt a bony finger poking her shoulder and turned round, all ready with her excuses as to why she couldn't give them any money.

'Good afternoon, Janice.'

Janice wanted to run but there was no way she could. She smiled as pleasantly as she could into Sister Nelson's gangy teeth and hurriedly dipped into her small store of cash. She could just feel Sister Nelson's eyes boring into her gold dress and her made-up face and over the top hairstyle. Now she would go and tell the whole church how Rose's daughter was dressed at the carnival. Sister Nelson smiled friendly enough, though.

'E-enjoying the carnival, Sister Nelson?' Janice ventured nervously.

Sister Nelson's smile faded slightly. 'No, dear, I didn't come to enjoy myself. I just came to see if I could collect a little money for charity.'

'Oh.'

'Anyway, goodbye, Janice dear. Say hello to your mother from me.'

'Sure, goodbye,' Janice said with relief.

The hip-hop was now getting a bit dry and the same songs were coming on again, so they wandered off in search of a new sound system. They had carefully studied the carnival maps in *The Voice* a few days before and had worked out which sound systems they were going to go to and exactly how long they were going to spend at each, but when it came down to it they couldn't tell where they were, where they'd been or where they were going.

They arrived at another sound system in a type of square, and some girls were dancing the butterfly in front of it. The three girls joined them and danced a little but

197

felt a bit self-conscious, dancing brazenly in the middle of the street while men and women looked on.

'YO! Paula!'

The shout came from the van behind the sound system. A tall lanky boy waved from behind the two great speakers.

'Who is he, Paula?'

'You know him. That's Damon, remember? My old boyfriend, before Michael.'

Shree took another picture, this time of the unsuspecting Paula doing the butterfly. She stopped for a minute to berate Shree for taking photos of her when she wasn't ready. Then she started dancing again.

'Hey, check what that girl's wearing?' A skinny girl walked by wearing a leotard and lace leggings and nothing else. 'How could she wear something like that?' exclaimed Janice.

'It's up to her what she wants to wear,' Shree said calmly.

'She's magar like I don't know what,' Paula said loudly.

'Paula, don't start causing trouble because you don't like what the girl's wearing. We're here to have fun.'

A little while later the three girls left the sound system since it was starting to get boring.

'Where's Westwood's sound system?' No one could remember so they walked up to a policeman to see if he knew where the road was. He gave them directions and they set off to try to find it but only succeeded in getting lost again. This time they found themselves at a reggae sound system. Tanasha and Tyrone, Elroy and Michael and their friends were there and –

'Tyrone, what the hell do you think you are doing?'

Tyrone quickly detached himself from the pretty young girl he had been slow-dancing with. And while the girl discreetly made her getaway Shree gave Tyrone an earful. However, Tyrone, knowing that she wasn't really cross with him, speeched his way out of it, so Shree softened up and danced with him herself.

'I don't even know why you're vexed, Shree.'

'Wouldn't you be vexed if you saw me whining up on some strange man?'

'Yes, of course I would, but it's different for me, I'm a man.'

'I don't see the difference.'

'Well, I'm sorry then, I didn't know you'd be vexed.' Shree humphed, but she let it go at that.

They stayed at that sound system for quite a while. Paula had a conversation with Michael. Janice just danced, although she was sure that Elroy tried to catch her eye on more than one occasion. At length they decided to move off and let the boys have their fun.

Walking down the street, Shree nearly fell over a troupe of very small boys dressed as pirates who were trying to catch up with their float and the rest of their parade. They were on their way to the loos since Paula needed to go and so did Janice. They turned round the corner and found themselves joining the end of a very, very long queue. There was nothing to do but hang around and wait.

'Please don't even mention the word "loo" to me again for the rest of the day,' ordered Shree as over half an hour later they finally made their way from the public toilets.

'What shall I take a picture of now?' she asked mournfully. 'I've taken so many pictures of processions and you lot but I've got loads of film left.'

Paula thought for a minute and then her eyes lit up mischievously. 'I dare you to find a fit boy and ask him to pose for a picture.'

'We aren't fourteen any more, Paula,' Janice began. But Shree agreed with Paula. 'Oh, don't be such an old woman, Jan. Come on, Paula, this will give us a joke.' They ran off down the road together. Janice shook her head regretfully and followed them.

'What about him?' Shree pointed to this boy who could see her pointing and hear what she was saying.

Paula shook her head in distaste. 'No, Shree, I don't know which part of him is fit, but it's not his face or his body or his hair, in fact, it's nothing.' They hurried past him giggling, while the boy looked embarrassed.

'Now, that boy is really beautiful.'

Shree looked to where Paula pointed. 'Oh yes!' She squealed with delight, now this one really was worthy. Janice looked at the handsome boy leaning against the wall, conversing in a laid-back way with some friends.

Shree walked up to the boy with her nicest smile. In no time at all his arms were wrapped around her and the picture was taken. The handsome boy wanted to carry on this encounter but Shree escaped quickly, giving the false impression that she was coming back.

'You made all that fuss about Tyrone and look at you, acting worse,' Janice said as soon as they were walking in the direction of the loud ragga. Shree just smiled smugly and said nothing.

Time had flown by. Most of the sound systems were packing up. When they couldn't find another one that was playing music the girls decided to follow the floats which were going up the hill, leaving the carnival area.

'Wanna jump on, ladies?' A man offered Janice his hand and she gladly jumped on to the slow-moving float. Shree and Paula quickly followed suit. There was just enough room since some other people were already on board. Several boys, seeing that there were some kriss girls on the float, tried to jump on too. When the float reached the top of the hill, Shree, Paula and Janice ran down again as fast as they could to catch another one. This time, however, they couldn't get on it but they joined the procession anyway. 'But why does it have to be soca and calypso?' Janice complained. However, since she was in the carnival spirit she didn't mind.

Different men tried to grab the girls in order to dance with them on the way up the hill. Janice was dancing with one man for ages, but when she turned around to talk to him, she found herself facing a really old and ugly man. Whirr, click! Janice was immortalized with her dancing partner.

'Now, see, whenever you're rude to me I'm gonna whip out this photo,' Shree threatened, laughing. 'You see your face?'

'Shree, you're so sad,' Janice said, sticking out her tongue.

The sun was setting and most of the sound systems were gone. The last of the floats were making their final circuits. People were heading towards the tube stations.

'Where are we?' Paula asked.

'Near Westbourne Park, I think.'

'Well, we'd better find the car now. We're raving at Shenola's, don't forget.'

'We've got to go home and get ready.'

'I've had a wicked day,' Shree said, putting one arm on Janice's shoulder and the other on Paula's.

'Yeah, it was good fun,' Janice said. 'Race you to the bottom of the hill!'

chapter eleven

'I don't know if I want to go any more. I feel like I'm spying on him.'

'Nonsense,' Paula said, striding towards the modern block of flats.

'Well, anyway, I think I should go into the flat alone.'

'Fine, but you are going to see him. We haven't waited a whole week for you to change your mind,' said Shree. They walked up to the security desk. The guard looked surprised to see Janice.

'Hi there, William, everything all right?'

'Fine, thanks, Janice,' replied the doorman. 'Is Mr Haccinene expecting you, Janice? I, er, don't think you should go up to Mr Haccinene's flat just now.'

'Don't worry, Maurice knows I'm coming round,' Janice said as the three girls swept past the doorman.

In the lift, Shree whistled at the mirrors and the red carpet. 'You weren't lying when you said he had money. His flat must be so nice.'

Janice did not say anything. The lift stopped at the fifth floor.

'It's flat 57,' Janice said, walking along the corridor. She stopped outside the door and motioned to the others to be quiet and stand to the side of the doorway so they wouldn't be seen.

'Hey, I can hear music,' whispered Shree.

'There's a woman in there, I can hear her laughing,' said Paula.

Janice's lips tightened as she knocked on the door. It opened almost immediately.

'Aaah, Janice,' said Maurice, who was wearing a bathrobe, 'I'm afraid you've caught me at a bad time.'

Janice pushed past him. 'I'll bet I have,' she said as she walked into the sitting-room and looked around. A bottle of champagne was sitting in an ice-bucket on the sideboard next to crystal glasses, clothes were lying on the floor and a Smokey Robinson cassette cover was on top of the hi-fi.

'So this is the project you've been working on,' Janice said, blinking away her tears. 'And where is the female accountant? In there?' She strode to the bedroom and pushed the door open. She looked blankly at the woman in the bed. Maurice gently pulled Janice away from the doorway and shut the door. She shook his hand off.

'This looks terrible,' he began.

'Maurice, I trusted you. Every time you told me you were working late, I believed you, but everything you said was a lie.' Janice turned her head away to hide her tears.

'I tried to tell you but you wouldn't listen.'

'What exactly did you try to tell me?'

'That we don't suit each other. I thought it could work but we're too different.'

'You said you loved me.'

'I thought it would give you more confidence.'

Janice slapped Maurice in the face. He put his hand to his cheek. 'I suppose I deserved that,' he said quietly. Janice put one hand on the wall to steady herself. 'Janice, I'll be honest with you. I saw you in the elevator and it was animal attraction from the start. I wanted to tear off your clothes, make passionate love to you and I always get what I want. The fact that you was, er, street and feisty made it all the more erotic. For a few weeks it was fantastic and I enjoyed spending time with you. Your ignorance fascinated me. But then you changed. You lost that ghetto charm and you wanted to be different and that wasn't part of the fantasy. I gave you everything you wanted, sophistication, money. I introduced you to new people and places. But you must have known it wouldn't last for ever.'

Janice wanted to run out of the flat. She tried to think of something strong to say, but her mind was a blank. 'But you met my parents,' she said weakly.

'That was all your idea. I never wanted to make things look so serious. It was never part of the plan to—'

'Go out with a black nobody?' Janice's eyes flashed fire as she faced him. 'You thought you could use me because I'm black. You treated my parents like dirt because we're not rich or anybody special. I've never heard you speak positively of black people, and let me tell you something you don't seem to understand. You are fifty per cent black. Do you think you can cover up your blackness and blend in with your white friends? They don't see you as half white, to them you're as black as me.'

'Janice, you'd better leave now,' Maurice said quietly.

Janice laughed sourly. 'You think you're so intelligent but you obviously don't know anything because you don't even know who you are.' With this she turned and walked out, head held high.

Shree and Paula followed Janice back to the lift in silence. Shree tried to tuck her arm through her friend's but Janice shook her off. 'Leave me alone, I'm not going to break down.'

'We heard every word. You told him good,' Paula said.

Janice thought about this, then grinned. 'You think so?'

'Yeah. He won't try that trick again in a hurry.' They went down in the lift and walked out of the building.

'Well, you two must be pleased with yourselves,' Janice remarked as they drove away.

'Janice, we're not about to judge you, but you're better off without Maurice,' Paula said.

'How does it feel to be young, free and single again?' asked Shree.

'It feels good,' Janice said emphatically.

Shree pulled over to the side of the road.

'What's wrong?' asked Paula.

'I don't know but right now I feel really ill. My stomach's turning over and I feel like I'm gonna puke.

Paula, you had better drive.' Shree got out and changed seats with Paula.

'What have you eaten today?' asked Paula.

'Just the usual things, urrgh.' Shree gripped her stomach.

'Paula, start the car, we'd better get Shree home fast.'

'It's okay. The nausea's gone now. I wonder what the matter with me is. I've been feeling sick for ages.'

'Maybe you should see a doctor,' said Janice.

'I hate doctors,' said Shree.

'I expect it's too much excitement for one day,' Janice said with a wry smile.

Shree had returned home to find her flat filled with boys, all drinking and smoking and lounging around wearing out her hi-fi with their loud jungle music. They ignored Shree while Tyrone just laughed and nudged one of his friends.

'Eh, pass me a can, star.' He held the can out to Shree.

'Tyrone, what's going on? Who the hell do you think you are?'

'Now stop your noise in front a me friends.'

'Do you really think I'm ramping wid you? Get them out of here now!'

Tyrone gathered that Shree wasn't in the partying mood so he motioned to his friends to chip. Shree held the door open for them and then slammed it really hard behind the last one.

'Don't turn my flat into a nightclub, Tyrone. This is

my home. You just bring your low-life friends a fill up my front room and then you come skinnin' teeth wid me and I can't even find a place to sit down. Look at the floor.' Tyrone looked. The sitting-room and hallway were a sorry sight, cigarettes and beer cans were strewn all over the floor.

'I've been feeling really sick again today and it doesn't help that I can hardly breathe in here because of all that unnatural t'ing you bring in here to smoke.' Shree opened the windows. Tyrone just stood there.

'It's me who has to clean up all your junk, every time. I'm sure you think you're living in a hotel. Just pass through wid your friends and every time Shree will clean up afterwards. I'm not your slave, Tyrone, or your lickle house rat.'

'I know you're not my slave. If you want me to help you, I'll help you.'

'You're so irresponsible. You're just like a chile, a lickle youth. You can't keep this place clean it's as if you think you're still in school. Why can't you be separated from your friends the whole time? You have a chance to be a good hairdresser, maybe start your own place, but you don't go to work full-time. You have no brains or you'd know where you're going wrong, but you wander from one rave to the next. You're nothing, Tyrone, you're less than nothing.'

'Oh, fuck you! So what if I'm irresponsible? If I had a kid or we were married then you'd have reason to talk, but you do this all the time, go crazy over stupid things. Yeah, I don't have full-time employment, so what? When I need money, I work. I'm not lazy. You've never done a day's work in your life and you always run to your daddy when you need cash, so don't run me down in front of my brethren and try an' manners me like I'm living off you. All you do is walk streets with Paula every day and then you've got the front to come and tell me what I do? If you're not happy with this relationship, Shree, just say so because right now I'm having doubts of my own.' Tyrone spun on his heel and walked out, slamming the door behind him.

Janice walked up the path to her parents' house. She paused before she put the key in the lock. She had decided to break the news that she was no longer going out with Maurice.

'Lord have mercy! What went wrong?' Rose left the dishes in the sink and quickly dried her hands on a dishcloth.

Janice tried to be off-hand. 'It just didn't work out, so it's over.'

'What's over?' Rio asked as he came strolling into the kitchen.

'I'm not going out with Maurice any more.'

'I see. How come?'

'Does it matter?'

'Yes, of course it matters, Janice. A nice boy like Maurice wouldn't break off a relationship without a good reason.'

'Actually it was me who broke it off,' Janice remarked acidly.

Rose shrieked in horror. 'How could you be so

stupid? You're stuck with that good-for-nothing Elroy for a whole year and then you get a man like Maurice. You don't know what you have.'

'Maurice is no better than Elroy.'

'Oh ho. I might have guessed that boy was at the bottom of all this. I can see where you are headed, Janice. I wanted the best for my daughter and she dashed it away. The first decent boy you meet and you couldn't care less.' Rose wiped her hands together. 'You're never going to get anywhere in life. I wash my hands of you.'

'You only care about the fancy cars and the smart suits and the City accent.'

'What's wrong with that? He was a mother's dream.'

'You know nothing about the real Maurice.'

'Couldn't you have stuck with it, held on? It doesn't have to be love at first sight, you know.'

'Leave the girl alone, Rose,' said Lloyd, who was now standing in the kitchen doorway.

'You're just glad to see him go because you is sweet on that stupid Elroy,' said Rose crossly. 'And me know why. Is because you two of a kind. Both lazy and stupid and irresponsible.'

Lloyd barely managed to hide a smile as he pushed Janice into the sitting-room, leaving Rose scolding thin air.

'Come and sit down, baby. I could see that you did like him a lot and all, but anyway, you don't have to tell anyone if you don't want to. It's your business.'

Janice smiled. 'Actually, we weren't seeing each other for a long time and then one day I went to see him and there was another girl there.' Lloyd didn't say anything so Janice carried on. 'I didn't ask him what she was doing there, I mean, that was pretty obvious, but I asked him why. It upset me quite a lot.'

'What did?'

'Just things. He basically said I'm not on his social level and that my ignorance fascinated him. Don't tell Mum. She wouldn't understand. Anyway, I got my own back.' Janice gave a wry smile.

Lloyd slapped Janice on the knee. 'At least you're not crying and acting silly over him.'

Janice was suddenly serious. 'In a way it was kind of a relief because all the time I spent with him I'd never been so bored in my entire life!'

'I knew he was bad news the minute he walked through that door.'

'Mum still doesn't think so.'

'I'll handle her.'

'Thanks, Dad. I really don't want Mum on my case, moaning about missed opportunities and Elroy.'

Lloyd got up and walked to the door. Before he left the room he looked over his shoulder. 'Is it really over with Elroy?'

'Yes. It's really over.' Janice lay down on the sofa and put her feet up. She would stay at home for a few hours and then maybe check Paula, see how she was doing.

The following Monday Shree woke up early. She took a small, empty jar from a cupboard in the kitchen and disappeared into the bathroom. A few minutes later she emerged, got dressed and put the jar, now containing a small sample of urine, into her shoulder-bag. Then she left the flat. She didn't bother to take the car as it was only a few minutes' walk to the chemist.

'Very pretty girl, how may I help you?' the grey-haired Indian chemist asked, smiling.

Shree swallowed. 'I'm here for the pregnancy test advertised in the window. The one with the instant results.'

'Do you have urine sample, taken before breakfast this morning?' Shree took the jar out of her bag and put it on the counter.

'I'm very cheaper, this will cost you only three pounds, ninety-nine pence.' Shree put a five-pound note on the counter next to the jar. The man gave her the change and then disappeared with the jar.

After what seemed like a lifetime he came back into the shop. 'Do you like the result written down?' he asked. Shree nodded. He scribbled the result on a piece of paper and handed it to her.

Shree looked at the piece of paper and gasped. 'Are you sure?'

'Only way you can be absolutely sure is if you see your doctor, but our results haven't been wrong yet,' said the chemist.

'Thanks,' said Shree.

'Velly nice meeting you.'

Shree left the shop in a daze. She decided to go for a walk and think things over. She was sorry she'd been so bad to Tyrone and she wondered where he was as he hadn't returned to the flat since their argument on Saturday night. She crossed the main road and cut through the park, walking aimlessly.

It was humid and Shree felt hot and sticky in her

baseball shirt. A squirrel shot out from a bush in front of her and then ran into the hedge on the other side of the path. Shree didn't notice. She walked the length of the park and came out the other side, still walking without any real sense of where she was going.

She kept walking. She wished she could go and talk to her father. He would know what to do. She wished she hadn't argued with Tyrone because now she needed his help. She carried on, engrossed in her thoughts, having a lot to think about. Shree was pregnant.

'Whaaat!!??' Janice nearly fell off her chair in excitement. Shree smiled weakly. Paula's mouth was hanging open, Janice's eyes were so big they couldn't get any bigger.

Shree nodded. 'Almost three months, I think.'

'Not *you*, Shree?'

'Why not me?' Shree asked shyly.

'For Tyrone?'

'Y-yes.' This time Shree's sad smile wavered and she burst into tears.

'Now look what you've done, Janice, with your foolish tongue.' Paula dragged Shree on to the sofa and sat down next to her while Shree cried into her shoulder. Janice came and sat on Shree's other side and held her hand.

'What's wrong, Shree? Don't you want to have the baby?'

Shree shook her head vigorously. 'It's not that. I love kids, I wouldn't have chosen to have kids now, but I don't mind at all.'

'Then what's the problem?'

'Tyrone—' began Paula.

Shree nodded, the tears in her eyes again. 'Tyrone doesn't want children. He hates kids. He's always said he doesn't want any kids until he's about thirty and that he can't understand why his friends boast about their kids all the time when it's just a – a burden.'

'Oh, that's just boys' talk,' Paula reassured.

'Tyrone's not even ready to be a father yet. He lives for his friends. He doesn't have a proper job, he never pays his bills and only cares about himself. He's just a little boy and we fight like cat and dog. He won't wanna know after I tell him I'm pregnant.'

'Maybe it won't be so bad,' Janice suggested but Shree just looked even sadder.

'It wouldn't be if I thought that he wanted him, or her, but he doesn't. He's told me and I don't know if I can have a baby without a father.'

'Plenty of women do,' Paula said.

'I don't care. I want a man who's gonna care for my kids the way my father cared for me. Someone who will be there for them if something happens to me, someone who will be there for me if something happens to them.'

'And Tyrone won't?'

'I don't know.'

Later that day when Shree got home from Paula's flat, she found Tyrone sitting alone in the dark. It was very quiet. She closed the door carefully and then walked along the hallway into the sitting-room where he sat, head in hands, staring at the window. She stood in the doorway, the light from the hall casting strange shadows around her, and said nothing.

'Shree, I've made a decision.' Shree went and sat down on the sofa next to Tyrone. She put her hands over his. His hands didn't curve around her as she expected but remained cold and still in hers.

'What kind of a decision, baby?' she urged softly.

'Shree, I was thinking that we should finish.' Shree had to feel her heart because she was sure it had stopped beating. She breathed deeply. Tyrone continued, 'I thought we had something together. You meant something to me, anyway. But if you don't feel that I mean anything to you—'

'No – I—'

'I guess those things which you said about me the other day was what you really felt deep down inside, and if that's the deal then it's best to finish now while we still have some good memories.'

Shree moved closer to him. 'Tyrone, I was tired and upset about something. I wasn't thinking straight and in any case none of it matters now.'

'But Shree, I—'

'Ssh.' Shree manouevred Tyrone's arm until it was around her and she was relieved to note that it stayed there. Then she leaned over and whispered into Tyrone's ear. For a while he froze. Then he untangled himself from Shree and stood up and went and looked out of the window. Shree sat very still but she was biting her lip so hard she could taste blood.

Tyrone turned away from the window, walked across the room and sat back down on the sofa. 'Shree, I'm sorry—' he began. As soon as Shree heard that she began to cry uncontrollably. 'Shree, stop acting stupid.'

'Go away, just leave me alone.'

'You're worrying me, Shree.'

'You don't care about me, Tyrone. You don't want to be a part of this family. You don't want to know, so why don't you just disappear?' she sobbed.

'Why do you think that?' he asked softly.

'Y-y-you just s-said—'

'Yes, Shree, what did I say?'

'Y-y-you said that you were sorry.'

'You didn't give me a chance to say what I was sorry for, silly girl. Why didn't you let me finish what I was saying?' Tyrone scolded lightly. Shree raised her tearful eyes to his. 'Shree, I was going to say that I was sorry for the ways in which I've treated you badly and that I'll never be the father that you must want. But I love you so much although I don't always show it and I'll always be there for you and our child even if we break up – *now* what are you crying for?'

'Because now I won't be alone and I know that you care.'

'Now, this one is really lovely,' Shree sighed, holding up the tiny puff of mohair for her friends to see.

'I swear your poor baby is going to have nothing but party clothes when he or she is born.' Shree shrugged in answer to Janice's comment. 'You're not even showing yet, but you're running to buy this pair of shoes, that silk dress, this mohair suit.'

'I *am* showing,' Shree insisted, opening her coat and lifting up her sweater so that her friends could see her thickened waist. They were not particularly interested and told her to pull down her sweater as other customers were beginning to stare. They wandered around the yardie shop, looking at other clothes, and after buying denim leggings for Shree and the little mohair suit that she had fallen in love with, they drifted off towards the arcades.

'Damn, it is freezing,' Janice said as she wrapped her thick cardigan tightly around her.

'Well, how did you expect October to feel?' asked Paula. Shree said nothing, snug in the leather coat and boots that Tyrone had bought for her.

'Chantelle has a next man,' said Janice in an important voice.

'A waa?'

'Is it?'

'What's he like?'

'Well, I haven't seen him but I've heard his looks are nothing to shout about.'

'Why is she dealing with him then?'

'She's just showing people that she's not brooding over Tanasha.'

'What happened with her and Tanasha?'

'I heard that Tanasha dumped her or something like that.'

'Why did he do that? I thought he loved her bad.'

'So did I.'

'We all did, but anyway, I think he said she was just after his money.'

'But everyone knew that already. That's old news.' Janice lifted her eyebrows and coughed to regain their attention.

'Anyway, they had a fist-fight.'

'Chantelle and Tanasha? But Tanasha is a big man, how could they be fighting?'

'Well, they're both bad-tempered and violent. Remember the fight Chantelle had with Donna?'

Paula and Janice tutted. 'I heard that she scratched up his face and that Chantelle has a nasty bruise on her cheek, all bluey-black where he thumped her.'

'No, that's terrible, I wouldn't take that,' said Shree indignantly.

'It's all right for you, Shree. No man would lay a finger on you because of your dad. He would kill them.'

Shree laughed. 'Forget my dad, I would kill them. But since I'm on the subject, he phoned me, y'know. He said he's been staying in Birmingham and he's coming back soon.'

'Oh, that's really good. I know how much you missed him.'

'But why did he go to Birmingham?' Janice asked, feeling the apples before paying the man on the fruit stall.

'He didn't say, I suppose all will be revealed when he comes back. He says that a friend helped him to get up there and got him somewhere to stay.'

'But what about Terror?'

'Didn't I tell you? Terror's gone back to Jamaica with his brothers. He took his main baby-mother and their pickanny and left. I heard that he was having too much trouble with his men and he had made enough money, I suppose, so there was nothing to stay for.'

'I wondered why I hadn't heard you talking about him for ages,' Paula said with a side-glance at Shree. 'You're looking much happier these days.'

'I must be happier because my hair is growing and my skin is clearer than a few weeks ago.'

'What it is to have someone love you,' Paula said wistfully.

'I need to pick up some clothes for work,' said Janice. 'It's getting embarrassing, always wearing the same skirts and shirts.' They trooped into a clothes shop so Janice could pick out a few things.

'How are you two enjoying single life?' asked Shree. Janice put her change in her handbag as they walked out of the shop.

'At least there's nobody to answer to.'

'But don't you two get lonely?' asked Shree. 'I'm all right, I have Tyrone.'

'I'm not alone either,' Paula insisted at once. 'I have—'

'Michael,' chorused Shree and Janice together.

'Well, I'm happy being young, free and single,' Janice said as they turned the corner into Brixton High Street and walked towards the tube. 'I'm so surprised Michael offered to look after Fabian for the day,' she added.

'Yes, Janice, that is the third time you've said that, but he is his dad. I don't know why you act so surprised when Michael helps me out.'

'Well, Janice does have a point, Paula. I mean it's

not like Michael is at your house every weekend begging to take his son out, is it?'

Paula humphed as they walked into Brixton tube station. 'Are we going straight back to Hackney?'

'Yeah. Get off at Highbury and Islington and take the overhead like we usually do,' said Janice.

'So what are we going to do when we get to Hackney?' Shree asked, looking at her watch. 'It's only three o'clock and I don't want to go home yet.'

'We could go and look around Dalston market.'

Shree and Janice shook their heads. 'How many times do we go down Ridley Road? I've seen all the clothes, all the shops.'

'Well, there's that new yardie shop in the shopping centre.'

'But I have no money left.'

'That's just as well where you're concerned,' remarked Paula.

'How about we pass through Chantelle's and get the inside story on the split?' Shree suggested eagerly.

'Look 'pon her!' Paula pointed to Shree's eager face and laughed. 'Still, I wouldn't mind going if we've got nothing better to do. We can see Chantelle after taking a quick look in Dalston market.'

'Hurry up,' Janice shouted. 'You two are so interested in Chantelle's business that we nearly missed our train. Come on!' The girls quickly got on the train.

'Oh, Paula, lend me some money to buy this top and skirt, please.' Shree was holding a red mohair jumper.

Paula shook her head. 'No can do, Shree. It isn't worth the money and I can't let you waste it on that.'

'Janice, sort me out.'

'No money I'm afraid, I spent it all in Brixton.'

'I can do it cheaply, cheaply.' The Asian man who owned the stall pushed the jumper into Shree's extended arms and grinned hopefully. 'All, best-quality wool. I make little money. Beautiful girls like my clothes, yes?' Shree smiled enthusiastically but when the Asian saw that he wasn't going to make a sale he retrieved his jumper quickly and turned his attention to a tall, middle-aged woman who was looking for a hat. 'Yes, plenty hats, plenty hats, madam.'

Seeing that they were being ignored and standing in the way of the man's trade, they made their way to the new yardie shop that Paula had mentioned. 'I've been here,' announced Shree, when they finally reached the shop. A couple of big men lounged outside. They nodded their heads at Shree as a matter of course before carrying on with their heated conversation as to why small-island people were small-minded, unlike big-island people who were broad-minded and generally easier to get along with.

Inside the shop were whole heaps of linen suits, batty riders, cat-suits, click suits, string T-shirts, leggings with chains on them, leggings with big holes cut out of them, leggings made up from just a few strips of shiny lycra. Paula and Shree chattered aimlessly in the shop with the shop assistants, while Janice fingered a few leggings and then flitted through the catalogues.

'Come on,' sighed Shree. They left the shop and

threaded their way through the noisy crowd of people and stalls. They quickly left the busy street behind and walked towards Sandringham Road. Shree ran ahead to where Chantelle lived and rang the doorbell.

'Hello, dears, is Chantelle you want?' Chantelle was the youngest of a long line of brothers and sisters, so her mum was quite old and grey. She smiled at Janice, Shree and Paula. The girls nodded. There was a thumping noise as Chantelle clattered down the stairs.

'What ya saying, girls?' Chantelle was pleased to have the company and she ushered them up to her room.

'You play your music damn loud, y'know,' Janice said, sitting on the side of the bed furthest away from the hi-fi speakers. Chantelle shrugged.

Shree kicked off her boots and jumped up on Chantelle's bed.

'So why did all you lot come round – oh no, let me guess.' Chantelle turned a full ninety degrees and glared at Janice. 'News travels fast.'

'You might as well tell us now,' Paula said, turning down the volume of the hi-fi.

Chantelle flung herself down on the bed between Janice and Shree. 'What do you want to know?'

'Well, for a start, tell us why you had the fight with Tanasha.'

'Oh, he's an idiot-bwoy, come telling me that I'm a gold-digger and that I mustn't treat people like that.' Looking at all the gold rings and chains on Chantelle's dressing-table, they were ready to agree with him.

'I didn't know Tanasha had that much money to spend. He's still at university, isn't he?' Paula said.

'Yeah, but his parents are loaded. His dad has his

own clothing company and because Tanasha's the only child they spoil him. This summer, Tanasha was helping his dad out too. He's studying marketing so he did stuff for his dad. Tanasha has money to play with, trust me.'

Shree nudged Chantelle. 'So after he told you that, what happened?'

'I gave him one slap in his face. Then we started to fight.'

'Yeah, but who got hurt in the end?'

'Well, maybe I did get hurt, but Tanasha can't chat to me like that, not now, not ever.' Shree looked at the bruise on Chantelle's neck. It wasn't as big as Janice had been making out but it was nasty all the same and it was purple. She touched it with her finger.

'Yooow!! What did you do that for?'

'Poor Chantelle.'

Chantelle shrugged her shoulders. 'It will be gone in a week.'

'Well, you must admit, Tanasha was right at least?' said Paula. 'You was blatantly after the man for his money, I thought he knew that.'

'He should be damn glad that I was after him for something, because that no-assets fool ain't got nothing else going for him.'

'Chantelle, you're out of order.' Paula laughed and shook her head.

'Yeah, Tanasha was so nice to you, he treated you so special,' Janice said.

'That's his problem,' muttered Chantelle, kissing her teeth. 'He thinks he's so kriss but I just told him those lies to get my Bally pumps.' The girls found this very funny, so Chantelle carried on, 'Oh, Tanasha, you're so kriss. I've never met a man like you before. Tanasha, I think about you all the time, you're so bad for me, I find it hard to concentrate on anything, even when I'm walking down the street I think of you.' She paused for breath as Shree, Janice and Paula howled with laughter.

'Stop, stop.' Shree held out her hand for Chantelle. Paula was already on the floor and Janice leaned weakly against the wall. They had watched Chantelle coo into Tanasha's ears for months and tell him how fine he was and they had watched the boy just lap it up. Chantelle really did know how to manners a man, the only draw-back was that when things went wrong like they had, they went wrong in a big way.

'So who's this new man you're dealing with?'

'He's a south London man called Tony.'

'Well, what's he look like?'

'Short, quite sweet. He's American, from New York.'

'Don't tell me you're trying it on somebody else.'

The corners of Chantelle's mouth curled up mischievously. 'He's got a wicked car and he has enough money.'

Janice shook her head.

'How old is he?' asked Shree.

'Oh, he's only about thirty-five.'

'Thirty-five?'

'What you wanna deal with a man that old for?'

'Do you need money that badly?'

'You don't need to get into them things, girl, he could be your dad.'

'Maurice was nearly that old,' Janice said.

'He's sweet and he looks young. I guess it's not that

224

old, it just sounds it,' was Chantelle's half-hearted attempt at speeching her way out of it, but the others left her alone, they didn't want to get involved in her problems anyway.

'Chantelle, Donna's at the door,' Chantelle's mother yelled from downstairs.

'Send her up then,' called Chantelle.

Seconds later, Donna came breezing into the room. 'Hello, everybody, I saw you lot down Dalston, but I was on the bus so I couldn't say hello.' She plunked herself down in the space that was left on Chantelle's bed.

'Mind you mash up my bed wid your mampee self,' warned Chantelle. Donna stuck out her tongue.

'Just mind your manners before I have to tell you about that growth on your cheek.'

'Yo, madam, don't get feisty,' replied Chantelle.

'So has she been telling you all about her man troubles?' Donna asked, putting her arm around Chantelle. The three girls nodded.

'I have a new man too,' Donna announced. The girls weren't that shell-shocked as Donna never settled down with one man long, her relationships lasted anything from four days to four months.

'Well, what's his name then?'

'Dean. He's from Brixton.'

Having listened to a good, lengthy description of Donna's new man, who sounded foolish, all of the girls except Chantelle, who was immune to it, had escape on their minds.

'We have to go now,' Paula said, cutting into Donna's flow. She wasn't going to sit all day listening to this girl chat stupidness in her earhole. The other two girls stood up, casting Paula grateful looks. Donna looked disappointed.

'Where are you going?' Chantelle asked.

'Probably back to Shree's place,' said Janice.

'All right then, I might call on you later or give you a bell.'

'Yeah, safe, Chantelle. Later, Donna.' They said goodbye and left the house.

The three girls were walking down towards the bus stop when a black Mercedes pulled up beside them. The driver's door opened and Nero stepped out. Shree shrank back between Paula and Janice.

'Wha' gwaan, Shree?' Nero leaned back against the car and stared at her.

'What are you doing down these sides?' Shree asked as casually as she could. She didn't love Nero or even like him, but she was deeply attracted to him, against her will.

'I'm just passing through, seeing some people.'

'Oh.'

'So you not going to introduce me to none of your friends.'

'We know who you are,' said Janice stonily. Nero laughed. Paula's eyes narrowed. Shree silently wished he would go away. Nero stopped laughing and looked at Shree. He lifted his index finger. 'Come here, cuteness.'

Shree moved a step forward but her friends pulled her back. 'Shree, where do you think you're going? Just stay right here and remember whose woman you are,' said Paula.

Nero stepped forward when he saw them holding her back. He took Shree's arm and led her round to the other side of the car. Shree tried to pull her arm away but Nero had a grip of iron. Nero opened the passenger door and motioned for her to get in. Shree shook her head and took a step back.

'Don't get in his car, Shree, don't be stupid,' Paula urged.

'Come back,' Janice said.

'I'm not getting in your car.'

Nero smiled. 'Are you afraid I'm going to take liberties?'

'No, if you touched me you wouldn't live to see tomorrow.'

'I'm not going to touch you, unless you want me to.'

'Why do you want me to get into your car anyway?'

'I want to talk to you.' Nero opened the door of the car wider and this time Shree got in. Paula and Janice pursed their lips together. Nero walked back and got into the driver's seat and shut the door. Then he leaned out of the window. 'Don't worry about Shree, I'll see she gets home all right,' he said before driving off, leaving Paula and Janice looking at each other.

'You want a sweet?' Nero offered Shree a tin with boiled sweets inside. Shree shook her head.

'So where were you and your two idiot galfriends coming from?'

Shree pursed up her mouth. 'I don't know who you're talking about.'

Nero giggled. 'Mampee and Magar, me t'ink say one of them call – Janice?'

Shree kissed her teeth, but she was smiling in spite of herself.

'But serious still, where were you coming from?'

'Nowhere special, we was just visiting a friend.'

'A boyfriend?'

'You're so foolish,' Shree said, laughing, but she didn't mean it. She looked Nero over. He was dressed quite yardie, in a red suit with his two heavy gold chaps on his wrist.

'You want to try them on?'

'All right. But they look so big.' He unhooked one and handed it to Shree. She ran her fingers over the choppy, rough surface, turning it over in her hands; rays of light caught on the uneven gold, making it glint.

'I'm giving it to you.'

Shree gasped and looked at Nero. He looked her in the eyes. He was serious. She looked longingly at the chaps. She loved beautiful things – but she knew that if she accepted this gift from Nero she could kiss Tyrone goodbye because Nero would be on her case for ever. If she wore his gold, that meant she belonged to him. She took the bracelet, put it on the dashboard and looked out of the window.

'No, Nero, and I want you to drive me home.'

'But—'

'Now.'

Nero, who had parked by the side of the road, started the engine and edged the car into the traffic. 'Why you wanna bother with them lickle youths, Shree?'

'Tyrone isn't a l—'

'No, no, no, Shree, stop that girlchild talking. Me

an' you, we're both from Yard. We know how t'ings run inna down here. I'm not one of them small-time England boys, Shree. I don't go running round checking nuff, gal. You won't see me pressing up on any loose girl in a dance. That's not me. See here, I'm a man with manners. I'll big you up and respec' you down to the ground. I'll buy you things, anyt'ing you fancy.'

'But Ne—'

'You see me? Me come from Yard a three year now. Me never come wid woman on my mind. I avoid that area. Me was just looking for a way to earn some money. But when I see you now, I see you as different from dem stupid girls who just run on the street noon till night and you can see them at any idiot dance, but you're not like that.'

The car pulled up at the edge of Shree's estate. She opened the door.

'Shree, make we chat some more.'

'What else is there to say?'

'Me an' you are the same. I'm a gangster an' I know your dad's a lickle yardie too. Your place looks nice. Me see your dad set you up well, with a nice flat, but I can do better for you than dis. If you come with me, you'll have everything. Big house, expensive car. Come back to Jamaica an' you'll live like a queen.'

'Nero, I have to go. You know what I'm going to say already.' Shree sighed. 'I have to clean up my home and wash my clothes and sort myself out. I don't have time for this.' She undid the seatbelt and put one leg out of the door. Nero put out a hand to stop her, and pulling her towards him, kissed her hard on the mouth. Shree didn't have the energy to start screaming him down. She was very quiet and avoided his stare as she got out of the car, shut the door and walked away without looking back. She didn't hear the engine starting up and when she reached the landing her door was on she looked down and saw the black Mercedes. She wished he would go away, because sooner or later he was going to cause trouble.

'Hi, baby.' Tyrone opened the door for Shree, just as she was turning the key in the lock. He enveloped her in a big hug and Shree absorbed the safety and happiness that his warmth meant to her.

Tyrone helped her to take off her coat. 'What's with the special treatment?' she joked as he hung it up in the cupboard. Tyrone put his hand over her eyes and guided her towards the sitting-room. Shree squealed in excitement and pretended to struggle to uncover her eyes.

'Be patient, woman,' commanded Tyrone. 'All good things come to those who wait.'

'Ooh, Tyrone, that's a lovely thing to do.' Shree wanted to cry when she saw the sitting-room all spick and span and roses in a vase on the table and a cuddly toy next to it. There was a meal prepared and laid out, ready to eat. A bottle of wine stood next to two wine glasses, and when she was sitting down, Tyrone dimmed the lights and lit the two candles in the middle of the table. He stretched out his hand to hold Shree's.

'Shree, when I said those things to you about loving you and always being there for you, they weren't just words, they were coming from my heart.' He made a sweeping gesture around the table. 'All this, this is only a drop in the ocean of what I feel for you, and even though I won't always have money to buy you them clothes and shoes that you like so much I'm going to treat you right, seen? You're my woman and you're gonna be the mother of our child and I'm looking to keep you, forever.' He searched around for some more words to add emphasis, but Shree leaned over and kissed him softly on the forehead. No more words were needed.

'No lies now, Tyrone. You got your mum to come over and cook up all that food, innit?'

They were lying on the floor side by side. Everything had long since been eaten. Tyrone shook his head and smiled a mysterious smile. He was letting nothing slip out, least of all the fact that he'd been asking just about everyone what her favourite food was, where to buy it and how to cook it. In the end, by a method of trial and error, he'd done it and Shree was happy. Tyrone really had undergone a change. It was as if the prospect of fatherhood had brought out his best qualities. He looked at her now: her skin was very dark and smooth and soft, and the small dips in her cheek trembled when she smiled. Her generous lips were dimpled, and her large eyes slanted upwards, almost as though she had Chinese blood in her. Tyrone knew he was lucky to have Shree, not just to have her but for her to love him as he knew she did. Many, many times Shree could just have got up and walked away from what they had, which at times hadn't been much. But she had always stayed and Tyrone was determined that there should be no cause for her to walk away again.

'Tyrone, don't stare at me.' Tyrone got up off the floor and pulled Shree up towards him with that well-known look in his eye. As they went into the bedroom, hand in hand, Tyrone thanked his lucky stars that he had remembered to take the phone off the hook early on in the evening.

chapter twelve

'**Hello, Janice,** looking as lovely as ever, I see.' Colin perched on the edge of her desk.

Janice gave an irritated sigh. 'Colin, I'm sure you have something better to do than breaking up people's furniture.'

He leaned over and peered into her face.

'Who do you think you're looking at?' she asked rudely.

'Naomi Campbell's twin sister,' sighed Colin. Janice laughed and waved him away. 'You're such a fool, why don't you go and distress some other poor soul?' She pointed to Elizabeth who was working at the other reception desk.

Elizabeth lifted her head at the mention of her name and waved at Colin who shook his head at Janice. 'Don't be silly, she wants my body so bad she might just—'

'Well, *I* don't want your body, Colin, and I have phone calls to take, so why don't you just disappear now, before the supervisor comes downstairs.' Janice picked up a phone. 'Good morning, Portman and Portman, Janice speaking, how may I help you?'

Colin sighed. 'So tell me what it is that I have done to deserve lunch with the nicest woman in the office?'

Janice didn't even look up from her message pad. 'Why don't you ask her?'

'Mmm, that sounds like a proposition.' Colin loosened his tie and fanned the air around him. 'I didn't realize you were so passionate, Janice.'

'Colin—'

'No, Janice, don't spoil the mood. What were we talking about again? Oh yes, passion and my sensitive, warm personality.'

'Elizabeth!' Janice shouted. Colin threw Janice a terrified look and fled quicktime. Elizabeth, arriving too late, leaned on Janice's desk. Janice smiled brightly. 'Are you hungry, Elizabeth?' she asked. Elizabeth shrugged.

'Lunch is on me,' Janice said as they signed out.

They found themselves seats in the crowded Burger King.

'Thanks for the lunch, Janice.'

'It's all right. I'm just grateful to you for rescuing me from Colin.'

'But how did I rescue you?'

'Er, well, um, you know how shy Colin is and all that.'

'Well, I think you're damn lucky to have someone as fit as Colin running after you.'

'As fit as Colin? He's not fit. He just about passes for all right.'

'I think Colin's lovely, the way his brown hair curls

around his ears, and his eyes are the deepest blue I've ever seen.'

Janice looked at Elizabeth's pale, acne-ridden, uninteresting face and shrugged. 'I don't know if I'd push it to lovely.'

'Oh, he's so sweet and funny and cute. The only reason you don't like him is because he's white, isn't it?'

'No, I like some white men, but I don't find him attractive.'

'You don't even have a boyfriend.'

'Who told you that?'

'Oh, come on, Janice. If you don't go straight home from work, you go to your mum's house or your friends come for you and you go out with them. Not like Natalie or Sanrishi. Their men come to pick them up at least once a week and they talk about them non-stop.'

'I went out with Maurice, didn't I?' Janice said crossly.

Elizabeth opened her eyes very wide. 'Yes, but how long did that last?' She sighed. 'No. We are just two girls on our own, you and I, still looking for Mr Right.'

'We'd better get a move on, you know,' said Janice. 'We've only got ten minutes to get back to the office. I've already had a written warning for lateness from that Yates woman. I don't need any more.'

'She's a bitch. I hate her too. She's always up on somebody. She's got it in for you because she fancies Colin,' Elizabeth said as they left Burger King.

'Good afternoon, Portman and Portman, Janice speaking, how may I help you?'

'Hello, Janice, sounding a little posh, aren't we?'

'What's up, Paula? You looking to make me get the sack?'

'Yes. Then you can come and keep me company during the day.'

'What's happened to Shree?'

'Nah, man. Shree's not the same. All she wants to do is cook and clean house nowadays. She's boring.'

'Poor Paula. All alone and nowhere to go.'

'Don't start dissing it now, Janice, or I'll ring up another receptionist and ask them to pass me down to, what's his name – Colin?'

'You wouldn't wanna try that one on me. Take my word for it, you really wouldn't.'

'You know you love him up really.'

'Ha, love doesn't come into this. That boy is so annoying. He's like an old dog who won't leave me alone.'

'Yeah, well, I didn't phone you up just to hear you cuss poor Colin into the ground, I came to tell you the latest news that's buzzing round London.'

'I didn't figure you for a gossip, Paula.'

'I have reason to be. Elroy has just broken up with Mona.'

'Is it?! – I mean, that's nice.'

'Yes. Elroy is free and single and living in Tottenham.'

'He's back with his parents?'

'He never moved, but he was at Mona's place a lot, I think. His dad's always at work and his mum does all the housework, so he didn't have any reason to move out.'

'How do you know so much?'

'Well, I phoned up Michael today, just to chat, you know the deal, and he told me that Elroy and Mona aren't going out – so you can go for it now, Janice.'

'Er, excuse me, "go" for what?'

'You know damn well what I'm talking about, so just admit that you're as craven for Elroy now as you ever was.'

'Why did they break up?'

'Well, I suppose – hell, I don't know, Michael didn't tell me and I didn't bother to ask. It's not my business, is it?'

'Well, who dumped who?' Janice asked eagerly.

'Janice! I swear you sound more and more like that eggs-up Donna everyday.'

'Who dumped who?' insisted Janice.

'Does it matter?'

'Yes.'

'Why? The point is that Elroy is yours for the taking. Go get him, girl. Don't be wasting your time with such minor details like who dumped who.'

Miss Yates, the supervisor, walked into the reception area and began talking to Elizabeth.

'All right, Mrs, er, Smith, what exactly is the problem?' Janice said.

'Oh, is the supervisor about again?'

'Yes. Come on, tell me, Paula, I mean, Mrs Smith. It's important to me.'

'I just don't know what the point is in telling you.'

'Then goodbye!' Janice replaced the receiver as Miss Yates walked across to her desk.

'I hope that wasn't a personal call, Janice,' Miss Yates said.

'No, it was a caller who was being rude.'

'Then I suggest you re-read the staff procedures to find out the *correct* way of dealing with troublesome callers.'

'All right.'

'Oh yes, and I've put your name forward for an evening secretarial course to start in January. I hope that's okay.'

'Yes, that would be great, thanks a lot.'

'Oh, don't thank me. David Scott the sales manager asked me to do it. He seems to think you could work in his group if your secretarial skills were a bit better. As far as I'm concerned your secretarial skills are fine, it is your communication skills that need improving.' Miss Yates marched off and left Janice muttering curses under her breath.

As Janice was unlocking the front door to her flat the telephone started ringing. She ran down the hall, leaving the door ajar.

'Hello.'

'Hi, Jan. You'll never guess. I've got the most exciting news to tell you.'

Janice sighed in disappointment. It was only Donna. 'If it's anything to do with Elroy, I already know.'

'Oh.'

'However, there is something you could tell me, that I want to know.'

'What?'

'Why did they finish?'

'I don't know that much, just what I heard from Ian, who goes out with one of Mona's friends. Anyway, I think that they were outside the train station and they were standing next to Elroy's car and when he told her it was over Mona got really angry and started to shout at Elroy but then she was just crying. Then she ran into the train station and he got back into his car and drove off.'

So Elroy had finished it. Somehow Janice was glad, because if anything did happen between her and Elroy ever again, she would know it was not because he was on the rebound.

'Oh well, I'll talk to you later, Donna, because I'm going somewhere and I'm late.'

'Where are you going?'

'I'll tell you when I get back, byee.' Janice hung up and rocked back and forward on her heels. She wasn't going anywhere but now that she had the information she wanted Donna was starting to bore her.

Janice was standing on a platform in Dalston station, looking at her watch. The train was late. She was tired and longing to put her feet up. She kissed her teeth when the fuzzy intercom announced that there was a delay due to signal failure. She was supposed to make dinner for Rio as her parents were going to a Pentecostal convention and her mother wanted her to stay home and make sure Rio didn't get up to any mischief.

'The train's rather late, isn't it? My name's Dave by the way.' Janice looked to her right where a very short man grinned up at her. Janice gave him a dirty look, then turned and concentrated on the platform directly opposite. Her eyes focused on a tall familiar figure in a dark Karl Kani suit. As she stared, wondering who it was, the head turned and she saw it was Elroy.

She didn't know what to do. She couldn't look away and neither, it seemed, could he. The looks were meaningful. Janice just knew this was it, that things were all right between them and that Elroy felt for her. Then the tube came rumbling in and stopped next to the opposite platform and she couldn't see Elroy any more.

A few minutes later the train sped out of the station, leaving an empty platform in front of her. Janice couldn't believe it, tears stung her eyes. They had something, she knew they had something, so how could he just leave like that? Why couldn't he have waited even for a few minutes to talk to her? She tried to tell herself that he must be going somewhere really important but it just didn't add up. He didn't care after all. Janice's own train ran into the station. She got ready to fight for a seat. Then, just when the doors had closed, Janice saw Elroy running along the platform. She gave a small cry. She watched as he ran along the carriages looking for her, but he ran straight past the carriage she was in without seeing her. Seconds later the train pulled out of the station and Elroy was left on the platform alone.

As the train disappeared into a tunnel, Elroy sat down on a bench and crumpled his baseball cap in his hands. Seriously shown up.

Another train came rumbling in and the platform was suddenly thick with confusion, a blur of people rushing around furiously, banging their bags against each other as they followed the migration towards the stairs at the end of the platform. Elroy held on to his baseball cap as the crowd surged and swayed and eventually swept out of the station. In all the chaos a young woman had dropped her briefcase and several magazines on the platform. Elroy walked over and bent down to help her gather her possessions up. She smiled at him.

'Oh, thank you. You don't have to do that, you know.'

'No trouble.' Elroy picked up the briefcase and magazines and handed them to her. The young woman blushed and gave him a shy smile before saying goodbye and walking off.

Elroy walked back to the other platform and caught the next train down to Hackney Central. When he arrived, Michael was waiting.

'Elroy, you're late, man. I've got a fine Nubian sister I have to check on.'

'Paula?'

'Don't be stupid, I met this girl yesterday. She's fit. She told me to come and see her. Don't tell Paula, though.'

'You're gonna break Paula's heart if you keep messing her around,' Elroy said shaking his head.

'Since when did you start worrying about Paula? Forget her, she's old news.'

'Don't disrespect her, she's your baby-mother.'

'Yeah, yeah. Let's hurry up before the record shop closes. What's the deal with the lateness man?' They walked up Mare Street.

'I had to go and see the owner of Equinox. He's offering me a deejaying job and the interview took longer than I thought it would.'

'I hear that's a good club. So how did it go?'

'It went well. They're offering big bucks.'

'So why are you so down?'

'It's a long story.'

'I'm not going anywhere.'

'I have just seen Janice but she was on the opposite platform. There was eye-contact. My train came in and I was going to get on but I couldn't bring myself to do it. I guess I'm still crazy about her. I just wanted to talk to her again so I went over to her platform but she obviously didn't feel the same way because she had got on her train and left.'

They reached the record shop. Michael stopped outside and laughed. 'I have to hear this. I can't believe you're worrying about Janice when you have Mona,' he said unsympathetically.

'Actually, I dropped Mona yesterday,' Elroy said, looking offended.

'What the hell did you go and do a stupid thing like that for?'

Elroy smiled. 'That's what Tanasha said when I told him.'

'Elroy, the girl is so pretty. She's got a wicked body, she's got the face and she definitely has the hair. Mona makes Janice look like a scarecrow. There's no contest, but then I never thought much of Janice, she's argumentative and thinks she's too nice. Look how she dumped you.'

'Yeah, I know what you mean.'

'So what's the deal with Mona?'

'I'm not ashamed to admit that I met Mona when I was on the rebound from Janice. I was doing the deejaying at a party for some mediocre modelling agency. It was really lame but while I was having a break this really beautiful girl came up and offered me a glass of wine. That was how it started. Mona looked exceptional and the devil in me took the bait. I thought that it would be a way to get back at Janice and keep face. It wasn't a question of loving Mona. I don't even find her attractive any more.'

'Well, you gave a good pretence,' said Michael, interrupting. 'You bought her a whirl of presents.'

'Yeah, it's true. Jewellery, clothes, and I took her to some really expensive restaurants.'

'Just to get back at Janice?'

'Yes. I know Mona is really nice but she's got no depth. She doesn't have any spirit and she agrees with everything I say.'

'But Elroy, that's ideal. You don't want a girl who argues, trust me. All a woman needs is to be good in bed and pretty. Did she meet the credentials?'

'Yeah, it was great.'

'So why are you worrying about her mind? Don't be a fool.'

'I'm not like you, Michael. I used to be when I was with Janice but now I appreciate her so much. She's smart and funny. She's argumentative but she's such an interesting person. You can't hold a conversation with Mona, she's just a showpiece and it was really starting to bore me.'

They moved away from the shop doorway to let some people through.

'So how did you break it to Mona?' Michael asked.

'Well, we met up at Highbury station yesterday

around lunchtime. She wanted to go shopping like she always seems to want to. I said I had a cold and that I was going home to lie down but she wanted to come home with me. I couldn't think of any more lies so I told her the truth, straight up.'

'How did she take it?'

'She was really quiet and asked me why. When I told her she banged the bonnet of the car and started yelling at me, telling me I'm treating her like shit and she's been wasting her time on me when she could have had her pick of a hundred men. Then she started crying really bad so I tried to comfort her, but you know what women are like. She wouldn't listen to me. In the end I got angry and yelled at her and she walked off, so I got in my car and drove away. We haven't spoken since.'

'You're an idiot, Elroy, that's all I have to say.'

'It's better like this for a while until I sort out what I want. Besides, I don't have much time for romance these days. I've got my deejaying spot with Choice FM coming up and this new job at Equinox. If Janice came back today, I'd treat her like a queen, but it's not likely.'

'You're a shame to the crew, Elroy. You used to be a regular gallis and now you're like an old man. Let's hurry up and choose your records. I can't stand your whining any more. I've seen this happen to both Darren and Tyrone and now you're following the same downroad.'

Elroy laughed and touched fists with Michael as they walked into the record shop.

*

Shree was the first to wake up. The bed was so deliciously warm and comfortable that she figured she might just go back to sleep, but, burrowing her head in her enormous pillows, she just couldn't. She looked across at Tyrone, snoring away with no shame in the world. She grabbed a fistful of his curly ski-slope.

'Oww, noo,' mumbled Tyrone. Shree twisted harder. A disgruntled Tyrone opened his eyes and gave her an angry look.

'What did you do that for, man? I'm tired, Shree.'

'You were snoring.'

'Allow me your foolishness at this time in the morning, idiot-gal. I never snore.'

'Who you t'ink you're talking to?' She pinched his neck cruelly. Tyrone had had enough. Thoroughly awake and seeking revenge, he caught Shree's arms and pulled her towards him.

She pretended to be scared. 'Be kind to me.'

'Only if you follow my orders.'

'What orders?'

'Well, treat me right and maybe I'll be kind to you.'

'Nahh!!'

'Why not?'

'I'm washing my hair.'

'Just a little bit of loving.'

'W-ell—'

'Please baby.'

Shree gave Tyrone one of her mischievous looks. 'All right, then.'

Tyrone made the mistake of letting go. As soon as her arms and legs were free, Shree jumped out of bed and ran out of the bedroom and into the kitchen. Tyrone followed and watched as she ate her way through a bag of crisps and half a tub of chocolate ice-cream.

'Tyrone, what are you looking at?'

'You have no shame.'

Shree gave him a dirty look. 'Is your baby me feeding so jus' rest your gums, star.'

'Looks to me like you're feeding yourself.'

'If and when I'm ready to munch, I'll munch. There's no point in starving myself, is there? My figure's long gone.' Shree raised her nightie to show Tyrone her thickened waist.

'All right, all right, I ain't saying nothing, but when you're three times the size of Paula don't come crying to me because I'll be with my next size ten girl.'

Shree flicked a spoonful of chocolate ice-cream at Tyrone. It missed. He came and sat next to her and kissed her.

'Don't get cross, Shree. You know I was just catching a little joke and that. Even if you was size twenty I'd still love you forever. I'm a one-woman man and you're the one.' Shree gave him a suspicious look but then she smiled.

'Damn it, I'm going to be late for work.'

'Yeah, you'd better hurry up.' Shree looked up from the tub of chocolate ice-cream.

'I'm going to come straight home.'

'Oh no you won't, you think I don't know what you're like?'

'I will.'

'At this rate, by the time you leave it will be time to come home.'

Tyrone ran into the bedroom. Shree picked up the tub of ice-cream and walked into the sitting-room. She sat down on the sofa, picked up the telephone and dialled Paula's number.

'Hi, Paula, how's it going?'

'All right.'

'Have you taken Fabian to nursery?'

'Yeah.'

'So how did the job-hunting go yesterday, did you find anything?'

'Well, I got this job in my local store.'

'Already? Doesn't it usually take a few days?'

'Yes, but the manager wasn't busy and I went into his office for a kind of on the spot interview and I got the job. You know him, the little old white man who always gives Fabian free sweets. I start tomorrow.'

'That's wicked!'

'Not exactly wicked, Shree. I wouldn't have minded a job in a clothes store where you get some discount off the clothes, but it's a bit better than my benefit and it will do until Fabian goes to proper school next year because I can't work the full hours now anyway.'

'Yeah, I see your point. Didn't Michael say that he was going to find you a job at the record shop his friend owns?'

'That's what I thought but that was weeks ago and he hasn't said a word since.'

'Well, he's working himself. Hasn't he given you any money?'

'Not a penny. Still, everyone's got their bills to pay.'

'Hold on a minute Paula. 'Bye, honey, make sure

you keep your promise to come straight home.' She kissed Tyrone who then hurried out of the flat.

'Was that Tyrone I heard you kissing?'

'Who else was it likely to be?'

'Just checking it wasn't that creep Nero.'

'Very funny, Paula. Actually he said something really funny about you and Janice.'

'I don't want to know.'

'He called you two Mampee and Magar.'

'And let me guess who was Mampee.'

'Oh, come on, Paula. It's just a joke. You're not really fat.'

'So what's the deal between you and this Nero?'

'The last time I saw him was when I was with you.'

'I know that. I mean, how do you two feel about each other?'

'Well, I'll be honest. Nero is crazy about me.'

'You're so vain.'

'It's true.'

'Do you like him?'

'I think he's sexy, I do find him attractive but I'm in love with Tyrone. I'm not going to do anything stupid.'

'It was stupid to get into his car that day. He could have raped you.'

'He's not like that.'

'You don't know him.'

'I think I do.'

'Does he know you're pregnant?'

'It's none of his business.'

'Oh, so now he isn't such a close friend.'

'Paula, what's your problem?'

'I don't want to see you making the same mistake that Janice made.'

'For God's sake! All I did was take a lift home.'

'He is never going to leave you alone.'

'Maybe I don't want him to.'

'You will lose Tyrone if you don't tell him to get lost right now.'

'Paula, don't tell me how to live my life. It didn't work with Janice and it won't work with me.'

'That was low, Shree.'

'You started this argument. You're jealous. Just like when Janice met Maurice.'

'Oh, I'm jealous now? Why? Because you're acting like a bitch on heat?'

'You're jealous because Michael doesn't love you and you can't get another man.'

'Don't call me until you're ready to apologize for that!' Paula slammed down the receiver.

Shree slowly replaced her telephone. She felt like kicking herself for that last remark. It was wrong but she wasn't going to apologize after Paula's insults. She walked into the kitchen, picked up *Ebony*, which was lying on the table, and flicked through it. Then she turned on the television and sat watching the morning programmes. The doorbell rang.

'Damn Tyrone, always forgetting things,' she muttered as she walked towards the door. The bell sounded again. 'Okay, okay, I'm coming,' she shouted.

'Oh!' said Shree as she saw who was standing on the

doorstep. The tall man, leaner than previously, but as immaculately dressed as ever, lounged at her doorstep, wearing that little half-smile well known to the women of his era. Derrick kissed Shree on the cheek before he walked past her into the sitting-room.

'Oh, my God! Daddy, you're back!' Shree stood in the doorway, still in shock.

'Are you happy to see me, baby?'

'Yes, I missed you so much.'

'I missed my little girl too.'

'Well, if you missed me why didn't you write or phone me for so long?'

'Er, I—'

'And when you did write, all I got was five lines, telling me you was fine and coming home soon.'

'Shree, calm down. I don't know what you're shoutin' for. Everyt'ing kriss. I'm gonna look after you, you know, there's no need to fret. You wasn't on your own. Those are Tyrone's trainers behind the door, nuh true?'

Shree nodded.

'See, he was here an' you had your friends, so you didn't get into any trouble. Don't worry, I'm gonna spend a lickle more time wid you an' take you shopping an' all. Everyt'ing kriss.' Derrick stood in the centre of the room and looked around. He took in the crisp packets and the tub of ice-cream on the floor. He looked at the copy of *Ebony* magazine lying on the sofa and then he picked up the book next to it; *The Last Five Months of Pregnancy*.

'Hey, Shree,' he yelled, 'Shree.' He stormed into the kitchen and found his daughter making a sandwich and watching the morning cartoons.

'Shree, you're pregnant?' Shree nodded like it was no big deal.

'Blouse and skirt! A wha' type of madness you carry on wid since me gone?'

Shree turned around and faced her father with the sweetest, most appealing smile she could conjure up. 'I don't know what you're worrying about really, Daddy. I know I can look after a baby, I love kids—'

'So this is the way Tyrone hangle me daughter? Jus' wait t—'

'Tyrone's not going anywhere and neither am I, so I don't know what you mean by "jus' wait". *You* "jus' wait". I'm not asking you for anything.'

'But why you couldn't wait till you settle down, till you reach older, find yourself a nice Jamaican man to look after you, not no smalltime English bwoy dem, who run up and down street all day looking woman?'

'Tyrone's not like that.'

'Well, what him like then? You tell me. Him a millionaire?'

'No.'

'Him a movie star?'

'No!'

'Him a member of – now wha' you call it? – him a Member of Parli'ment?'

'No.'

'Den why in God's name are you having baby fe dat ruffneck?'

'I love Tyrone and Tyrone loves me.'

'Dat street tramp couldn't give love to a dog, a' so me tel you. Him couldn't even hangle a *dog*, so wha' him do wid my daughter deh? Cha!'

'You haven't been home for months but you think you can start running things twenty-four-seven the minute you come back.'

'Don't back-answer me! I just want the best fe you.'

'Well, we didn't plan for the baby but it's here now. Do you want me to get rid of it?'

'No daughter of mine ever gwan murder a yout' —'

'Then there's no more to be said.' Shree turned off the television, snatched up the sandwich and went into the sitting-room. 'Bring the television in with you,' she ordered over her shoulder.

Derrick picked up the television and carried it into the sitting-room. 'You have all the answers, Shree, but I haven't even started to deal with Tyrone yet.'

'So are you going to tell me where *you*'ve been all this time, or must I guess?'

Derrick scratched his head. 'Just me went to that place, down Beck-no Bexley, an' I was just chillin' low, seen? Then, ahm I was staying at the house of this funny landlord. But the man carry on too nasty, plates nuh wash, floor nuh wash, bedclothes nuh wash. Me couldn't deal wid that so me did call a brethren who tell me say he will meet me an' tek me to a next man who lives in Birmingham and das where me been all this time.'

'So you could call a brethren and you couldn't call your own child?'

'It's not like that. It was business, I couldn't be calling up women to hangle my business.' Derrick sat back. 'Lord God, me tired. That was a long drive.'

'Well, if you must be running up and down country you must be tired, no? Too tired to phone an' ask if me and Paula all right after we nearly cut slice up by dem gangster friends of yours.'

'What's this? Terror lay him hands 'pon you? Raasclat, if that soldier ever harm you me gwan follow him back a yard and chop off him foot, so me tell you!' He went over to Shree and looked at her. 'What him do to you?'

'It was my fault. Me and Paula went to your flat and I think Terror and his friends were in the building because when we left the flat they blocked our way in the car park.'

'Go on.'

'Nothing happened. It was just scary but we kept our cool and ran away from them.'

'Don't lie to me, Shree. I know Terror wouldn't just leave it at that.'

'Calm down. I'm all right now, so don't go running off into any more trouble.'

'Was the flat in good condition when you went there?'

'Yes, but me and Paula might have messed it up a bit.'

'Me notice you took a couple of photos and letters and the money.'

'Yeah, I did. Can I keep the photos? The letters are around somewhere.'

'Sure, but how you find the combination?'

'It was on the back of a photo.' Derrick smiled, but then he grew angry again.

'But me nuh no how a chile of mine come out so hard of hearing. Me tell you not to go to the flat. A' wha' me tell you?'

'Yes, yes, I know, I know, but I needed the money.'

'So what's Tyrone there for?'

'Yeah, but them times, we wasn't getting on too well and I didn't feel to ask him.'

'I'm not sure about this baby business at all, me tell you, at *all*!! If my daughter have to be breaking into people flat and doing all kinds of dangerous things for a few dollars and her baby-father right next to her and him cyan sort her out, that no seen right. Me t'ink say me better have words wid this Tyrone who thinks he's such a *don gargon* to be fathering this one, fathering that one.'

'Daddy!'

'No, no, I'm not going to do anything to him serious but I have to sceer him a lickle, just let him know it's not anybody's daughter him dealing wid, it's mine.' He folded his arms and sat back on the sofa beaming at Shree who just glared back. She gave an exasperated sigh and changed the subject. 'I saw Pearl doing her Saturday shopping in the market the other day. She was asking after you.'

'Yes, me must pay her a call soon. She is one of the first people I have to see. Do you know how her holiday went?'

'Not really, but she said she had a good time, you know, the usual things. I was supposed to drop round there to see the photos but I haven't got around to it.'

'Well, I can drop by. I just have to see to some business but I want you to see someone first.'

'Who?'

'She's waiting in the car. I'll go down and get her while you tidy up a bit. I'll be about five minutes, so clear away these crisp packets, open the windows and let some fresh air in, and put something clean on and do your hair.'

'All in five minutes?' asked Shree, laughing.

'It's not a joke. I want you to make a good impression.'

Shree put on some clean clothes and tidied her hair and straightened up the room. Ten minutes later the doorbell rang. Shree opened the door. Derrick had a tall, very dark-skinned and fattish woman with him.

'Shree, this is Andrea.'

'Hi, come in.'

Derrick took Andrea by the hand and led her into the sitting-room. The woman was more handsome than pretty, with a large, open face and big lips. The texture and length of her hair suggested she had Indian blood.

'So you're the Shree I've heard so much about.'

Shree noticed the soft Birmingham accent. 'Would you like a drink?' she asked, smiling.

'Oh no, we're not staying,' Derrick interrupted. 'Andrea and I are going back to my flat. I just wanted you to meet each other.'

'Well, I'll probably see you another time, Andrea,' Shree said.

'Yes. 'Bye.'

Derrick and Andrea left the flat and Shree sat down again in front of the television. Although she tried not to, she kept thinking about Paula and their argument. She leaned over and picked the telephone up from the floor and dialled Paula's digits.

'Hello.'

'Hi, Paula, it's Shree.'

'So, what do you want?'

'Look. You're right, I didn't have no right to say what I did, so I'm apologizing.'

'That's good.'

'You should apologize too. You called me a bitch on heat.'

'I never called you any such thing.'

'Yes you did.'

'Well, if I did, I'm sorry too.'

'Still friends?'

'Yeah, we're safe.'

chapter thirteen

'**I think** I should start maternity classes so I can learn how to breathe and stuff.' Shree was lying on Paula's bed, flicking through Paula's old baby books and Mothercare catalogues.

'Breathe how you want, it won't make any difference in the real thing,' said Paula grimly, as she cleaned out her wardrobe.

'You're such a bringer of bad news, Paula.' Janice was painting her nails with Paula's gold gloss.

'Yeah, and I heard that it does make it easier,' said Shree.

'All right, all right.' Paula held up her hands. 'Then when it's time for you to have the baby you start breathing away and see if it doesn't hurt.'

'I don't have to have it in a bed, you know.' Shree held up a picture of a beaming woman sitting in a bathtub. 'I can have it in a water bath. See here. The woman says it was – um, better than eating chocolate.'

Paula stood up, took the magazine and scrutinized the picture. She handed the magazine back. 'I think you should see how much she paid for all of that and then tell me how wonderful it would be.' Shree read the paragraph Paula pointed to and her face fell.

'Is it really that painful, Paula?' Janice asked with curiosity, reaching for a nail file on Paula's dressing-table.

Paula glanced at Shree. 'I can't lie. It is really painful because unless your labour is really long or difficult they don't encourage you to have painkillers any more. At first it's not so bad but then it is tough.'

'Did you scream like they do on television?'

'Why are you asking me these questions all over again, Janice? You kept pestering me every five minutes when I had Fabian, I would have thought you could remember.'

'I'm just interested.'

'Listen, look how many kids there are in this world. Look how many women have three up to six children. Yes, it's pain but if they go through it time and time again then perhaps it's not that bad.'

Shree looked up. 'What's the date, Janice?'

'Ten days before Christmas!' said Janice excitedly.

'Calm down, you idiot,' said Paula. 'You're in *my* house now.'

'Yeah, where's the excitement? We're only going to do the usual things, buy up a whole heap of Christmas presents nobody wants, go t—'

Paula held up her hands. 'Hol' on. Stop right there. I ain't buy jack for nobody. I haven't got money to waste this year, especially on people I just say hello to in the street. I'm buying for you and my son.'

'Well, what about Chantelle and Donna?'

'Times are hard. They can have a card and maybe something small.'

'What about Michael?'

'What about Michael?'

'I'm sorry, not this time. I've given enough.'

'Are you serious, Paula?'

'Yeah, this is *Michael* we're talking about. The one and only.'

'Oh, I don't know. Maybe I will buy him something small.' Janice and Shree groaned and resumed their various activities.

'It will be good to see everybody again,' said Shree.

'It's all right for you,' said Janice. 'I won't be able to go to Tanasha's get-together, I'll be forced to stay at home, just as if I was Rio's age.'

'Well, it's probably just as well, because Elroy will be there and that will only make you miserable. Don't worry, we'll tell you how it went,' said Paula.

'I think we should go out and buy presents today,' Shree said enthusiastically.

Paula gave a sarcastic snort. 'Just another Shree-excuse to spend money,' she remarked drily.

'Yeah, come on, Paula. We've all got a little money now, me with my job, you with your job, Shree with her dad back.'

'Hey, don't try it now, Janice,' Shree said smiling.

'All right, I'll come with you, but I'm not buying a single thing and neither are you, Shree,' said Paula firmly.

*

'Ahh, Fabian would love that,' said Paula, flinging the puzzle into her basket. The other two looked at each other. Five shops and three shopping bags later, Paula had done more shopping than both of them put together.

'Paula, I think you've passed the limit now,' said Shree anxiously.

'Listen to you, the girl with *no* shopping limit,' retorted Paula.

Shree leaned over to Janice's basket and drew out a bottle of aftershave. 'Whew! That looks expensive, girl, who is that for?'

'Oh-er-oh yeah, my dad.'

'But your dad wears Quorum, not Joop,' Paula said. 'I remember you told us that you hate the smell but that he hasn't worn anything else for the past fifteen years. So who is this Joop for, Jan?'

'Well, if he didn't wear it before he does now.' Janice said. 'Come on, Shree, you're next. Empty your basket, you're holding everyone up.'

'Where to now?' Shree asked enthusiastically.

'Don't you think you've done enough shopping for today, Shree?' asked Janice wearily.

Shree shook her head. 'Well, I do have a few more things I want to look at—'

'Then do it with Janice. I've got to go and get Fabian.'

'Sorry, I can't. I have to help my mum with the er, Christmas tree and um, everything.'

'You two are being so unreasonable, I only want to look at a few more things.' Shree paused, waiting for the other two to change their minds. 'All right then, I'll just go home. I'm feeling a bit sick so I should probably go lie down anyway.'

Ten days later, Fabian opened his eyes big and wide and looked around the room. He'd been lying awake for some time, just waiting for the right moment. He looked at his toy box and then at the window-sill. His small forehead creased into a worried frown. This wasn't right. He sat up and wiped his eyes hastily as he could feel a tear coming. Then, as he pulled the duvet up to cover his face, he noticed some strange shapes at the bottom of the bed. He flung the duvet on to the floor.

Paula, in her bedroom, hugged her knees and smiled to herself as she heard the squeals of delight coming from the small bedroom. She didn't need a man to make her Christmas right. She had the person who meant more to her than anyone else in the world right next to her.

'Thank you for the presents, Mummy,' said Fabian, running into the room and jumping on to the bed.

'That's all right baby, I just hope you like them.'

'Did Daddy give me a present?'

'No, he must have forgotten.'

'Is he coming to visit me today?'

'I don't think so, honey, but he may telephone.'

'Does Daddy love me more than Shree or Janice?'

'Yes, deep down, he loves you better than anybody except Mummy.'

'What are we going to do today?'

'We are going to have breakfast and then you can play with your presents and if you're good we will go to Tanasha's house for a party.'

'Are we going to see Granny?'

'Do you want to?'

'No, Granny shouts at me an' she doesn't have any toys.'

'Well, don't worry, you won't have to visit Granny today.'

'I wanna go to McDonalds.'

'Fabian, it's Christmas Day. McDonalds will be closed and you're going to a party.'

'Will Daddy be there?'

'Maybe.'

'Well, I said to her, why do you want me to wear the dress, and do you know what she said?'

Shree shook her head vigorously.

'I don't think Shree wants to know, Mum.'

'Ssssh!' Shree waved Tyrone away. 'Come on, Cherry.'

'She turn to me and tell me that I am prettier than her so it should really be me.' Shree smiled. Cherry got up, still chattering, unlocked the old chest of drawers in the corner of the sitting-room and took out a pile of ancient photos. 'You see, I wasn't always as old and ugly as I am now.'

'You don't look very old and there's no way anyone could call you ugly!'

Cherry reached over and squeezed Shree's hand. 'I hope Tyrone takes care of you.'

'You know I do!' said Tyrone indignantly.

'So when are you two going to get married?'

'We don't want to get married just because we're having a baby. We think it means a lot more than that.'

'Yeah, that's just what I was going to say,' added Tyrone.

Cherry kissed her teeth at him and turned her attention back to Shree. 'Has he offered?'

'Yes,' lied Shree.

Cherry looked at her son proudly. 'My Tyrone always knows when to do the right thing.'

Tyrone looked at Shree quizzically.

'Are you sure you don't want to come back later to Christmas dinner?' Cherry asked for the fifth time as Tyrone and Shree rose to go. 'Well—'

'No, no, no, we don't want to sit round the table with all your made-up friends, thank you – ow, whad'ya do that for?' Shree had reached out and smacked Tyrone around his head.

Cherry smiled approvingly. 'Well, thank you for the flowers and the chocolates and the shawl. They're really lovely,' she said as she reached over to kiss Shree.

'Yeah, yeah, 'bye, Mum, happy Christmas.' Tyrone gave his mother a bear hug and then dragged Shree out of the house.

'You're so rude, Tyrone. How can you treat your mother like that? Suppose she's lonely?'

'My mother? Lonely? You must be talking about someone else, honey. She's got all my goofy brothers and sisters coming round, how can she be lonely? And what do you mean "treat my mother like that"? I treat her good.'

'So you should, she's wonderful.'

'I'm glad we agree, now can we get home? You didn't let me finish my breakfast.'

Janice mumbled and grumbled as she reluctantly followed her mother around their spacious kitchen.

'No, Janice. Don't cut your eye at me or no one is getting any breakfast today. You have ears, you can hear me, nuh?'

'Yes, Mum.'

'The truth is, you think you're so smart, well, let me tell you something, pickanny. You're too smart for your own good. You t'ink you can just waltz down here for Christmas and be waited on hand and foot. I already have your father, who nuh even understand to pick up him socks dem whenever he take off his shoes. Me also have your lickle brother who always outta road but expect him dinner on call whenever he get back. Me is not a slave, me is not going to be your slave.'

'God, I'm not asking you to be, am I?'

'A' who you t'ink you talking to like that? I don't want to hear you taking the Lord's name in vain in this house on this day, young lady.'

Janice glowered at Rose and then stamped out of the kitchen. 'I should have stayed at home,' she muttered.

'No bodder, go back to bed, Janice, a' so me warn you,' Rose called after her. 'Me is not cooking a slice of toast until you come back down here and cut up the plantain, so just hurry up yourself.'

Janice stamped her feet all the way up the stairs. On the landing Rio opened the door to his bedroom. 'What's all the noise for, you fool? Can't you let a man get some sleep?'

'Happy Christmas to you too!'

'Eh?' Rio was not impressed by Janice's sarcasm. 'Just go back downstairs and earn your Christmas dinner and stop being feisty, seen?' He grinned and quickly closed the door before Janice could retort.

'Janice! Why you disturbing everybody?' Pops called out sleepily from another bedroom. 'You cyan let your brother get some sleep but you must go making hargument with everyone? You're supposed to be downstairs helping your mother, nuh true?'

'Janice, me gwaan count to t'ree,' yelled Rose from downstairs.

'Yeah, slave. Get downstairs and cook my breakfast,' Rio hissed from behind his bedroom door.

'Cook it yourself, you nasty tramp,' spat Janice going downstairs.

'And nuh bodder talk to your brother like that,' shouted Pops testily. 'It's Christmas!'

'Yes, well, it's lucky for some, isn't it?' Janice grumbled down the phone, much later.

'What's up with you, bad girl?'

'Oh, Shree, I had to wake up at the crack of dawn and make breakfast for my whole family – yes, that includes that dried-out bean bag, Rio. He's been so feisty to me ever since he got up I would just like to fling him into the oven.'

'So if the work's done, what are you complaining for?'

'What do you mean – if the work's done? I still have to wash and cut up all the vegetables for the salad, hoover out the front room and wash up the lunch dishes before any of my mum's church cronies get here, or any of my aunts, or anyone else in need of food.'

'So who's supposed to be coming, exactly?'

'Oh, I don't know, I lose track. I know Auntie Nesta is coming down with her kids and her ugly husband. I know that Mum's church people will at least pass through to say hello, that could be any number from one to fifty-one, oh yeah, and my other uncles and aunts and cousins will most likely be coming for dinner too.'

'Whew, sounds like quite a party. What's the crew doing?'

'My dad's watching the television. Rio's getting dressed, you can probably hear the music, and my mum's taking the clothes off the washing line.'

'Leaving everything to the last minute.'

'Leaving it to *me*, star. Well, you might as well tell me what a good time you're going to have today with Mr Loverman.'

Shree giggled. 'You're such a joker. Actually, we visited his mum early this morning. Now I'm gonna be on my own for the rest of the afternoon. Tyrone's gone off to console those two broken-hearts, Tanasha and Elroy. I've got a few things to do anyway, then I have to meet everyone at Tanasha's place about six, seven o'clock. His parents have gone visiting so the house is going to be empty.'

'Who's everyone?'

'Oh, you know Janice, the full crew. Paula, Chantelle, Donna, Tamara—'

'Which boys?'

'Tyrone, Tanasha, Elroy, Michael, Darren, Aston, everyone. Why can't you come?'

'How am I supposed to get there?'

'Oh, I would come and get you but Tyrone's taken the car.'

'It's all right, maybe one of my relatives will give me a lift.'

'Give you a lift where, Janice? Today is a family day. The only place you gwine go is back inna de kitchen to finish cleaning them carrots. Just remember that!' Rose said sharply, passing Janice on the way to the stairs.

'Then again, Shree, maybe not.'

'Janice! Get off de phone!'

''Bye, Janice.'

'Later on, Shree.'

Shree put down the receiver, shaking her head. She reached over and turned off the television and then lay down on the sofa. She figured she was lucky. Even though she wasn't with the millionaire she had dreamed of when she was much younger, Tyrone was a million things to her and being pregnant was one of the best things that had happened to her. She drifted off into a dream where she was back in Jamaica, sitting under a palm tree with a baby in her arms on a deserted beach.

The doorbell rang, waking Shree up. As she walked along the hall to open the door she wondered who it was who had rung the bell. She opened the door.

'Oh, hello, Nero. H-happy Christmas.' She gave Nero a curious smile, but the door knob stayed in her hand as she waited for him to state his purpose.

'Eh, Shree. How you keeping?'

'I'm all right, thank you.'

'Well, I was passing and I thought to come up and talk to you, you know. I'm not going to try anyt'ing, Shree. You know me an' you are safe, but I understan' if you cyan let me in. It's just that I don't know many people dis side of the Atlantic an' I was spending Christmas alone but if your man will go on arms-house then it's understood.' He dug his hands in his pockets and turned as if to go.

'Nero.' He turned to see the door open and Shree waving him inside with a smile. 'Come in, man, and have something to drink.'

Nero walked into the flat, sat down on a chair and looked around the room. On the way to the kitchen Shree kicked her pregnancy books underneath the sofa. She returned and handed Nero a Tennants. He nodded his thanks. She sat down opposite him.

'You look tired,' she said.

'I've been working hard,' he replied.

'Doing what?'

'Dealing mostly, you don't need me to tell you.'

'So how are you spending your Christmas?'

Nero shrugged. 'I went to a couple of silly dances that really never had nuthin' in dem and moretime I stayed in my yard.'

'You have any family down here?'

'A' what dem supposed to come over on, the banana boat? Them too poor, man. They're dirt poor. I just come over here to see if I can earn a few dollars to take home. Me know my brother's ol' baby-mum move here wid her son, my nephew. You've seen him, but dat's all.'

Shree had already smelt the expensive aftershave and

seen the car and the gold. 'Have you made enough dollars?'

Nero looked at her unblinking. 'Enough to take care of you.'

Shree broke up into giggles and punched him on the shoulder as if he'd made a good joke. She opened her small bottle of Babycham and sipped it slowly.

'So what have you been doing these past few weeks that I haven't even seen you outta Dalston posing wid your style crew?' Shree just smiled mysteriously. Nero looked her up and down. He grabbed her ankle and squeezed it.

'You puttin' on a bit of weight there, nuh? You don't think you should cut down on de akee an' saltfish?' Shree gave him a sour look. 'But you look cute still,' reassured Nero. 'None can test.'

Shree looked down at her plump ankles, then she launched into a colourful account of her escapades over the last month or two. Nero smiled from time to time. When Shree had finished talking, he stood up and walked around the sitting-room, picking up framed photographs and looking at the paintings on the wall. On the television was a photo of a really beautiful young girl, about the same age as Shree, with slanted eyes and a creamy brown complexion, leaning against a palm tree on a deserted white beach, hugging a bunch of tropical flowers to her chest. Nero looked from Shree to the photo. 'When did you get this done?'

Shree gave a quick smile. 'That's my mother. She was my age at the time the photo was taken.'

Nero picked it up and examined it closed. 'Dead-stamp,' he murmured.

'Yeah, it's true,' agreed Shree. 'Except that I have darker skin.'

'Ah, she must live a' J. A. because me never seen her in London.'

'No, my mum's dead.'

'A' true? Anyway, me sorry to hear dat.'

'She died when I was four.'

'Was she sick?'

'She was hit by a drunk driver.' Shree bit her lip. She blinked away the tears before they grew visible and went into the kitchen.

'So what are you doing tonight?' she asked as she came back with another Tennants.

'Oh, I don't know. Stay in my yard most likely. It's too damn col' to do anyt'ing else.'

'But it's Christmas! Your friends nuh invite you anywhere?'

'Yeah, yeah. My good brethren Skins did invite me roun' to his family party to celebrate, y'know.'

'You might as well go. How can you stay at home alone today?'

Nero shrugged. 'There are things worse than loneliness to bear in life. But you're a woman, you wouldn't understand.' He drained his Tennants with a gulp and stood up. 'Thanks for the drinks and the company, I'd better be going now, you mus' have places of your own to go to.'

'Yeah, I am supposed to be somewhere else, in fact I think I'll leave with you.' Shree went to get her coat and her keys. 'I hadn't noticed how late it was getting.'

When Shree had put on her boots and buttoned up her coat, she followed Nero to the door. On the landing he felt around in his jacket pocket and took out a small velvet case and gave it to her. She was acting cool and ladylike but she was burning to get the box open. She loved presents and she knew that Nero was no cheapskate. She pressed a tiny button and the case flew open. Inside on the soft silk was a little West Indian bangle with her name on the side in diamonds. Shree gasped. She knew it was very wrong but this was one present she couldn't bear to give back. It was beautiful and expensive.

'I didn't get you anything. I'm sorry!'

Nero put a finger on her lips. 'Where are you going?'

'Oh, I'm going to a friend's place. There's going to be a small get-together with a few friends.' She slammed her front door shut and locked it.

'I'll drive you there, young girls like you shouldn't be outta road when it's so dark and cold.'

'I could easily get a cab, but thanks.'

Tanasha staggered out of the off-licence carrying a box full of bottles of wine, cans of beer and packets of crisps and sweets. He'd been out for ages looking for a place that was still open. Now he slowly made his way back along the road, humming the new beats Elroy had brought round for him to listen to.

'So there are rich black people in London,' Nero chuckled as he drove along Tanasha's street with its large houses and tall, bushy trees.

Shree laughed too. 'Not every homeboy's like me

an' you, gangsta.' They touched fists as Nero stopped his car outside Tanasha's parents' house.

Tanasha, coming round the corner, was intrigued to see a large Mercedes outside his parents' house. He walked close to the kerb and tried to see inside as he passed.

Donna opened the door for Tanasha. 'Where have you been? We've been getting thirsty.'

'Shut up. It's Christmas Day and I had to walk miles to find an open shop. Has Shree arrived yet?'

'No. Tyrone telephoned her a few minutes ago and there was no answer so she must be on her way. Why are you so worried?'

'Well, I'm sure I've just seen Shree outside in a big Mercedes with someone who looks like a yardie.'

'Oh, really? I'll go and tell Tyrone.'

'Mind your own business. Here, take this into the kitchen, I'll find Tyrone,' Tanasha said as he handed Donna the box.

'God, this is heavy,' Donna said as she staggered off towards the kitchen.

Tanasha went to find Tyrone who was surrounded by girls to whom he was boasting about how he was going to be a father soon. Tanasha took Tyrone upstairs to his parents' bedroom, from where he could see the Mercedes, and left him there. It was up to him to sort out his woman.

Shree thanked Nero again for his present, and before getting out of the car, raised her face to kiss him, partly out of pity, partly because she was so happy with her present. However, Nero grabbed her arms and pulled her to him and plastered her with kisses. 'C'mon, Shree, I've never made love in a car before. Make we do it now.'

'Nero, leave me alone, who the hell do you think you're trying to feel up?'

Nero ignored her. 'I've waited so long,' he whispered. Shree backed up against the door but she could feel his hands dragging down her leggings.

She slapped him. He stared at her in confusion. She pushed her little clenched fist right up against his face. 'No man takes liberties with me,' she said with deliberate slowness. 'You lay one hand 'pon my body again and you gwaan feel my papa's kitchen knife. I swear to God he will tear out your eyes and cut out your heart.' Then she turned, pushed open the door and got out of the car. Taking the small velvet box from her pocket, she hurled it back into the car.

'I'm not a whore!' she shouted as she slammed the car door shut. Whipping round, she walked off without looking back.

Nero started the car and drove off slowly. His face had a blank expression. Shree had just blown him out in a big way, but no one would be able to tell and he wanted to keep it that way. Shree was no different. By the time she knocked on Tanasha's door, there wasn't a hair out of place, not a tear in sight. She had tucked her T-shirt in. Shree was going to go into the party like nothing had happened and she was going to fool everybody.

Although it was dark, Tyrone saw Shree tumble out of the Mercedes and then fling something back into the car. As the car drove off he watched her hastily fixing her clothes and her hair.

'Aaah, happy Christmas, girl!'

Shree blinked in the bright lights. Loud music assailed her ears as Chantelle and Donna hugged her. Shree laughed and hugged them back. They dragged her towards the sitting-room.

'How come you're so late? We were about to send Tyrone out for you.'

'Yeah, Paula's here and even Janice managed to come.'

'Oh, by the way, thanks for my present, I haven't opened it yet. We're all doing that later.'

'Yeah, thanks for mine too, yours are under the tree.'

'There's a tree?'

'Yes, and holly and decorations and mistletoe—'

'So you and Tyrone can get busy.'

'Speaking of which . . .' Shree turned to see Tyrone coming down the stairs. She wanted to run into his arms and burst into tears, but she smiled and gave him a little wave. Tyrone gave her a sort of sad look but then he smiled. As soon as Shree saw the sad look she knew he knew. She didn't know how he had found out or how much he knew, but she knew Tyrone.

'Eh, Shree, you feisty wretch, how come you don't phone me to find out how I'm doing or nothing?'

'Elroy, if you honestly believe that I have time or money to throw away, you need to come off the cloud.'

Elroy waved her away like she was speaking rubbish. The full crew was definitely in the place. Paula waved to her to come over to the corner where she was sitting. Fabian sat at her feet, chatting away to Janice who kept casting sidelong glances at Elroy. Alisha and Natelle were howling with laughter at some joke Tanasha and Aston had just told them. Nicola crossed the room, carrying drinks and crisps for her and Tricia.

'Happy Christmas, Nicola. Where have you been hiding out?'

'I've been around. You just haven't been in the right places.'

'Where's my present then, Shree?' Darren Marshall shouted from behind Tricia.

'What do you mean, where's your present? Where's mine, honey?' Shree rested her hand on her hip.

'Er, um, okay, okay, rude girl, I'll allow you, this year, just this year, mind.' Shree kissed her teeth jokingly.

Asher reached out and slapped Darren on the head. 'Hey, idiot-bwoy, rest your gums now before you make an even bigger fool of unno.' Then he nudged Michael and Jason and all of them laughed at Darren.

Shree sat down next to Paula. 'Oh, I'm so tired,' she complained.

'You look as though you've had a few drinks already,' said Paula.

'Well, give me another one. After I've had a few more, I'll perk up.' Paula passed a Babycham to Shree which she quickly drained. 'So how come you made it here in the end, Jan?' Shree asked, hauling Fabian on to her lap.

'I think it was my Auntie Nesta that did it. The woman is so boring, all she wants to talk about is her wonderful son who's going here and coming there. Anyway, my dad just stood up and said that he had to drop me somewhere.'

'That was good of him.'

'I don't think he could take it any more,' Janice sighed. 'But anyway, I managed to reach before you, you chief.'

'Yeah, Tyrone said you would turn up about six or seven o'clock but you didn't get here till about eight.' Donna said.

'Oh, a friend came round, that's all.'

'Anyone we know?'

'No, I don't think you'd know him.'

'Him!' Donna's voice was loud enough to attract passing male interest. Michael picked up Fabian and joined the crowd.

'What's this, what's this about a man?' he asked eagerly. 'Hey, the girls are talking about some man.'

'So tell us which man came to your house today then, Shree,' said Donna.

'Eh! Eh! Tyrone, I'm hearing the whirl of things about your girl tonight,' said Michael.

'No man came to my house.'

'Don't try it with me, Shree. You did say a man came to your house.'

'No man came to my house.'

'No, I heard you – ow! Janice, watch where you put your elbows, please. No, Shree, I know—'.

'Listen to me, you loud-mouthed fool. I'm not in the best of moods right now, so if I say that no man came to my house then you'd best agree with me, right?'

'I was only joking, Shree.' Donna got up. 'Damn, some people are miserable this Christmas.' Then she stomped out of the room.

'Yo, pass me that Canei over there.'

Tricia handed Shree the bottle. 'Are you sure you should?' she asked.

Shree poured herself a full glass, then drank it quickly. 'I'll worry about my family, you worry about yours.' She wiped her mouth with the back of her hand, then refilled her glass.

'Hey, I've got a wicked idea,' Elroy said. All the company turned to him.

'Well, roll wid it, rude bwoy,' urged Aston.

'Let's switch off all the lights in the house and play hide-and-seek.'

'Better to find yourself another house, dred. This one ain't available,' Tanasha said, but he was accosted by all the girls.

'Oh, go on, T,' begged Tricia.

'Yeah, it will be a laugh.'

'Yeah, yeah, all right. But if I find anyone in my parents' room it's going to be a cold, cold Christmas.'

'Understood.' Elroy turned down the hi-fi. 'So come on, girls, how are we going to do it?'

'Let all the girls write down their names and all the boys write down their names and put them in two separate boxes, mix them up and pair them off,' Chantelle suggested straight off.

Paula turned to Janice. 'Now just watch the fool I get paired off with,' she whispered.

Janice nodded. 'Yeah, that's a def idea. There's the paper over there. Everyone get to work.'

Bits of paper and a pen were passed round. Although some people had looked upon this game with some scepticism, all were now getting excited. Paula gave Michael sidelong glances which he pretended not to see.

He knew she was just waiting for an opportunity to ask him why he hadn't bothered to telephone and say happy Christmas to his son. Enough of the females there smiled suggestively in Elroy's direction. He was a free man now and he was extremely kriss.

Alisha and Natelle stood shivering on the doorstep, waiting until the two minutes had passed.

'Trust us to get landed with the job of looking for people,' Natelle complained.

'Yeah, I'm sure that pairing business was rigged.'

'It's true. What a coincidence that Janice gets put with Elroy.'

'That is so unfair. They don't even talk to each other.'

'It's just a waste of a good opportunity.'

'Innit. The man's so fit and I had so much to tell him.'

'Words are cheap, I had so much to show him.'

'Oops, Natelle, they've had about three minutes.'

'Come on, then.' They slowly opened the door and went back into the now pitch-black and silent house.

'Coming!' they yelled.

'You have a wicked body, Donna,' said Michael as he moved his fingers along her leg and up her thigh. He moved closer until his face was right next to hers.

Donna kissed her teeth. 'Michael, you're such a womanizer.'

'When I see a good thing, I take it.'

'What about Paula?'

'That's my old beef. What are you busying yourself with her for? It's me an' you.'

'How can you be so offhand? She's your baby-mother.'

'Nah, nah, don't get me wrong.' Michael was quick to repair the mood. 'My son is everything to me. I love him more than anything in the whole world. It's just that Paula, she's not like how she is when we're in public. She doesn't want me to be near him. All the money I give her, she just spends it on herself, she buys clothes and make-up and then she comes and asks for more. Yeah, it's true. If it wasn't for Paula's lies and her selfishness, I'd still be with her today, but she drove me away.' When Michael had finished his fairytale, he glanced at Donna and she smiled back suggestively. Michael reached over and kissed her. 'Such pretty breasts,' he murmured softly, 'and so little time.'

Elroy and Janice were the last ones to run for cover when the game began.

'Mind that box,' he whispered. By now the house was nearly silent. All the good hiding places seemed to be taken.

'What about the kitchen?' Janice suggested, but muffled giggles proved that the kitchen was already occupied. They went into the back room. There didn't seem to be anyone in there, but then there didn't seem to be anywhere to hide.

As Alisha and Natelle tumbled back into the house, Elroy dived behind the large chintz sofa, pulling Janice down on top of him. So close to his chest, she could hear his heart beat as clearly as her own. She could smell his aftershave. It brought back good memories. She couldn't help herself. She kissed him. Elroy's arms tightened around her and –

'Oh no you don't!!' They looked up to see Alisha, Natelle, Michael and Donna laughing down at them. Janice felt blood rush into her cheeks. She rolled off Elroy and got up quicktime. She didn't dare look at Elroy, which was a pity because he wore an expression of bewilderment and happiness.

'Okay, Natelle, that's four down. Where to now?'

'Well, we could always go to the bedrooms, eh, Elroy,' Michael said and everyone groaned.

'Michael, you're so disgusting,' said Natelle, laughing.

'I think there must be a lot of people upstairs,' said Elroy, so off they went.

'Ow!!' Shree slammed up against a wall. She heard Tanasha laughing to himself. Normally she would have cursed him off but this evening Shree was not herself. She had had too much to drink and she could hardly walk and in the dark she couldn't see anything, everything was a blur. Tanasha eyed her contemptuously. It had given him a kind of satisfaction to let Shree walk into that wall. She was going to pay for cheating on one of his brethren.

'Yeah, we can hide in here, slusher.' He pushed Shree behind the Christmas tree in the sitting-room they had all just been in a few minutes ago.

'Sh-Shasha, don't call me dem names.' Shree burped

noisily and then giggled. Tanasha put his arm round her. 'G-go 'way, you idiot-bwoy.'

'Nah, nah, come on, yard gal. Give me some of what you was giving that other idiot-bwoy in the car outside.'

Shree freed herself and peered at him. 'I thought you was my friend?' she said before sinking to the floor.

Tanasha looked down at her. His tone was hard. 'I'm no friend of yours.' Shree was too drunk to reply. 'Look at you, you nasty—'

'There's no point hiding behind that tree, Tanasha, we can see you two clearly,' said Janice. Tanasha smiled and came out to join the hunt, leaving Shree sitting on the floor.

Tricia could tell that Tyrone was not in a good mood. They were the ones hiding in the bathroom shower cabinet.

'I'm not going to ask you what the problem is, Tyrone, but I know how much Shree loves you and I think you should trust her. After all, she is carrying your child so it's in her best interests to stay with you, isn't it?'

'Yeah, it's true. You know you're all right – for a married woman.' They both laughed. 'Darren's lucky to have you.'

'I think we've been found.' The clatter of footsteps towards the bathroom grew louder and then everyone burst in. Tricia was dragged away by Darren. Tyrone looked around for Shree.

'Where's Shree, Janice?'

'Downstairs behind the Christmas tree. She's really drunk, you should take her home.'

'Hey! I thought I heard something in there. Get the

hell out of my room!!' Everyone turned to see Tanasha turning on lights and waving a fist in the air.

'So that's where they were,' exclaimed Alisha and Natelle simultaneously, as out from under Tanasha's duvet crawled Aston and Nicola.

'Just look what you've done to my room!'

'Jus' cool, star.' Aston made haste to pacify Tanasha.

'That's a wicked place to hide,' remarked Alisha. 'I walked past that room without seeing you.'

'It was easy. We just threw the duvet on to the floor with a heap of Tanasha's clothes and hid underneath.'

'That's liberties, though. I'd be so vexed if anyone did that to me,' said Paula.

'It's just a bit of fun. What's wrong with that?'

By now everyone was back downstairs in the sitting-room, talking about the wicked New Year's rave that Elroy was going to hold.

'Well, I think some of us have had more than enough Christmas. Does anyone need a lift?' Everyone was having too much fun to go so no one took up Tyrone's offer. 'Yeah, well, happy Christmas and all.' Tyrone walked out of the house with Shree propped up against his large frame.

By the time they reached their estate, Shree was totally out of it and Tyrone had to carry her upstairs. It had really upset him to see her drink like that, but as she lay on the bed, senseless, he decided that it would do no good to start an argument, so he pulled off her socks and boots, unclasped her jewellery and put her to bed.

chapter
fourteen

Shree unenthusiastically laid out her clothes for Elroy's New Year's party. Tyrone was just about talking to her. He hadn't asked, but she had told him everything about Nero anyway. He'd listened with tight lips and then he'd got up without a word and gone about his business. That was the worst thing. Shree wouldn't have minded if he'd started shouting or cussing, but he didn't tell her how he felt. Nothing. Shree could feel the suspicion and accusation in his eyes whenever he passed her. An unspoken sadness which cut her to the bone.

She couldn't fit into any of her dresses. She had some maternity dresses but they weren't appropriate. She put on an orange legging-suit and then went over to her dressing-table to do her hair. She decided to wear it in a high pony-tail. When her hair was done and she had put on some earrings, she put on her coat and her shoes and left the flat. She definitely wasn't in a New Year's mood. In fact she had a really bad feeling about the party tonight, she didn't know why, but she did.

'Oh, at last. You're damn lucky to find us still here. We were just about to call a cab.'

'Good for you if you're looking to pay their sky-high prices.'

Janice and Paula looked at each other. 'I hope you're not going to be in this mood all night,' Paula said crossly.

'Evening, Rose,' Shree said as Janice's mother came downstairs.

'Hello, Shree dear. He's sleeping now, Paula.'

'Thanks so m—'

'Don't say another word. You know I love Fabian like he was my own grandson.'

'So how do we look, Shree?' Janice was dressed in a long red velvet dress. Shree turned to Paula who was wearing a black lace jacket with a short skirt to match and a beaded bra-top underneath. She glared at them sourly.

'Don't you think you're a touch overdressed? It's only *Elroy's* dance.'

'This is the dance of the year, everybody will be there.'

'Well, you two will definitely be the odd ones out, trust me.'

'Well, what are you wearing then?'

'This.'

They looked at Shree's orange baggy legging-suit and then at each other.

'Shree, you look fine, but aren't you going to dress up even a little?' asked Janice. Shree just gave her a dirty look.

'Just because you're pregnant, y'know, doesn't mean you have to dress like you're going jogging.'

Janice elbowed Paula sharply.

'Yes, well, nothing else fits!' snapped Shree.

284

'Don't be stupid, you haven't put on any weight.'

'Isn't it obvious?'

'Shree, you can't see anything!'

'Anyway, I'm not going anywhere, so you'd better call that cab.' Shree plumped down on the stairs. Janice turned and ran past her upstairs.

Paula sat down next to Shree. 'Now, how about you just tell me what the real problem is?'

'I don't know. I just don't feel like going. I've got a really bad feeling about tonight, my hair looks terrible and I can't fit into any of my clothes any more.'

'Shree. Just because you're stomach's a bit bigger, it doesn't mean nothing will look good on you. Anyway, when I was pregnant, didn't you say if you've got it flaunt it?'

Shree cut her eyes at Paula and looked away.

'Come up here,' called Janice, standing at the top of the stairs. 'I didn't take all my clothes over to Aunt Sarah's flat and I'm sure I've got something you could borrow, come on.'

They went upstairs to Janice's bedroom. Shree and Paula sat on the bed while Janice looked through her wardrobe.

'What about these black trousers and the jacket?'

'Janice, trousers are definitely out where my waistline is concerned, and anyway your legs are much longer than mine.'

'Well, how about this blue dress with the crinoline bottom?'

'Don't be stupid, Janice, you wore that when we went to Roseberry's, everyone will remember it.'

'Shree, I'm trying to help you.'

'Then show me something sensible!'

'Well, this is the only other thing I have,' said Janice, showing Shree a yellow silk dress and jacket to match. Shree looked at it with hatred.

'I suppose it will have to do then,' Shree said, taking the dress from Janice. She changed into the dress and then looked at herself in the mirror. 'Well, what do you think?' she asked.

'It looks kriss, one hundred per cent,' Paula said.

'You don't think my stomach sticks out too much?'

'You can hardly see it, Shree,' assured Janice.

'But my hair still looks a mess.'

'So what are we here for?' said Janice, smiling. Shree sat down at Janice's dressing-table while Janice plugged in her curling tongs. She undid Shree's pony-tail so that the hair fell to her shoulders.

'Why did you hide your lovely hair in that pony-tail?' asked Paula.

'Do you think that was a bad idea?'

''Course. A few curls at the ends and your hair is going to look great,' Janice said, as she began to roll a strand of hair around the barrel of the curling tong. When she had finished curling Shree's hair, Janice sprayed her head with sheen spray and hair spray.

'Oh, Shree, you look really pretty,' said Janice.

'Was this the girl who told me she wasn't going anywhere because she didn't look nice?' said Paula. Shree smiled shyly and put her shoes and coat on.

''Bye, Mum.'

''Bye, dear. Have a nice time.'

Janice, Paula and Shree hurried down the garden

path towards Shree's car. 'It's really cold tonight,' moaned Janice.

''S true. Look, those trees and bushes are white with frost. Maybe it will snow,' said Paula.

'It would be really pretty,' Shree added as she unlocked the driver's door.

They all got in and Shree started the car.

'I've never seen the streets this empty before,' Janice said, looking around.

'Well, check the degrees, star. It's too cold for walking,' said Paula.

'This year's gone so fast,' said Janice. 'Shree's birthday's coming round again.'

'Don't remind me. I feel 'nuff old,' said Shree.

'Imagine. Nineteen is a safe age to be but once you hit that two zero, you're in big women's league,' said Janice.

'I think we should do something special. When was the last time us three held a small party?'

'You two are mad,' exclaimed Shree. 'If you think there are going to be any celebrations while I look like this, you better just rethink.'

'Calm yourself. You look fine now and you're not going to look like an elephant by February. You'll only be seven months,' Paula said reassuringly.

'Talking of parties, how come Elroy can use his parents' house tonight?' Janice asked.

'Tyrone told me that his parents are in Nottingham visiting cousins. They said Elroy could have a little party because they're planning to recarpet and repaint the downstairs rooms anyway.'

'Yeah, well, that don't look like no little party to me,' Paula pointed out as they drove down Elroy's street.

'Look at how many people have turned up,' exclaimed Shree. 'Where am I going to park?'

'Try and get really close to the house. It's too cold for any big-time walking,' said Paula.

'I didn't know Elroy knew so many people,' said Janice.

Shree parked the car quite close to Elroy's house and got out as a group of yardie-looking girls passed. 'Eh, Shree. So you cyan say hello to your longtime friend?'

Shree was cuffed roughly on the shoulder by a grinning yardie girl. She smiled back and they exchanged a few words before the girl chased after her companions.

'Who was that?' asked Janice.

'Oh, that's Jacqui. Her dad and my dad are good friends. I used to see a lot of her when I was little.'

'*Interesting, interesting*, but could we get a move on before my toes freeze off?'

'Well, that's what you get for coming outside with a flimsy lace jacket on,' Shree said unsympathetically.

Elroy's party was drawing a lot of attention. Neighbours peered from behind curtains or blatantly hung out of windows, watching. Even though it was still quite early, some people had already had enough and were cooling out on the front porch, standing around or sitting on the front steps and front wall. Among them were Alisha and Natelle whom several men were trying to persuade to come to a "next" dance just down the road. Shree, Paula and Janice gave them knowing smiles as they passed by.

'Whirl 'a gals!!' Elroy and Asher touched fists as the

three stepped up to the house. Attracted by the sound of fresh voices, a number of males surged into the hallway. The girls smiled their sexiest smiles right on cue. As they went up the stairs the other girls, making space for them, eyed them viciously. Clothes, shoes, hair, everything had to undergo examination.

'Yo, baby. Just let me take that and put it somewhere safe so me and you could, um—'

'Just leave it where you see it, rude boy. Too damn fast!' Paula pulled her jacket back from the hands of one eager young man. Paula had few words for the kind she knew would go up to anything in a skirt, so she sent them all packing and waited for Elroy to come and take care of their coats. As soon as he did so, Shree and Paula hurried downstairs and Janice was left in the bedroom with Elroy.

'You look really wicked in that dress.'

'You don't look so bad yourself, baby.'

Elroy opened the door for Janice. Just as he switched off the bedroom light he whispered, 'I know who left me that Joop underneath the Christmas tree at Tanasha's place.'

Janice looked him straight in the eye and said nothing.

'Well, thanks.'

Elroy had set up his deejaying equipment at one end of the large ground-floor sitting-room. The turntables were placed on a table with the speakers stacked up on either side, and the records in boxes on another table running parallel to the first, forming a barricade between the deejay and the rest of the party.

'How's it going?' Shree had to repeat what she said

five times before Tyrone, who was deejaying, realized that someone was speaking to him.

'So you made it then.'

Shree shifted impatiently. 'I thought Elroy was deejaying tonight?' she said.

'We're sharing it. He's on a break now.'

'What are you looking for?' she shouted.

'"Rhythms of Romance". Some girl requested it and I had it just a minute ago but now I can't find it anywhere.' Tyrone turned sideways, bending over the table with the boxes of records.

'Is this it, on the speaker?' Shree waved it in her hand. Tyrone nodded gratefully and reached for it but Shree pulled it back, a serious look on her face.

'Give it to me, Shree, stop messing around.'

'Only if you promise to talk to me, Tyrone.' Tyrone gave her a dirty look and turned his back on her. 'Tyrone, why are you doing this? You know there was nothing between Nero and me.'

Tyrone put the headphones on. There was nothing Shree could do except put the record down and walk away to find a drink. Fighting her way through the crowd, Shree met up with Chantelle and Donna who offered her some spliff. She refused the joint but stopped to chat with them.

'Did your mother let you leave the house like that, Chantelle?' she asked.

'She's used to it by now,' Chantelle said, shrugging.

'There are a lot of girls looking at you. I think they're worried about the male attention you're stealing.'

'Actually, there's one man I really like, over there.'

'Tell me another time, Chantelle. I'm trying to find Janice and Paula,' Shree said as she moved on.

'Where did you get to?' Paula and Janice were in a corner when Shree finally found them.

'I was talking to Tyrone and then Donna and Chantelle.'

'Meantime, we were waiting to put our dancing routine into effect,' said Janice.

'Sorry, I forgot, can't we do it now?'

Paula and Janice gave her a withering look. 'Not to hardcore hip hop.'

'I – I guess not,' Shree conceded. They were being jostled and jumped on by the men in the room who were throwing themselves around to the wild rhythm.

'Let's get another drink and then go outside for a few minutes,' Paula said.

On their way out they saw Elroy at the door.

'Wicked party, Elroy,' said Shree, kissing him on the cheek.

'For some,' said Elroy.

'What's up?'

'Darren was supposed to have taken over the door ages ago. Man, I need a break.'

'Go get yourself a drink and then join us outside,' said Shree smiling.

'Safe. Let me find Darren first.' Elroy disappeared into the room where everyone was dancing.

The cold air hit the girls as they went out of the front door.

'It feels nice and fresh out here.'

'Yeah, it's so hot and sticky inside.' They sat down

on the front wall. 'But we mustn't stay outside too long or we'll miss the beginning of New Year.'

'It's way too cold to stay out here long. Anyway, it's a wicked party,' Paula said, kicking off her shoes so her feet could get some air.

'Elroy's planned it really well,' said Shree.

'At least there's no trouble,' said Janice. 'I hate that.'

'Well, don't speak too soon.'

'Oh, come on, Shree, Janice is right. What can possibly go wrong? Everyone knows everyone and the boys are manning the door.'

'All right, all right.'

'Drinking again, Shree, are you sure you should?' Janice asked.

'I can take care of myself,' said Shree, kissing her teeth in annoyance before taking another sip of her Canei. 'I wish everyone would get off my case. It's not as if I'm drinking hard spirits.'

'Did you see what Chantelle and Donna were wearing?' Janice whispered.

'It's hard not to. They do kind of stand out from the crowd.'

'They look ridiculous, they must think they're on a beach.'

Shree laughed. 'Oh, come off it, Paula. They don't look that bad, it's just hotpants and a beaded bra-top.'

'It just looks so slack. I don't know why you insist on knocking heads with them, Shree. Chantelle isn't so bad but Donna's an airhead and I don't like the way she's hanging around Michael.'

'Eh, nice an' decent girls.'

A small man with an unkempt appearance who had

obviously had too much to drink stood grinning at them. He made a very wide gesture with his bottle of Sisco. 'Only ten seconds ago I saw you and I just had to come and chat to you.' He leaned over Shree. All three girls cringed as his foul breath hit them. Shree covered her nose with her hand.

'Best-looking girl I've seen at the party tonight, face like sunshine and shape like – like the US dollar.' Janice and Paula dashed back into the hallway where they collapsed in giggles. Shree glared after them.

'I'm Clem. What's your name, cutsie?'

'E-er, Denise.'

'Well, Denise, there's a petrol station at the end of the road and I wondered if—'

'Yeah, yeah, my friends are calling me. See ya.' Shree got up and started walking away.

'I'll talk to you later, catch a dance maybe.' Clem then leaned towards some other girls sitting on the wall but they also disappeared. A few minutes later, Clem heard the cheers and the laughter as friends hugged strangers and lovers kissed and toasts were made to the New Year. Then a black Mercedes pulled up in front of the house. Clem looked at it with curiosity.

'Is this some yout' call Elroy's party?' someone from the car shouted. Clem nodded.

'You know if a girl call Shree is in there?' asked the same voice.

Clem shook his head and shrugged his shoulders. 'No, I don't know her.'

A large, dark-skinned man with dreadlocks and a gold chain got out of the car. 'Go where you want to go but meet me back here 'bout ten minutes. Understood,

Skins?' The large man ran up the steps and disappeared into the house, as the Mercedes drove off.

The party tempo was slowing down. Exhausted by the pumping hip-hop tunes and the fast ragga tracks, couples were starting to move in slower circles. The tunes being played by the deejay were creating a more romantic atmosphere as late night drifted into early morning.

Janice was making her way to the kitchen to get more drinks when she stopped by the turntables.

'Yo, Tyrone, seen Elroy? He was supposed to have been minding the door.'

'There's a lot of things that Elroy was supposed to take care of. I've been deejaying non-stop.'

'He went off to look for Darren.'

'Darren's another one who's been hiding from me.'

'Well, if I see either of them, I'll tell them to come and help out.'

'Thanks,' Tyrone said wearily.

Janice moved off. She was slowly working her way through the crown when suddenly two arms grabbed her waist and spun her around. Her expression changed from one of confusion to one of joy. For, as her head had touched his chest, Elroy had whispered softly. 'I love you, Janice.'

'They're so right for each other,' sighed Shree.

Paula nodded. 'They're never going to break up now, you can just see it.'

At the turntables, Tyrone was also looking wistfully at Janice and Elroy. For a brief second his eyes met with Shree's before she turned away, this time with a sad sigh. She looked around. Everywhere, someone was with their man. Jacqui and her friends were slow-dancing with men. Darren was dancing with Tricia. Alisha and Natelle were dancing with Asher and Aston. Donna and Chantelle were dancing with their men. Paula had been whisked away by a handsome young man. Shree twisted her rings uncomfortably. She looked towards the decks again. Tyrone had disappeared. Stumbling backwards, she fell into someone's arms that closed around her and held her tight. Shree smiled. It was Tyrone. She knew he couldn't see her alone on the dance-floor and not come and dance with her. She closed her eyes and leaned back until she was resting on his chest. They whined together slowly.

'Let go of my woman now!'

Shree was roughly pulled away from her dancing partner by Tyrone. She fell to the floor. It was only when she scrambled to her feet that she saw she had been dancing with Nero. He reached out and grabbed Shree's left arm, pulling her back next to him. Holding on to Shree, Nero faced Tyrone. A ring of people quickly formed around the three.

'What the fuck are you doing? What are *you* doing?' Tyrone put the question first to Nero and then to Shree.

'Tyrone. I – it was just a dance. I m-made a mistake. I – I thought it was you.' Tyrone seized Shree's right arm, dragging her back towards him. Nero let her go.

'This is going to be sorted out now. I saw what happened in the car the other day. I know—'

'All right, rude bwoy. I'm not going to trouble your t'ing again.' Nero spoke mockingly and made as if to move off, but Tyrone barred his way.

'Let it go, Tyrone. It's finished.' Shree tried to put herself between them but Tyrone pushed her firmly out of the way.

'Like hell it's finished. Shree, just back out of it, you don't understand shit. True say, I don't even know what's down with you two, but you're my woman and you're having *my* baby. You heard right, Nero. Shree's having my baby or didn't you know?'

Nero looked shocked. Dealing with someone's woman was one thing. Dealing with someone's baby-mother was a whole new ball-game. Nero glared at Shree. The way Nero saw it, he was being made a fool of. First incredulous, then angry, he slammed Tyrone on the chest. 'For the last time, move out of the way, rude bwoy!'

Suddenly Tyrone and Nero were rolling over on the floor and hitting each other. Tyrone scrambled up and kicked Nero in the stomach again and again, but then Nero caught his foot and dragged Tyrone down and slammed his head against the floor.

Outside, as Clem finished his bottle of Sisco, the same black Mercedes pulled up in front of him. 'Ah where him deh?' the driver asked, cigarette dangling from the side of his mouth.

'Oh, yeah, your pal went inside. Sounds like there's a fight.' The driver listened. The music had long since stopped and screaming and shouting had taken its place. The cigarette flew out of the driver's mouth as he jumped out of the car, motioning to his brethren to follow him into the house quicktime. Clem watched them pile out of the car, open-mouthed. He had seen enough gangs in his time but this was a posse to be reckoned with. He chuckled to himself, then stumbled off into the frosty night before the police arrived.

As Skins and his crew burst into Elroy's house, the place erupted into chaos. Elroy, Tanasha, Aston, Asher, Darren and Michael immediately took Tyrone's back. They had been ready to carry Nero out but now it looked like Nero had brought company and there was no way they were going to let them come rioting in like they were running t'ings. Others joined them as they stepped forward as a body to meet the enemy. Everyone was getting involved. As Skins held Michael up against a wall, ready to stab him, Paula picked up the nearest wine bottle and smashed it against Skins' head. Tricia yelled to Darren to watch out as a man approached him from behind. Janice, along with Alisha and Natelle, was trapped at the wrong end of the room. Something flew from nowhere and hit the wall just above Janice's head. The lights went out. In the dark it was hard to see who was who but the violence continued. A window was smashed and furniture was broken. Then, over the din, the wail of sirens could be heard.

As the police burst into the house Michael cursed. He had a packet of weed on him. He looked around wildly, then dropped it on the floor, and quickly moved to the other side of the room.

Skins, as soon as he saw a policeman, lept through a window, only to drop down into the arms of a waiting constable. Two policemen grabbed Nero, threw him to the floor and handcuffed him before dragging him out of the room. Tyrone hadn't needed to be dragged off, kicking and screaming. He had just walked off with the police in a daze, he could hardly stand up straight.

In the kitchen Elroy was being handcuffed. The police had found Michael's weed and were threatening Elroy with a possession charge. Paula was screaming at a policewoman. 'You're not taking me anywhere. Take your hands off me or I swear to God I will kill you.'

'I have to warn you that you will be charged with assault on a police officer along with being drunk and disorderly,' said the policewoman, trying to grab her wrists.

'I've got to get home to see my kid. There's the baby's father, he'll look after me,' Paula shouted, pointing towards Michael.

The policewoman looked at Michael. 'Excuse me, do you know this woman? Did you see what happened here?'

Michael just looked blankly back at Paula and then the policewoman and shook his head.

'Okay, now, that's enough. You're going down to the police station and you'll only make things worse for yourself if you resist.' The policewoman dragged Paula out into the street.

Having just put in a new lightbulb, Janice was able to see the extent of the damage. She looked around as if she couldn't quite believe it. Then she turned to Darren, Tricia, Alisha and Natelle.

'We'd better start tidying this lot up,' she said. Broken chairs and glass covered the floor. 'Where are all our friends when we need them?'

'In the police station.' Darren's joke sank like a

stone. 'Did Shree go down to the station with Paula?' he asked as he left the room to find a broom.

'Oh, no. I didn't see those two leave together, I would have noticed.'

'Oh, well, she must have gone with Tyrone.' Janice began picking rubbish off the floor.

'No, she didn't. Tanasha went with Tyrone,' Darren said from the doorway. 'I remember it clearly.'

'The car's still outside so she didn't go home . . .'

'Shree can take care of herself, man. She probably went to Chantelle's place, innit?'

Tricia nodded. She crossed the room to look at the decks. The speakers had been knocked over and one of the turntables was on the floor. The table with the records on had been overturned and there were records everywhere, most were damaged.

Then she saw Shree, half-covered by a speaker.

When they heard Tricia yell, Darren, Alisha, Natelle and Janice came running.

'Oh, God, is she dead?'

'She's not breathing,' whispered Darren.

Tricia knelt down next to Shree and put her head on her chest. 'She is breathing, but you'd better call an ambulance fast, Darren.'

Shree was so still, so silent. Janice knelt down and smoothed her hair away from her face. Her skin was bruised but it was hard to tell if anything was seriously wrong. Darren came running back into the room. 'The ambulance is on its way.'

When the ambulance arrived the paramedics took charge. 'So what happened here?' one of them asked as Shree was strapped into a stretcher.

'There was a fight and I think she must have come behind the table to protect herself but a speaker fell on her,' said Janice.

'Is she going to be all right?' asked Darren.

'It's too soon to tell,' was all the paramedic could say. 'Does anyone want to come with her to the hospital? It's North Middlesex.'

'Yes, I'm her friend, I'll come,' said Janice.

'Okay, let's go.'

As the ambulance disappeared, sirens whirring, lights flashing, Tricia started to cry. 'All the time, no one wondered where she was, most people just went home,' she said quietly. Nobody said a word. Everyone was thinking the same thing. Tyrone was going to have to be told that his girl and his baby might not see in New Year's Day.

chapter
fifteen

At the police station Tyrone explained what had happened. He was lucky, the two policemen interviewing him were sympathetic. He was given the regulatory warning about causing a public disturbance but as he had a clean record and hadn't broken any laws, he was then allowed to go. As Tyrone left the interview room, one of the policemen handed him a slip of paper.

Tyrone Dennis,

Please come urgently to North Middlesex Hospital.
Shree is in casualty.

Janice.

As it had been his house and his party Elroy was having a harder time. He was sitting in another interview room opposite two tired and bored policemen. The middle-aged overweight man in charge of the interview sipped black coffee from a plastic cup while his younger assistant sucked nervously on a cigaretté.

'Now, let's go over your statement again,' said the

older policeman. 'You say you didn't know there was any cannabis at the party.'

'That's right.'

'How can you expect us to believe that, when you had several known drug dealers at your party?'

'I told you they—'

'They gatecrashed. Now, that's not very likely is it, with all of you strong lads in the house?'

'That's why we were fighting.'

'That's your story is it?'

'Listen. You can't touch me,' said Elroy. 'You don't have anything to link me to that weed. All you have is your imagination.' The policemen looked at each other and said nothing.

'Interview terminated at ten past six on January first,' said the young policeman. He turned off the tape-recorder and then leaned across the table and snarled, 'We may not have anything yet, but as soon as we do, we'll be on your case like flies on shit.'

The older policeman put his hand on the other man's shoulder. 'That's enough, Dave. Actually, Mr Richardson, I believe your story. Obviously there was a fight and those yardie thugs don't look like your type somehow.' He paused and sipped his coffee. 'I shouldn't tell you this, but we have been looking for the man who calls himself Skins for some time. As a result of your party we not only have him under lock and key but we also have most of his gang, a very unpleasant group, I can tell you. As an added bonus we have also detained a dealer known as Nero. It turns out that this Nero has long overstayed his visa and his welcome and it is my guess that he will shortly be back in Jamaica. So, Mr Richardson, I'd like to thank you for indirectly helping us start the New Year in such a successful way. I am pleased to be able to tell you that no charges relating to this incident will be made against you and that you are now free to go.'

At that moment Paula was also being released. As she signed out her hand shook. She had been really scared. In a cell with two drunk old women and three hard-faced prostitutes, she kept recalling Michael's blank expression when she had asked him to help her. The last four years of Paula's life had gone up in a puff of smoke.

As she approached the door, leading through to the reception area she heard a familiar voice. 'Michael Vichy. Yes, V-I-C-H-Y. You're holding Paula Thomas here, I'm a – a – friend here on her behalf. I need to know if you're going to charge her.'

Paula pushed the door open and walked towards Michael. She was desperately trying to fight the rage that was building inside her. Michael took several steps backwards. She lunged for him, only to find that Elroy, coming out after her, had clamped her arms from behind. She strained to get at Michael but Elroy was stronger.

'I'm gonna kill you, Michael. I'm gonna find you and cut you down like the dog that you are,' she hissed through clenched teeth as Elroy led her back towards their friends.

They were all waiting there. Darren, Tricia, Tanasha, Aston, Alisha and Natelle. They looked strange, still in their flashy party clothes, a splash of colour in the dull, grey world of the police station. Tricia's head rested on

Darren's shoulder. Aston looked around the busy police station nervously. Tanasha's folded hands rested on his knees and he stared at a spot on the floor.

'Is it sorted?' asked Aston.

'Well, they're not charging me with anything,' Paula said, looking at Tricia's tear-stained face. 'What's up?'

'You'd better come and sit down, Paula.'

The hospital waiting-room was quiet. Tyrone sat there, head buried in his hands.

'Has Miss Nelson's father arrived yet?'

Tyrone stared at the man in the doorway. He gulped before speaking. 'I – I can't reach her father, I've tried several times but there's no one in.'

The man looked at his notepad. 'You are Tyrone Dennis?'

'Y-y-yes.'

'I'm Mr Phillips, the duty gynaecologist. Will you please come with me, Mr Dennis?'

Tyrone stood up and followed the man into a small, cluttered office.

'Please sit down.'

'How is she, doctor?' Tyrone blurted.

'I know this must be hard for you, Mr Dennis, but I would like you to sign consent forms on behalf of Miss Nelson who is still comatose despite our efforts to wake her. Unfortunately she has started to bleed and the situation is deteriorating quickly. It looks as though she has gone into very premature labour. I'm going to be frank with you. We need to operate now otherwise complications may develop and we could lose the baby.'

304

'Lose the baby?'

'I need to perform a caesarian section to remove the baby and to stop the bleeding. It's the only chance for either of them.'

'I'll sign, but I want to be there.'

'Very well. However, you will have to leave the theatre at the slightest complication.'

'Of course,' said Tyrone.

The doctor handed him a clipboard with a form and a pen. 'Sign at the bottom.' Tyrone signed his name. 'Okay, quickly now, follow me.' Before he entered the operating theatre, a nurse gave Tyrone a surgical gown and a mask which he put on.

The theatre was very quiet. Shree lay on the operating table, surrounded by monitors. A thick tube disappeared into her mouth. The gynaecologist began the operation. Tyrone found himself pushed back against a wall. Everyone seemed to be doing something. A nurse wheeled in an incubator for the baby. When Tyrone saw it, he felt his heart leap with excitement. This was the moment he and Shree had been waiting for. He was going to be a daddy.

Then he saw it. A tiny baby, smaller than anything he had ever seen. His emotions bubbled up inside him. He stepped forward but was restrained by a nurse. Then he couldn't see the baby for all the nurses were crowding around it. When he reached them, the nurses melted away. He looked down at the tiny, tiny body. 'Do something,' he whispered. The doctor shook his head sadly. Tyrone bent over and touched one of the baby's little feet. Tiny, but everything about it was perfect. It was a little girl.

'I'm sorry. There was nothing we could do. Twenty-six weeks is very premature, Mr Dennis, and the baby was already suffering from a lack of oxygen due to her mother's accident. Please, Mr Dennis.'

Tyrone stared at the doctor, dazed. He hadn't been a father for five minutes. He wanted to look at his baby some more, to hold her, even to pretend she was breathing. They couldn't expect him to just walk away.

'Cardiac blood-pressure fifty over zero and dropping.'

'She's still bleeding, doctor.'

'Get him out of here!' the doctor said, gesturing at Tyrone. A nurse led him out of the room. He tried to look through the doors as people hurried in and out but he couldn't see a thing. In the end Tyrone took off his mask and gown, leaving them on a trolley in the corridor, and wandered back to where his friends were waiting. As he neared the door, his footsteps slowed. How was he going to tell them that his baby was dead when he didn't want to believe it himself? Tyrone kept walking, straight past the door. When he reached the corner, he stopped and looked back down the hallway. He couldn't do that to his long-time friends, Janice and Paula would be in there, Shree's best spars. It was hurting everyone. Not just him. He had to be strong and tell them.

His hands sunk deep into the pockets of his baggy trousers, Tyrone told them what was down. There was a long silence. Paula bit her lip as her tears spilled out. Shree was a sister and she'd just lost her baby and she still had to fight for her life. Janice crossed over. She held out her arms and they hugged each other. Elroy chewed his nails. He didn't know what to say but his heart went out to a long-time brethren. Tanasha sighed sadly. He looked over at Janice trying to comfort Tyrone.

Several hours later Tyrone was the only one who was still there, curled up in one of the waiting-room chairs, half-sleeping. He had refused to leave the hospital until Shree woke up. One arm hooked over the back of the chair, one leg trailing on the floor, he drifted off into the happy times they had had together.

A month or two ago, he and Shree had gone over names. 'What about Sanchez?' she had said, poking him in the back.

'No, I prefer Tyrone.'

'Well, you would, stupid.'

'It might be a girl.'

'I'd like it to be a girl.'

'Well, what shall we call it then?'

Shree had been really quiet for a long time and Tyrone thought she had gone to sleep. 'If it's a girl, then I'm going to call her . . . Carina.'

'Why? I've never heard that name before.'

'Because that was my mother's name . . .'

'Well, then we will call her Carina.' Shree had felt for Tyrone's hand under the covers and held on to it in the darkness.

'I love you baby.' . . . Tyrone blurred back to the painful present. It was no use trying to think about good things. The memories just amplified his misery.

It seemed a deathly silence hung over Hackney, like the lull after a storm. Everyone had heard about the fight at the party and what had happened to Shree. There was relief that she was out of danger and sadness at her loss. New Year celebrations continued but a pall hung over proceedings.

Paula placed the tray on the table and took off Fabian's coat. He picked up his hamburger and bit into it. Paula just sipped her extra-large milkshake. They were on their way to the hospital to see how Shree was doing. Paula listened to her son's happy prattle, without anything really registering. She looked around. The McDonalds was busy.

'Well, I know I'm reaching the barbers tonight if it's the last thing I do.'

'Michael, you know you don't need to go to the barbers. Your hair looks kriss just the way it is.'

Paula choked into her milkshake. She didn't need to look over her shoulder. She had already seen Fabian's eyes light up and now he was getting ready to jump down and run to his father. She restrained him with her hand, he wasn't going anywhere. Then Michael was at her table with four or five of his friends and Donna on his arm. Paula fixed two vicious eyes on her. Michael reached over and pinched Fabian's cheek. His friends sat down at a nearby table, but Michael and Donna sat down on the other side of Paula and Fabian's table. Paula began getting her things ready.

'Yeah, I have to be getting myself to a barbers before six.' He grinned at Paula. She turned away from him. Michael threw an arm along the top of the seat that ran behind Donna. He looked from Donna to Paula.

'How come I don't hear you two saying hello to each other?'

'Do I have to say something to every slusher you take out?' Paula stared Donna down. Michael laughed like it was all some big joke. He slapped hands with his friends who thought it was all very hilarious too. He put his arm around Donna's shoulders. But Donna pushed his arm away.

'Hey, who are you trying to diss? No, no, it's no use trying to keep up appearances, baby. Everyone knows I'm sexing you so don't try an' manners me.' He started to whisper things in Donna's ear.

'Fabian, can't you eat a little faster?' Paula said.

'I'm eating fast as I can Mummy,' said Fabian. Michael started to kiss Donna. Paula was getting angry. It was one thing to do that in front of her, it was another to do it in front of his son. Fabian's eyes were getting wider and wider.

Paula smashed her fist down on the table to get Michael's attention. Donna broke away from him instantly. Michael looked at Paula, still with an infuriating half-smile.

'I hate you Michael. I hate the way you look, the way you talk, I can't stand being near you, you make me sick.'

'Paula, if it's about the police thing, I'm sorry, how many times do I have to say it? I'll never do anything like that again. I'll make it up to you. Trust me.'

'This time you're not playing me like a fool, Michael. I'm telling you straight. I gave you everything and you betrayed me. I had a son for you, remember? You must have thought that I was going to take the shit you've handed out forever. Well, I'm going to be blatant with you. I'm not your bitch. I'm not your whore and I damn sure ain't one of your girls. So when you start treating me worse than that slusher sitting next to you, it makes me so fuckin' angry. I'll admit, your games worked well. All those times, you said you loved me. Jesus! Love is blind.'

'Oh, come on, Paula. I don't know what you're trying to play the big woman for. I know you care about me.'

'Care about *you*.' Paula was shouting now. 'When did you ever care about *us*? Me and Fabian? When did you ever do anything for *us*? I was blind but I see it now clear as day. You used us, you fucking bastard. You treated us like dirt. All the times you came round to my flat, it wasn't to see us, it was because you wanted something. You have ignored Fabian for years. You don't have any other responsibilities, you have so much time on your hands. Time for all your friends but not five minutes to phone your son on Christmas Day. There's a little boy out there who needs so much loving and he has a father who only knows how to love his clothes. Well, the bank's closed.'

Michael looked around nervously. No one was laughing. His crew were shaking their heads and Donna looked disgusted.

'I'll give you all my money, I'll help you out, I'll do anything you want.'

Paula grabbed Fabian and their things. 'I wouldn't touch your money. This is how it is, Michael, but you're too immature to see it. Man enough to make a baby but not to take care of one? No, I don't think so. You see, Michael, you've never been anything but a little boy.' Paula did the buttons up on Fabian's coat and picked up her bag, ready to go.

'What did you ever give me?'

Paula had been picking up her rubbish to throw away and her fingers had just closed around the extra-large milkshake as Michael had thrown his final blow. She hurled the milkshake at him. The top came off as the paper cup hit Michael's shoulder. The remains of the milkshake sloshed up into Michael's face and splattered all over his suede jacket. A stunned silence was broken by a few gurgles from Michael's friends who ineffectively hid their laughter behind their hands.

Paula gripped her son's hand, as she looked down at Michael. 'I gave you the best years of my life and I *gave* you your son.' Then she walked out. The cold air stung her cheeks but she was too exhilarated to notice.

The atmosphere at the hospital had always troubled Paula. Fabian stared and pointed as they passed Casualty.

'Why does that man have blood all over his head, Mummy?'

'Because he fell over, Fabian.'

'Why is the woman crying?'

'I don't know, perhaps someone she loves has hurt himself.'

'What are those people in the corner doing?'

'They're praying for everything to be all right.'

They found Tyrone in the cafeteria, picking at a sandwich. The eyes he raised to them were sad and strained. Paula bent down and kissed him on the cheek. He lifted Fabian up on to his lap.

'How are things going, Tyrone?'

'She isn't conscious yet but they've put her in a proper room. They said they can only wait and see. She could come to in five minutes – or five months.'

Paula sat down opposite him. 'Is it very hard to bear?'

'It's hard. They say that I have to bury my little girl in the next few days. I can't wait for Shree and I can't do it alone.' He looked across the cafeteria to the windows. 'Are either of you hungry?'

'No,' said Fabian. 'We went to McDonalds.'

'Really?'

'Yes, we saw Daddy and Daddy's friends.'

Paula snorted and Tyrone looked up. 'Problems?'

'Not any more.'

'You're well rid of him, Paula. He's still my friend, but he hasn't been good to you.' They were both quiet.

'Can I see her, Tyrone?'

'Yeah, but she won't know you're there.'

Tyrone led Paula and Fabian up some stairs and along a corridor. They passed a room where an Italian woman was praying loudly.

'That man's going to die for real. The doctors have given him forty-eight hours to live, so she's praying for his soul.'

Paula gulped as she followed Tyrone. 'How can you say that so calmly?'

'If this experience has taught me anything, it's that no one is too special to have an accident, we all die in the end.'

'What does die mean, Mummy?'

'I'll explain later, baby.'

'But what does it mean?'

'It's a long sleep, Fabian. A very long sleep.'

'Here we are,' said Tyrone as he opened a door. The nurse monitoring Shree's heart rate smiled at them and picked up her file. 'I'll come back in about ten minutes.' She left, quietly closing the door behind her.

'Everyone's done so much for her, you know, Paula. The doctors and nurses worked flat out to save her and even the relatives of other patients, they're so supportive.'

'Mummy, why isn't Shree moving?'

'Because she's not well.'

'But why isn't she speaking?'

'If she speaks then it might hurt her.'

'But why does she have tubes in her nose and on her arms?'

'They help her to breathe.'

'But why?'

'Fabian, come with me. I'll show you all the toys in the waiting-room,' said Tyrone.

'Oh, yes please.' Paula smiled gratefully. 'There are a lot of flowers,' she said, looking around.

'Yeah, most people from the party came round with flowers or cards or something. Alisha, Tricia, Darren, Natelle. That massive bunch over there is from Tanasha, that really surprised me. My mum came round, with my brothers and sisters. It was hard for me to explain to them but they're helping me with the – the—'

'Yeah, I know.' Paula looked down at Shree. Tyrone left the room with Fabian on his shoulders. Paula pulled up the chair close to Shree's bed.

'How ya doing, Shree? Maybe you can hear me. You're gonna be all right, you know. One day you're going to wake up and see all our faces staring down at you. You know how long we've been best friends, me, you and Janice? Since second year junior school when you had just come over from Jamaica and we all got into trouble for cussing in the patois you taught us. We've been like sisters to one another, but me an' you have been the closest because we've never had much of a family, either of us. We've had to look out for ourselves. I've finished with Michael once and for all, you would have been proud of me, I really gave it to him because if what's happened to you has taught me anything, it's that life is short. If you have something to say or do, you'd better get it done before it's too late. Sometimes I thought maybe us three would have broken up. Especially over Janice's Maurice, but we got through. You're a part of me and I'm a part of Janice and we're a part of you. If you go away, I won't have anyone's hair to do and Janice won't have anyone to do her hair.' Paula smiled through her tears. 'And you know that Janice doesn't know what a comb is.' She leaned over and kissed Shree on her forehead. 'I love you.'

Elroy and Janice stopped by Janice's parents' house. When Rose opened the door and saw Elroy standing behind Janice she looked surprised and then her eyes narrowed.

'Hello, Janice, come in.'

'Hi, we're on our way to the hospital. Didn't you

say you had some gifts for Shree? We thought we'd take then for you.'

'Oh, yes. I've got some lovely plants to brighten up her room. Well, if Elroy doesn't mind waiting in the sitting-room, I need to talk to you about something.'

Rose bundled Janice into the kitchen and slammed the door. 'What is he doing with you, Janice?'

'We're together again, Mummy,' said Janice, laughing.

'I saw him down Dalston not too long ago with another woman, Janice.'

'That's all over.'

'Janice, what do you see in him? I thought we had gone over this and you promised.'

'I did no such thing.'

'He's a rake, Janice. It's not going to last.'

'Yes it will.'

'Well, you just try explaining this to your father. I really feel like boxing your ears. Elroy, of all people, the deejay. I am going to be the laughing-stock of my church. Maybe Lloyd can talk some sense into you.' As Rose approached the sitting-room door she heard loud laughter. She stuck her head around the door. Lloyd and Elroy were laughing and touching fists. She frowned in disapproval. 'Lloyd, I need your help in the kitchen.'

Lloyd waved her away. 'Ask Janice to help you, nuh.'

'Lloyd!'

'Can't you see that I'm keeping Elroy company?'

'Oh, I'll do that, Dad,' said Janice, coming into the sitting-room. Reluctantly Lloyd rose, walked into the kitchen and sat down at the table.

'Lloyd, she's going out with the deejay again,' Rose hissed.

'Well?'

'Lloyd, you talk some sense into her. She's your daughter too.'

Lloyd sighed. 'Janice knows what she wants. It's none of our business.'

'Then whose business is it if not ours? Aren't we her parents?'

'Janice is a big girl now. We can't dictate to her any more.'

'We can advise her *strongly*, we can point her in the right direction, we can show her where she is going wrong!'

'Yes, but there's nothing wrong with Elroy. I like him. He's full of life, he's good for Janice.'

'He's good-for-nothing and so I warn you. He's lazy and ignorant. What can he do for my little girl?'

Lloyd stood up and taking Rose's arm, he led her towards the sitting-room. 'Come and see, old woman.' Outside the sitting-room door he signalled to her to be quiet and pointed to the crack in the door. Rose peered through. She could see Elroy talking to Janice who was sitting on his knee. Her eyes were bright and her face was flushed. Then Rose understood. Janice was happy and in love. There was nothing she could do to change that and as she looked she wasn't sure that she wanted to. In fact it evoked old feelings and memories in her. She rested her head on Lloyd's shoulders.

'Now do you see?'

'Yes, I'm sorry.' Rose stood on tiptoe and kissed her husband. Lloyd looked at her in surprise and then he kissed her back. In Janice and Elroy he had always seen himself and Rose and now it seemed Rose could see it too.

Tyrone watched the television in the waiting-room. It was the end of the day. He was waiting for the doctors to finish more tests. That was all they ever seemed to do. The results were still the same. Nothing. He switched television channels back and forth, uncaring. He glanced over his shoulder at the Italian woman at the back of the room. She was asleep in a chair.

'Mr Dennis?'

'Yes, what is it?' Tyrone asked, turning around to see a doctor standing in the doorway.

'Mr Dennis, Shree could regain consciousness any second, we need you on standby.' Tyrone knocked over the chair in his hurry to stand up.

'Mr Dennis, you can't just rush in there. You have to be calm. Shree doesn't know anything.'

'What shall I say?'

'There is no right way to tell a mother that her baby is dead. I'm sorry, Mr Dennis. Just break it to her gently. Remember she's still living on the edge.'

Tyrone walked into Shree's room as quietly as he could and sat down in the chair beside the bed. He took one of her hands in his own. She looked so peaceful. Tyrone leaned forward and started to sob. Shree opened her eyes and turned to see where the noise was coming from. She tried to comfort Tyrone but found she couldn't move. Alarmed, she put a hand underneath the covers. Around her waist, all she could feel was bandages, so many bandages.

Tyrone looked up. All he could do was shake his head at her sadly and from his eyes she understood her baby was no more. No words were needed. Staring at the ceiling, tears coursed down her cheeks. She opened her mouth to scream, but no sound came out. She felt herself being lifted. She tried to push Tyrone away, striking out with her arms because she couldn't bear to be touched, but soon Tyrone was holding her, stroking her hair, and she was crying on his shoulder, just crying for a long, long time while Tyrone gently whispered the special words which only he could say to her.

'Shree. There's nothing more precious to me than you. The baby, it meant so much to me but I still have you. What would I do without you? Remember what I said to you, the night you told me you was pregnant? I love you so much and I'm here for you. Remember all those things I said when I made you that meal? I'm a one-woman man, and you're the one. You're the only person I've ever loved and I'm gonna spend the rest of my life beside you, making sure you never get hurt again. I blame myself for what's happened. If I hadn't been so angry and started fighting then perhaps . . . I should have listened to you, Shree, I just don't know what happened next. From now on I'm gonna protect you and listen to you and we're gonna get married, Shree, and we're going to have other children – there, don't cry. Our baby's in heaven, she ain't never sinned so she's gone to God. Listening darling?' Shree gave a small nod.

Derrick walked into the hospital weighed down with flowers. He had been angry when he had heard. Janice had been the one to phone him but he hadn't been able to get two straight sentences from her, or anyone else. Tyrone seemed to think that hiding out in the hospital would keep him safe, but someone was going to pay.

Derrick strode up the hallway. He had always known Tyrone wasn't good enough for his daughter. Wait till he saw him, he was going to string that boy up, he was going to beat him until . . . Derrick walked into the waiting-room, put down the flowers and literally dragged Tyrone up from his chair and flung him against the wall.

'What have you done to my girl?' Tyrone's chest heaved. He did not try to fight back because he understood that it was his fault.

Derrick studied Tyrone. He took in the style growing out in his head, the growth about his chin, the crumpled clothes, but what he noticed most was the eyes. There was genuine unhappiness in those eyes and he remembered a time long ago, when his eyes had looked like that but worse. He crossed over to Tyrone again but this time he helped him up.

'Shree's going to be all right, you know. She's conscious now,' said Tyrone.

'But how is she feeling?'

'She's still in shock. She doesn't want to eat, she hasn't said a word, I think she blames herself. She cries a lot and she won't see anyone except me.'

Derrick went into Shree's room. The two of them were shut up in the room for hours. No one ever knew what was said. Shree didn't tell Tyrone and he never asked, but after Derrick's visit Shree started seeing people. Janice and Paula before anyone else and only a few at first, but after that her room was always crammed with well-wishers, even though she didn't say much and was sometimes too tired even to smile.

Tyrone would sit there all day. 'I'm a one-woman man, and you're the one,' he said again one day.

Shree squeezed his hand. 'I love you, Tyrone,' she said softly.

'Well, I don't think I've changed one bit!'

Paula and Shree looked at each other and then at Janice.

'But I *haven't*!' Janice protested.

'No, not much,' Paula said sarcastically.

Shree giggled and then winced. 'Hey, don't make me laugh or the nurse will come in and send you away,' she said.

'Well, I would say that if anything I've become more mature,' Janice said as she sat back on Shree's bed. 'Yes. I now know what I want in a man.'

'Not money?' Shree asked softly.

Janice hesitated. 'Elroy has enough for me, so that's not a problem, but I don't love him for that.'

'Why do you love him?' Paula asked.

'Because he's honest and kind and responsible and he loves me. He brings out the best in me. Maurice made me bitchy and deceitful. Elroy makes me feel special without me thinking I'm better than anyone else.'

'God, you sound like something off Oprah Winfrey,' said Paula.

'What about you, Paula, how have you changed?' asked Shree.

'Well, it took a long time, but I've finally realized I don't need Michael or owe him anything.'

'Are you sure? I remember a time when Michael could do no wrong and everything was, my Michael this, my Michael that,' said Janice.

Paula smiled bashfully. 'It's true, but I think it was Christmas Day, when Fabian was asking why his dad hadn't bought him a present, that I felt I had to stop making excuses for him.'

'Good for you,' said Shree. 'You really don't need him, you know. You have a job now and you're such a good mother to Fabian.' There was an awkward silence so Shree continued, 'I know a few days ago I wanted to die but now, I'm so glad I survived because I have so much to live for. Although I blame myself for the fight, I think it's made me a better person and Tyrone too.'

'But Shree, you was always a good person. You are the glue that has held the three of us together!' said Janice.

Shree looked happy. 'Really?'

'Of course. We would have split up over Maurice if it hadn't been for you, giving me a lecture about friendship being bigger than boyfriends,' Paula said. 'And we would have broken up over Michael if you hadn't been so unselfish as to apologize even though I insulted you.'

'Well, if it wasn't for you two, I would have never made it through my troubles. My dad going away and the arguments with Tyrone. However, I see what you're saying about me being the glue, I really am special and kind and sensitive.'

'Hey, don't get feisty now, Shree, or we'll smother you with one of your pillows,' Janice said, grinning.

Paula and Janice helped Shree down the front steps of the hospital towards the car which Tyrone had driven round to the front entrance. It was bitterly cold and the clouds obscured the sun.

'Shree, you're supposed to lose weight in hospital, not put it on.'

'Paula is right, you weigh so much the steps are sagging.' As her friends moaned and complained about everything from the cold to hospital food, Shree threw back her head and laughed. Paula looked at Janice over Shree's head. It was the first time they had heard their friend laugh in a long while.

They had to be doing something right.

Suddenly the sun appeared from behind the clouds and its glorious rays shone over the three girls as they descended the stone steps. One was dark and tall, another light-skinned and plump, and between them, one was slim and petite. Laughing together they looked as if they hadn't a care in the world. Best friends since the beginning of time.

All Pan Books are available at your local bookshop or newsagent, or can be ordered direct from the publisher. Indicate the number of copies required and fill in the form below.

Send to: Macmillan General Books C.S.
Book Service By Post
PO Box 29, Douglas I-O-M
IM99 1BQ

or phone: 01624 675137, quoting title, author and credit card number.

or fax: 01624 670923, quoting title, author, and credit card number.

or Internet: http://www.bookpost.co.uk

Please enclose a remittance* to the value of the cover price plus 75 pence per book for post and packing. Overseas customers please allow £1.00 per copy for post and packing.

*Payment may be made in sterling by UK personal cheque, Eurocheque, postal order, sterling draft or international money order, made payable to Book Service By Post.

Alternatively by Access/Visa/MasterCard

Card No. ⬚⬚⬚⬚⬚⬚⬚⬚⬚⬚⬚⬚⬚⬚⬚⬚⬚⬚⬚⬚

Expiry Date ⬚⬚⬚⬚⬚⬚⬚⬚⬚⬚⬚⬚⬚⬚⬚⬚⬚⬚⬚⬚

Signature _____

Applicable only in the UK and BFPO addresses.

While every effort is made to keep prices low, it is sometimes necessary to increase prices at short notice. Pan Books reserve the right to show on covers and charge new retail prices which may differ from those advertised in the text or elsewhere.

NAME AND ADDRESS IN BLOCK CAPITAL LETTERS PLEASE

Name _____

Address _____

_____

_____

_____

8/95

Please allow 28 days for delivery.
Please tick box if you do not wish to receive any additional information. ⬚